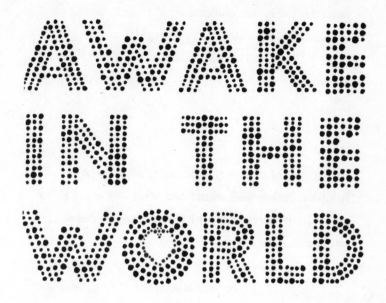

AWAKE IN THE WORLD

JASON GURLEY

USBORNE

Even if it's very late at night.
Someone's always awake in the world.

Ann Druyan,
A Famous Broken Heart

I believe that it is very difficult to know who we are until we understand where and when we are. I think everyone in every culture has felt a sense of awe and wonder looking at the sky.

Carl Sagan,
The Varieties of Scientific Experience:
A Personal View of the Search for God

I don't think I'll ever see Carl again. But I saw him. We saw each other. We found each other in the cosmos, and that was wonderful.

Ann Druyan,
"Ann Druyan Talks About Science,
Religion, Wonder, Awe…and Carl Sagan,"
Skeptical Inquirer, November/December 2003

AWAKE IN THE WORLD

For Connie and Seth,
without whom this book simply wouldn't exist.

PART ONE

SEPTEMBER 2012

ZACH

Top three unluckiest things to happen to me this week:

1. I dropped my house key into a storm drain.
2. Ms Grace informed me that I'm one credit short for graduation next spring.
3. I tore Dad's hoodie.

And it's only Monday.

The hoodie pissed me off the most. The impound lot is fenced in with chain-link, and the twisty-tie barbs atop the fence are as sharp as upturned ice picks. I dropped to the other side of the fence and examined the rip. I could see my jeans through it. *Damn.*

I hefted my backpack and moved through a thicket of rusted Hondas and forgotten Toyotas towards the lot's oddest resident: the fishing boat. Behind it, a sign hung on the impound lot's fence:

SMILE,
YOU'RE BEING WATCHED

Below the words was a picture of a camera with an eyeball for a lens.

But there weren't actually any cameras. I was certain of that. I'd managed to escape detection all this time, despite some close calls, but I sometimes wondered if it was because I was just that stealthy...or if I was fooling myself. Maybe everyone knew about my secret pre-dawn infiltrations. Maybe they left me alone because they felt sorry for me. It's like this: sometimes it feels like the whole town is waiting to see what wallop of bad luck will hit me next; other times, I can feel them quietly rooting for me. I'm never certain which is true when.

On the boat, inside the wheelhouse, I sank into the old captain's chair and snapped on the deck lantern. The warm orange glow chased the shadows from the walls, where my father's face stared down at me from a hundred tacked-up sketches.

"Morning, Dad," I said softly.

I opened my sketchbook and returned to an illustration in progress. Sometimes this was my only time to draw, these early hours on an impounded, slowly rotting boat. Between school and my job at the market, and the girls and their homework, and their bedtime stories – well, I didn't have space for much more than that. Quietly, I roughed in the structure of my father's boat on the page. It peeked through the haze of the marine layer, the shroud that blanketed the sea on early summer mornings.

The sketchbook was a gift from my father four years back – in 2008, which had been a good year until it wasn't. "Things are going to change," Dad had said to Mama after the promotion at Bernaco. And he was right: they had, although not exactly how I think he'd intended. He'd given me a stack of sketchbooks like this one: bound in leather, or something like it; expensive, toothy paper. "I'm tired of seeing you draw on the gas bill," he'd said with a wink. Between then and now, I'd filled every inch of every page of each book, except this one. This was the last of them. Nothing I'd drawn in this book seemed good enough.

Not for the last thing my father ever gave me.

The pencil broke, etching a dark gash on the page. I sighed. I could fix it, but…The weight of the previous day had settled on me, and I was tired. I went to the window and pulled back the blanket that hung across it. From here I could see the credit union sign announce the time: 3:35 a.m.

I bagged my sketchbook, extinguished the lantern, and closed the wheelhouse door. When I dropped to the ground beside the boat, my ankle rolled beneath me, and I clapped a hand over my mouth to stifle a cry. I tested the foot gingerly. It wasn't serious – not a break or a sprain – but it qualified, I thought, as a small warning from the universe.

Remember whose side I'm on.

Yeah. Not mine. Got it, universe.

I tugged my hood over my head, then carefully scaled the fence and limped home, aware, as always, that when luck goes bad, it tends to stay bad. Some things just don't change.

2

VANESSA

The stranger rolled his ankle when he landed, and I cringed. I'd done that a few times, back when Mom and I played on the Santa Barbara public tennis courts. Those memories always ended with Mom helping me to the car. But the stranger limped away, and I reviewed my notes: I didn't know who he was, or why he broke into that lot a couple of times each week, or what appeal that old boat held. And yet, we weren't so different, except maybe for the breaking and entering. Two souls, wide awake in the most wee of hours.

I'd found him entirely by accident, of course. Mom and I had just moved into Aaron's house in the hills of Orilla del Cielo. From the window of my new room, I had a panoramic view of Orilly and the Pacific beyond. (That's what everyone calls the town, I quickly learned. As in *O, RLY?*) The vista was lovely, but it held secrets, too. Aaron had pointed out the scars left by a severe storm that hit the coast years before: an abandoned trawler, mouldering on the rocks, saw grass growing through holes in its hull; the rubble of an old stone pier that had collapsed, dumping Aaron's favourite seafood restaurant into the sea. And despite the million-dollar view, Orilly is an oil town, strictly blue collar. Bernaco Oil, where Aaron works, owns most of the land, and its drilling platforms stand like sentries offshore, watching the townspeople. It's the polar opposite of Santa Barbara, where I'd lived before and where one might bump into Rob Lowe at the supermarket or sell Girl Scout cookies to Oprah. Orilly has no such glamour. There isn't even a movie theatre. Highway 1 serves as a neat seam, separating the town into two halves: the hills, where Aaron and the rest of the oil executives live among bright lawns and lush eucalyptus groves, and the lowlands, where the oil workers are stuffed into little boxes among nail salons and strip malls.

But that view. The sunsets, practically nuclear, transform the ocean each night into a shimmering golden blanket. The grimy, bulky oil rigs become blazing, floating cities, strung across the horizon like Christmas lights.

That view is the reason OSPERT has a permanent home in my window, and the reason I spotted the stranger. OSPERT is my Orion SpaceProbe Equatorial Reflector Telescope. He's got an aluminium Newtonian optical tube, a rack-and-pinion focuser, and two Kellner eyepieces. All of which means he's exceptionally good at tracking anything that moves: comets, the International Space Station, Mars.

And strangers who break into the police impound lot.

I found him because of Twylight Guy, a weekend stargazer who keeps an amateur-astronomy blog. That night, weeks and weeks ago, TG was all lit up about a supernova: *Supposed to be a real light show*, he'd exclaimed. And that was good for me, because if TG could see something, then I probably could, too; he blogs from Monterey, just a short hop from Orilly. You'd expect an exploding star to dominate the night sky, but alas, even the brightest supernovae are hardly more than a pale smudge among the stars. The magic, though, isn't in what they *look* like, but in what they *are*: the final echo of a stunning symphony, performed a million miles away, a thousand thousand years ago. They're a flourish of history, preserved against the cape of night.

Unfortunately, while TG is a perfectly competent astronomer, he's a shitty meteorologist.

Supernova a bust
by Twylight Guy | June 23, 2012 • 1:48 a.m.

Sorry, folks! Low pressure system from the northwest made its way down the coast late last night, effectively ruining any West Coasters' chance of seeing PSN J11085663 + 2635300. Major bummer. International folks, send your own photos so those of us in the dark (LOL, *in the dark*) don't miss out!

Major bummer, indeed. I'd loaded up on caffeine and couldn't sleep. So instead, I turned OSPERT towards the earth, adjusting the finderscope until I found the oil rigs, glowing in the dark. Even that late, they were alive with activity. Eventually, I turned the telescope towards Orilly itself. And that's how I spotted the stranger. He was practically the only thing moving at that hour. He wasn't hard to spot.

Jesus, if Mom knew I was spying on people…could just imagine the headlines.

LOCAL VOYEUR STRIKES AGAIN
Peeping teen allegedly points telescope down,
not up; neighbours scandalized

But Orilly was dead tired, everyone asleep. Nobody would know.

Anyway, Mom already felt scandalized by OSPERT. And the stars, and the Carl Sagan posters, and the Cornell pennant tacked to my bulletin board. Though, of course, her true feelings had nothing to do with any of those things, and everything to do with my father.

Who I don't think about.

Below me, the stranger limped into shadow. With a yawn, I covered OSPERT's big glass eye with the lens cap and dragged myself to bed.

3

ZACH

The administrative office of Palmer Rankin High School hummed to life around me. Derek – my older brother – was somewhere in the back offices, meeting with Ms Grace, my adviser, about that missing course credit.

So I waited.

Always with the waiting. When you're a kid, that's just the way it is: you wait for the bus. Wait for the bell. Wait for summer, the weekend. Wait to grow up. Except then you do grow up, and you realize adults are always waiting, too. Waiting for a pay cheque, for a letter from the lawyer, for your food stamps. Waiting forever for that moment when something just *clicks*, and your life finally turns into the life you *thought* you'd have.

You wait and wait and wait, and then, as you wait some more, you die. It's morbid.

While waiting, I opened my sketchbook. As I worked, the world went out of focus, until there was just me and the page. Me and the eraser, reminding the clock of the gash

I'd created the night before. Drawing was always like this for me. It opened a tiny rip in the universe. Time didn't exist there. Except time kept on existing for everyone else, and that fact had gotten me in trouble more than once. Most of my parent-teacher conferences, at least in my younger days, had been about my attention span.

Well, except one of them. The inciting event happened during lunch period in fourth grade. I'd filled a sheet of notebook paper with graphite, save a little twisting ribbon of white in the middle: a firework, captured in the moment of its unfolding, streamers of negative space rippling out from its warm heart. And then Bobby Longdale poured a carton of milk onto the drawing, destroying it. It was lasagne day, which is important because Bobby wound up wearing his, and I wound up in the principal's office, waiting for my mother. Dad had the car for work, which meant that Mama walked a few miles in the heat because of my stunt. And though I knew that, I still snapped at her when she reached for my hand on the walk home. I don't remember what I said, but I remember what Dad had to say when he came home later. He put away his dive gear, then came to my room, sat on the bed, and explained the difference between being human and being angry. He wasn't mad that I'd acted out at school; I'd done so with cause. He was disappointed that I'd taken it out on my mother. *Recognize the people in your life who give you love*, he said to me that afternoon.

Give love back. Just love.

Wait for your father to come home, Mama had said.

Remembering that day hurt. I blinked to clear my eyes.

I wish I could wait, Mama. I'd wait a thousand years for him. I'd take a thousand lectures.

Derek's lectures weren't quite the same, though he tried. Right now he'd be listening to Ms Grace say something about not applying myself. *Please*, Derek would sniff. *The boy applies too much of himself. He works two jobs. I can't stop him. I've tried. What do you want from him?*

None of this was new territory for me. For us.

Outside the office, the rest of the world swam past. Students chattering excitedly. The same conversations every day. Back and forth, wielding their opinions like knives, jabbing one another to see who bleeds more for the things they love. *Stab, stab.* Mama would have taken a lighter view: *Maybe they're just passionate about things.* But I'm less reasonable, especially on days that begin with Ms Grace reporting about my squandered potential.

Potential is for people who are going places. But where am I going?

I fanned through the pages of my sketchbook. Page after page of intricate illustrations. Dense clouds spilling over mountain tops; a tree, split by lightning, smouldering. I was good, I knew that. But it didn't matter. You can't support a family with nice drawings. And anyway, artists were supposed to know what they were *about*. I had no idea what my art was about. If someone asked me to make an artistic statement, what could I say?

My father gave me this book, and I loved him.

I leaned back in my chair. For the first time, I noticed the fine layer of white dust on the other chairs in the waiting area, heard the din of power tools somewhere above. The ceiling tiles vibrated as I watched, coughing up more dust, and a piece of paper fluttered down from one wall and came to rest at my feet. It was bright yellow, with screaming type.

PLEASE EXCUSE A MESS; CONSTRUCTION!!!

"Our educators commit the most grievous grammatical atrocities, don't they?"

I glanced up to see a girl standing near the door. She raised one eyebrow in disapproval, and the corner of her mouth turned up slightly.

Palmer Rankin doesn't get many new students. People aren't exactly flocking to Orilly. So when someone transfers in senior year, just in time to mount a serious valedictory challenge to Cecily Vasquez – who was labelled "most likely valedictorian" at my kindergarten "graduation" – it's difficult not to notice. The new girl and Cece were straight AP kids – except for health education, the random-ass elective that everyone puts off until they can't any more. Which makes it the one class I share with both of them.

Despite all that, I couldn't remember her name.

Thump. Above me, a square ceiling tile bucked and clattered back into place.

"Maybe you should scoot over a few seats?" the girl said, casting a critical eye at the ceiling. Her dark hair fell away, revealing small-gauge eyelets in her ears – I could see right through her earlobe to the hollow behind. I'd never noticed a girl's jawline before – my observation skills aren't terrific, except when I'm bent over my sketchbook – but I noticed hers, and the way her neck sloped up to meet it. Over one shoulder she carried a messenger bag; strapped to its buckle was a bicycle helmet. Each of her fingers bore a different ring, sometimes two. Nebula-print leggings, a strappy top, shoulders *everywhere*.

"So you don't get hit."

"What?" I said.

"I said maybe scoot so the ceiling doesn't squash you."

I looked up at the tile. It was motionless. "It…seems fine."

She shrugged, then lifted one hand dramatically. "Alas," she said, projecting like a theatre student. "How little I knew the young man. A bright future in the arts he might have had." She dropped the act and grinned. "Or not. I mean, I've only seen the one drawing."

"What?" I struggled to parse her words; she was talking on some frequency that hummed beyond my ability to hear, or maybe faster than I was able to sequence.

She sighed and pointed to the sketchbook. "It's nice. Your drawing."

"Wh—" I stopped, realizing I'd been able to keep up with her that time. "Oh. Thanks."

"I mean, it's nice for a *delinquent*," she added.

"What?" *Oh, Zach, goddammit.*

She unfurled a hand, gesturing at our surroundings. "The administrative office," she intoned. "Court of the detestable and ill-behaved. The fuck-ups, if you will. So what did you do wrong?"

"What?"

This time she looked at me as if she thought I might really be dumb. Some invisible wire strung through my chest twitched. I'd never felt *that* before. But I didn't have time to examine that feeling more closely.

"Good morning, Zachariah," chirped Mrs Rhyzkov, one of the school's guidance counsellors. "I just saw your brother. Such a pleasure when he comes back to visit. He always was such a determined student, that Derek Mays."

"It's Zachary," I muttered, but the counsellor had already turned to the girl.

"Miss Drake, Vanessa, dear," she said, and I thought, *Vanessa, that's right, I knew that.* "Why don't you come on back? You must be so excited about the college fair this week…"

Vanessa adjusted the bag on her shoulder and waggled her fingers at me. "Zachary," she said primly, and her lips parted into a genuine smile.

I almost said *What* again, but she was gone before I formed the word. After she'd disappeared into the back with Mrs Rhyzkov, I tried returning to my sketchbook. But the pencil wasn't moving right, so I closed the book and leaned back in my chair. I watched the ceiling apprehensively.

Vanessa. Okay.

4

VANESSA

"Here's the thing," Mrs Rhyzkov said, leaning across her desk and clasping her hands. "With your GPA, you'll essentially have your choice of schools. I don't understand why you would limit yourself to just one."

"But with my GPA, wouldn't I get in?" I asked.

She sighed. "Students who put all their eggs in one basket make me...uncomfortable. Can I ask a personal question?"

"Okay."

"Is it just that Cornell is far away?" She gestured towards a map on her office wall. "Because I can say with certainty there are many other schools equally far from home. It's wise to apply to at least a few more. To be safe."

It wasn't just that Cornell was far away. Cornell was... well, *Cornell*.

When I was small, my father would wake me in the dark. "Cass," he'd whisper. (He'd wanted to name me Cassiopeia, but Mom wouldn't agree to it.) "You've *got* to see this."

He'd bundle me outside, blanket and all, to point out the streaking light of the Perseids or Venus drifting like a champagne bubble.

My father talked about space in awestruck but rigid terms. For me, however, the sight of such things created an indescribable feeling in my chest. When I was nine, I found words for that feeling: I saw Carl Sagan for the first time. He spoke about how small we were, yet how grand our aspirations; he spoke of the universe like a poet. My father grumbled about Sagan; he despised the easy popularization of science that Sagan represented. My father was a devotee of more *serious* scientists. It occurred to me, at that young age, that my father believed himself to be smarter not just than me, but everyone. The accessibility of science, of knowledge, somehow threatened him.

As a teenager, I smuggled home an old issue of *Popular Science* beneath my jacket, as if hiding a porno. Its very title was an affront to my father's sensibilities, but I didn't mind. That issue had a feature about Dr Sagan and changed the shape of my future. Dr Sagan, I learned, taught astronomy at a university in Ithaca, New York. A university called Cornell. To my father, I'd fallen prey to the siren call of "science for idiots". He wasn't proud; he was disappointed. "You're only about ten years too late," he said. I would never forget the smug contempt in his voice. "Your hero's been dead since you were a baby."

Later, after he'd left us, I learned that my father's heroes were no different from Carl Sagan. Richard Feynman, Stephen Hawking – in their way, they too made science essential to everyone. But it was too late to fashion that knowledge into a retort, and my father wouldn't have heard me, anyway. He was already gone.

That was the thing, though. He wasn't *gone* gone. His face stared back at me from my own features in the bathroom mirror.

I looked so much like him, sometimes, that my mother would look away. It wasn't only the shape of my nose or the way my eyes crinkled like his; it was what he'd left within me, this devotion to the stars. Sometimes I wondered: were the stars something I loved because *I* loved them?

Or was it just *him*, still taking up space in my head?

Cornell wasn't just a top school for astronomy students. It was a rejection of everything my father represented. Choosing Cornell sent a message: Y*ou're wrong about me*, it said. *Wrong about* everything.

"Okay," I lied. "I'll pick a few backup schools."

"Wise choice. You know, you and Ms Vasquez, you're my legacy," Mrs Rhyzkov clucked. "The first female chief justice, and the girl who named a star after me."

And named a black hole for her father, I thought.

In the hallway, I was nearly bowled over by a tall, red-haired man. "Pardon," he said with a quick glance to make sure I was all right. He passed through the waiting room and beckoned at Zachary, the artist boy. Zachary stood up and took a single step, and a ceiling tile cracked and fell onto the chair he'd just vacated. It detonated in a puff of white dust and tile fragments.

Zachary blinked, as if he couldn't believe he'd escaped unscathed, then looked around and saw me watching. His face changed – was that relief ? Gratitude? His hood had fallen down, revealing thick red curls that dangled over his brow. The hoodie had seen a few years; the knees and thighs of his jeans were worn thin. I was struck by how tall he was – well over six feet – and lacking in any sense of physical confidence. He was…*knobby*, I thought. Hands too large for his slender wrists. Shoulders so sharp I could've hung a hat on them. The boy was a walking coat rack.

I waved, and that seemed to snap him to attention. The smile that bloomed on his face was the most unreserved thing about him. I couldn't help but smile back. He dipped his gaze, almost bashfully, then limped out of the office, following the other man.

Limped.

I went after him, then stopped in the crowded hall, watching as Zachary pushed through the doors. It was windy outside, and he tugged his hood over those curls. As I stood there, Cece sidled up to me. Her eyes were glassy, her smile half-drunk. *Was* she drunk? I sniffed, then watched Zachary again. The boy in the hoodie.

But not just any boy.

My stranger.

5

ZACH

Each afternoon, I left Palmer Rankin and walked three-quarters of a mile to Maddie's Market. My title was "associate", but that just meant I did it all. On this particular afternoon, I was the associate in charge of collecting carts. I'd found them at all ends of the parking lot, but our customers didn't always stop there. I'd found one parked in a grassy median in the middle of the road. I'd found one tipped over on an apartment lawn when I walked home at the end of my shift. I'd even spotted one at low tide, wheels rusted and clogged with grit, mostly buried in the sand. I didn't retrieve that one.

By the time I'd finished gathering them today, the sun had leaked out of the sky. Past the market, I caught a glimpse of the oil rigs, like campfires on a vast prairie. Derek, I knew, was probably out there right now. I understood why he was, but I never asked him what it felt like. Suiting up. Inspecting pipelines, welding joints, handling drilling assists. Working the same rigs that took away our dad.

Everybody around him knew the story. But they wouldn't ask why he did it. They knew why.

Above the water or below, we carry the wrench. It's what we know.

The lament of the working-class man. I'd heard Dad recite it a hundred times. The first time I drew him, it was as that working man, at the end of a day: slump-shouldered, sunken-eyed. An enormous wrench dangling from his fingers. Derek looked just the same when he came home these days.

And one day, I knew, that would be me.

The girls were still up when I came home. Leah heard me shut the front door and came out to meet me. "Oh, thank goodness," she said, sounding harried. "Derek isn't home yet. I'm running late for a patient."

"Evening shift?"

"This kind of work is all hours, Z, you know that."

I dropped my bag beside the couch. "I'll take over."

"Thank you," she said. She kissed my forehead, then gathered her things and disappeared through the door in a rush.

I didn't know what we would do without Leah. She was practically family. The girls wondered, but didn't ask, why she wasn't *actual* family yet. She and Derek had dated all through high school and broken up when he went away for college. Despite that, she had stuck around: helping Mama prepare Thanksgiving dinner, buying presents for the girls. After we lost Dad, Derek dropped out of school and came back to Orilly, and Leah was right here, as if he'd never left. They fell into their familiar rhythms again. But Derek is a steam engine, desperately moving forward, trying to fill Dad's shoes. Leah doesn't complain, just gives and gives. I worry sometimes we've taken advantage of her big heart.

I went to Mama's door and cracked it, just a sliver. Inside: darkness, stillness. The steady rhythm of her breathing. "Night, Mama," I whispered. I closed her door again, and for a moment I just stood there, feeling the house. The girls giggled in their bedroom. The rude thump of a stereo from our duplex neighbour rattled the plastic sheet that covered the door to my former bedroom.

The girls feigned sleep when I peeked in, until I snapped off the light. Robin cranked out a fake snore, and Rachael couldn't hold back her laughter. They were nine, the only twins in the fourth grade. Redheads, like me and Derek, but more freckled, and sparky, like neither Derek nor I had been for a long while.

"Past bedtime," I pointed out.

"Leah didn't read to us."

It was late. But I couldn't say no. We'd been reading our way through A Wrinkle in Time and its subsequent books.

And not for the first time, either. This was our second lap through the series. I picked up the third book, *A Swiftly Tilting Planet*, and began to read. It was my favourite of the series, and I read longer than I otherwise might have. Two chapters later, Robin was asleep, and Rachael blinked sleepily at me.

"Sing?" she whispered.

My voice was nothing like our father's. He'd had a rich baritone, clear and strong, even at a whisper. I didn't have to ask Rachael which song; there was only one. Dad's father had sung it to him when he was young, an old folk tune about a frog who romanced a mouse and married her.

I put my hand on Rachael's cheek, and she closed her eyes.

"Froggie went a-courtin' and he did ride, mm-hmm," I sang softly. I'd hardly made it to the second verse before she was asleep as well.

I slipped quietly into the hallway. Derek wasn't home. Our neighbour's music had stopped, though I heard the murmur of a television through the walls now. I had a slice of toast, then brushed my teeth and unfolded my blanket onto the couch. Before I fell asleep, I thought of Vanessa, the new girl. I'd embarrassed myself today; next time I'd have to think of something better to say.

I worked on that for a while, until sleep came.

6

VANESSA

Cece was still distracted. Not glassy-eyed – but off her game. She was uncharacteristically resistant to my subtle attempts to extract an explanation, so I had to go for the direct approach.

"What's up?" I said.

"Nothing."

"Girls," said Mr Herrera, our AP Spanish teacher.

I looked at Cece. "*¿Qué pasa?*"

"*Nada,*" she said back.

Mr Herrera looked satisfied and went back to his desk work. I lowered my voice and said, "So – what's *up?*"

She narrowed her eyes. "I don't know what you're talking about."

"You're all spaced-out."

"No, I'm not."

"You're lying to me. I don't believe a word you're saying."

"Climate change is real," she said.

"Fine. I believe *some* of the words you're saying."

With a coy smile, she returned to her notebook. She'd been doodling for most of class, but I resisted the urge to snatch it away from her. She wasn't herself, though. Until recently, Cece had been laser-focused on college. Her life revolved around test scores and her GPA – which at the moment was, I thought, about a tenth of a point higher than my own.

Not that I was counting.

She spotted me looking and curled the cover of her notebook to obscure her work. Then she changed the subject. "I saw you," she said. "Staring at Zach."

"You weren't even there."

"Yes, I was."

I amended my statement. "You were there. But you weren't *there*."

"I can keep a secret," she said, undeterred. "Besides…"

I lifted one eyebrow. "Besides what?"

"If you get distracted, maybe your grades will suffer."

"Because that's how you want to win, huh? By hoping for your enemy to trip and fall on her own mechanical pencil?"

"Did you know there's a betting pool?" she asked.

"Jesus. It's not a competition."

"*Everything* is a competition."

"Well, fine. I withdraw," I said. "I'll bomb the next exam, and you can be Queen Vale*dick* of 2013."

"No fun if you throw the game."

"But it's okay to wish for me to blow it," I said. "Anyway, it's not a game."

"*Everything*—" Mr Herrera shot Cece a stern look. When he returned to his work, she hissed, "Why were you watching Zach? Did you talk to him? You didn't tell me."

"I didn't know I had to."

"Um," she said, adopting a Valley-girl lilt. "Like, we're *besties*, like."

"I thought we were at each other's throats."

"Eh," Cece said dismissively. "Better for the pool if we play it that way, maybe. It's up to seventy bucks."

"Who gets the money?"

"Not us."

"Unless we place bets."

"Ooh," she said, picking up the thread. "One of us takes a dive…"

"We split the winnings…"

"This is good."

"How do we decide who dives?"

"You dive, of course," Cece said.

"I already said I don't care."

"Yeah, but you're a lying liar." She wore a sly smile. "Who lies. About lying."

The bell jangled overhead. We filed into the hallway together. "Why did you ask if I talked to him?"

"I saw him before. He was looking at you."

33

"He doesn't know me."

She shrugged. "Put a pair of tits on something, boys are all about it."

I looked down at my chest. "My body missed the memo."

"I saw him," she said. "Before. You were in the office, and he was...I could tell he liked talking to you. You, I couldn't tell so easily. I just..." She hesitated. "I don't want you to be collateral damage."

"Please. He's a person, not a bomb."

Cece swapped books at her locker; then we exited into the gravel courtyard between buildings. It was cluttered with discarded cigarettes and old potato chip bags and skinny freshmen who lumbered about in a fog of body spray. "They seriously need to clean this shit up," she muttered disdainfully.

"Don't change the subject."

"Look," she said. "He's a sweetheart. Seriously. I've gone to school with him my whole life, and you'll never meet a nicer kid. I swear."

"Collateral damage, though? Come on."

Cece sighed, then turned to a knot of seniors who leaned against the wall, passing a cigarette. "Hey, Boyd," she said. A boy with a scraggly topknot looked up, smoke leaking from his nose. "Zach Mays."

Boyd shook his head, waggling the topknot. "Abandon hope, all ye who—"

Cece didn't wait for him to finish. "See?"

I was unconvinced.

"Freshman year," she said. "Someone hacked the district computers, erased a bunch of records. Kid from the hackathon group got caught and expelled. They got all the records restored, except one. Guess whose."

"That's awful. What happened?"

"They held him back."

"That's messed up. It wasn't his f—"

"Sophomore year," she went on. "Zach got tall over the summer, so he got roped into basketball try-outs. He's no athlete, but he tries. Takes one shot. Nowhere close to the basket. Hits those big metal things that hold up the whole backboard, right? *The whole goal* comes down. Like, falls off the ceiling, shatters on the floor."

"So he's a little unlucky. Nobody believes in luck."

"He slipped on a dry floor, then fell down a flight of stairs and broke his arm," she said, ticking off the episodes on her fingers. "Junior year, he worked at the Dairy Queen. He was robbed, like, four times. *Nessa, the Dairy Queen had never been robbed before.*"

"So he's—"

"He got his driver's licence," she went on. "His brother bought him a little Geo Metro. You know, those death traps you can buy used for, like, fifty dollars and a sandwich? It spontaneously combusted. In the parking lot. It caught a bus on fire, too." She put her hands on my shoulders. "Collateral. Damage."

"Bad luck isn't contagious," I said.

"What if it is?" She was serious. "What if it rubs off on you?"

"Cece."

"Look," she said. "Zach's sweet. He's just had…a really hard life. I don't think he quite knows how to *be*. So…just be careful. Okay?"

"Good thing I only talked to him *one* time. Overreact much?"

"It's not that you wouldn't be the best thing to ever happen to him," she said, ignoring me. "You would be. For sure. But I don't know how he'd handle something good happening to him. Nothing ever has."

"That's a little melodramatic," I said. "Can we just—"

The bell rang, silencing me. None of the kids in the courtyard moved except Cece, who held the door for me. Our next class was health ed, and we took our seats at the front of the room as Mrs Harriman tried gamely to stuff plastic organs back into a model of a torso. The late bell rang a couple of minutes later, and Zach plunged through the door. His sketchbook fell out of his bag. When he reached for it, he kicked it by mistake. He retrieved it, then limped towards his desk, pausing long enough to smile – a little – at me.

I smiled back.

Cece clucked at me.

ZACH

"Yo," Vanessa chirped. She came from nowhere and slid into a perfect pose, reclined against the locker beside mine. "Zach."

I shut my locker and slipped my backpack on. "Vanessa."

"Good!" She clapped once. "We know each other."

"Yes."

"Mrs Rhyzkov said your name," she explained, walking beside me. "I think she got it wrong."

"Yeah, but you knew my name already. From class."

Vanessa shrugged. "I'm bad with names."

"Maybe you're bad with *uncool* people's names."

"Touchy."

"I think it's pronounced *too-shay*," I corrected.

"Nope. That's *tushy*." She pivoted and lightly tapped her butt with one hand. I must have coloured slightly, because she laughed. "That was my butt," she said. "I just touched my butt."

"I think only grandmas say *tushy*," I pointed out. "Maybe

Southerners. Are you from the South?"

"Santa Barbara. So…technically, yes, though that's not what you meant."

It didn't occur to me until we'd arrived in the main hall that she'd somehow taken control of our destination. I'd started walking, but now she was leading. I couldn't figure out how she'd done that. But: I also didn't stop walking with her.

"College fair is Friday," she said. My response was a grunt. "You're not turning backflips."

We passed a flyer, one of a hundred pasted up around school. Vanessa tore it from the wall. "Have you looked at this thing?"

"Not really."

Day-Glo yellow paper. Huge black letters.

CLASS OF 2103
COLLEGE FAIR

She flicked the paper with the back of her hand. "You see what I see?"

"I see I'm stuck here a hell of a lot longer than I planned."

"Ninety *years* longer."

"So we can skip college fair Friday, then," I said. "We've got, like, eighty-nine years before we need to figure out our futures."

She laughed. Not the kind of laugh I expected to fall out of a face like hers. No, this was the laugh of a woman who'd smoked three packs a day for at least fifty years. Throaty, deep.

I liked it.

"I mean, just imagine what it'll cost in the twenty-second century," Vanessa said. "Probably a hundred million in annual tuition. *Per student.*"

"Not even close," I said. "By then we'll have achieved enlightenment. Education is a human right. You can't charge for human rights."

Vanessa directed us to B wing, and I waited while she popped her locker open. She pulled out the messenger bag and her bike helmet. She rapped on the helmet with one knuckle. "My stepfather says I should earn the money for my first car on my own," she said. "So I bike."

"Because you disagree?" I wondered what that was like. The ability to save money for anything at all.

Another shrug. "Driving seems…less fun."

"Than what?"

"The wind in your hair. Coasting down a long grade." She buckled the helmet to her bag. "Besides, if I got a job, my grades would take a hit."

"The valedictory pool," I said. "Yeah. I've heard about it."

"Cece can have it."

"Not in it to win it?"

She shut her locker. "I keep the grades up for other reasons."

"You've got a dream school," I speculated. "You *are* excited about college fair." She began walking again, and my feet – mind of their own, those things – joined her. "What school?"

"Cornell," she said, eyes glittering. "What's yours?"

"My dream school? I...don't have one." Suddenly I didn't want to have this conversation any more. "I hear Santa Barbara's really nice. I hear a lot of famous people live there."

"Katy Perry had sleepovers at my house." She lowered her voice to a whisper. "Farts. In her sleep. A *lot*."

I rolled my eyes. "I can't imagine why you left."

"My mom got married. And here we are."

I walked with her to the bike racks, where she paused beside the most elegant contraption I'd ever seen. "What... is that?"

"It's a Kestrel," she said. I detected a hint of embarrassment. "My stepfather bought it for me."

"I used to have a car. I think your bike *helmet* cost more than it did."

She fastened her helmet strap. "Do you ride?"

"I don't."

"Hey…" She looked at the empty bus lanes. "Did I make you miss your bus?"

"No, I walk."

She blinked. Palmer Rankin wasn't exactly in the heart of Orilly. "Is it a long way?"

"It's not bad."

"How far to your house?"

"I'm not going home. I have one of those things. A…job, I think you call it?" I was mildly amused by her discomfort. She was different right then, which made me wonder how much of the sliding-up-to-the-locker thing had been an act. "Don't forget your mirror," I added.

She touched the folded mirror attached to her helmet, then blushed. "I feel like a walking cyclist-hipster catalogue in front of you."

"You'd have to be wearing bike shorts under your clothes to achieve that," I said. She looked mortified. "You are, aren't you. You're totally wearing spandex shorts under your clothes. Were you just planning to strip down right here in front of—" The turn of her smile said it all. "I get it. You're fucking with me."

"You're an easy target." She threw a leg over her bike. "See you at college fair, yeah?"

"Next century," I said. "Sure."

"Grammatical *atrocities*!" she howled as she pedalled away. I watched her go, then turned towards Maddie's Market. Though it wasn't far, my ankle throbbed uncomfortably by the time I tied my apron on.

I'd live. Always managed to.

41

8

VANESSA

Orilly didn't rate its own college fair, so we were off to San Luis Obispo. I boarded the old bus behind Cece. Zach was already there, a sketchbook open across his knees. He was working on something serious, frightful: the ocean, ominous and dark, rising up against a little seaside town. The curl of the waves looked like fangs, white and hard and cold; the sliver of moon above like a heavy-lidded eye.

This was a boy who needed some cheering up. As I passed him by, I tapped the tip of his nose with my fingertip. "Boop."

He flinched, then gave me a shaky smile.

By the time the bus chugged out of the parking lot, Cece was prioritizing the schools she planned to visit at the fair. I bumped her elbow – I'm a pest when I'm bored, what can I say? – and sent her pen looping across the page.

"*Stop* that," she chided. "I'm busy."

"You've already gone over that list fifty times."

"Listen, just because some of us have safety schools and backup plans…"

"Don't start," I warned. "Anyway, you can't work. We have to talk."

She shook her head, still bent over her list. "No, we don't."

"Yes. I think you're not telling me something. So we do."

At that, she did look up. Her cheeks had flushed pink. "No," she began, but I cut her off.

"You know exactly what I'm talking about. Couple of days ago. You had this – I don't know. This *look*. So let's hear it. What's the big secret?"

"I don't have a secret."

I tapped a finger against my chin and stared thoughtfully at the ceiling. "High school girl…easily embarrassed. Has a secret but can't confess it. I mean, there's only one thing it could be."

She caved remarkably quickly. With a look left and right, she said, "You can't tell *anyone*."

"We're on a bus full of kids. Nobody here knows how to keep their mouth shut."

"Forget it, then."

"Except me. Spill it."

"No."

"Fine," I said. I raised my voice: "Cecily Vasquez, you have a crush, and if you don't—"

"*Knock it off*," she hissed. When she was certain nobody was paying attention, she curled back the cover of her notebook, like a poker player on TV. Written over and over on page after page was a single name.

Ada Lin.

Oh my god, I mouthed.

I know, Cece mouthed back. *I don't know.*

I mean, she's beautiful.

"She *is,* isn't she?" Cece whispered, breaking our silence. Her voice was so soft I could barely hear her over the rumble of the bus. "She's my partner in AP English. I start sweating any time she looks at me."

"Does she know?"

"No." She blanched. "I don't know."

"Maybe when you look like Ada, you just assume everybody's into you." I raised my butt off the seat and peered over the head of the boy in front of me. "Is she on our bus?"

"Sit down. Right now."

I did, grinning. "She is. She's on our bus."

"She's not."

"She's sitting right next to Zach."

Cece sighed. "Well, there goes *your* crush. Sorry about that."

"My crush?"

"Yeah. He'll have eyes only for her by the time we get to SLO."

"Wait. My *crush?*"

She laughed at me. "You forget how well I know you."

Cece and I had met at Aaron's company barbecue last summer. As he'd taken Mom around, making introductions, I'd searched for faces my age. There had been plenty of kids: playing Frisbee, knocking a volleyball around. But I'd spotted a girl beneath a sprawling oak, reading a book. I'd sucked in a deep breath and tried to be confident, like Mom.

"You're Mr Bartlett's new wife's kid," the girl said, after I'd introduced myself.

"That's my name. It was a little hard to fit on the birth certificate," I said. "And even harder to time travel in order to make it happen. But I pulled it off."

"You're a smart-ass," she said. "That's too bad."

"Why?" I blurted.

She shrugged. "One smart-ass is the limit to every friendship. If both people qualify…"

"You're messing with me."

"I am."

I sank to the grass. "I'm Vanessa. Which is your parent?"

"Like you know anybody here."

"I don't," I confessed.

"Then it doesn't really matter." She put out her hand. "I'm Cecily Vasquez. Ernesto's my dad."

"Is your dad a lawyer, too?" I asked. Aaron was Bernaco Oil's in-house counsel.

"Just your average hard hat."

She was reading a book about the Supreme Court. Not exactly summer reading, I thought. "But you're into law?"

She shrugged. "I'm into a lot of things. Law's one of them. You?"

"Space."

"Going?"

"Looking." I leaned forward until I was uncomfortably close to her and stared.

She pulled back. "What are you doing?"

"Looking," I said. "I like your eyes. They're like Japanese pears."

"You're a serial killer."

I mimed plucking and eating one of her eyes, and, happily, she laughed. We'd hung out the rest of the summer, and through Cece I'd met a few dozen seniors before the school year began.

And now here we were, on a bus to college fair, our respective crushes possibly crushing on each other.

"I don't know what it is," I admitted to her. "Zach's... interesting. Like you."

"I think we're both idiots," Cece said. "High school's almost over. Afterwards, you're off to New York. I'm off to..."

"Harvard. Columbia. Alpaca college."

"That's not a thing."

"Might be."

"It's not. I promise."

"Takes all kinds of people to make a world, Cece."

"My *point*," she continued, "is that we'd be stupid to *act* on our crushes. I can't exactly see Ada at law school. Or Zach at Cornell."

"So we'd be signing up for heartbreak. That's your point?"

An emphatic nod. "I say we focus on college. Ignore them both. Let Zach fall for Ada. That's probably happened already, actually. We just move on and preserve our exciting futures."

"I dunno," I said, casting another glance towards Zach. "I'm...intrigued."

Cece grabbed my arm. "Don't go towards the light, Vanessa."

"Whatever. You're intrigued, too."

She deflated. "It's true." Then her eyes narrowed, and she said, "Subject change: You're a moron."

"*What?*"

"You *have* to have a safety school. At least one."

The bus lurched to a stop in front of the Madonna Expo Centre, and my stomach swayed. "Tell me something nice," I said. "I am nerv."

Cece thought for a moment. "Less than a hundred yards from here sits a Cornell goddess who wishes to talk to you, and only you."

47

I buried my face in Cece's dark hair. "More."

"Someone," she went on, "from the very halls where Carl Sagan once walked –"

"Dr Sagan," I corrected.

" – from the school where the mythic, *mighty* Dr Sagan once enlightened the unwashed peoples of the world," she continued, "stands just inside this hallowed hall, waiting to sweep you away to the sparkling green hills of Ithaca, land of starstuff, where you, too, will navigate the solar tides in your sturdy Viking longboat—"

"Okay," I said, lifting my head. "You're overdoing it."

"Good. I was running out of purple words."

"They'll want me, right?"

She wrinkled her nose. "Well…you are more emotionally flimsy than their usual applicants…"

I thumped her shoulder. "*Right?*"

"I promise they'll save a brochure for you," Cece said, standing up. "A postcard, at least."

9

ZACH

Oh, man, did I ever not want to be at a college fair.

I'd barely had time to take in the layout of the expo centre before I was swept along by a river of students rushing from booth to booth. The safest place in the building, I soon learned, seemed to be the outer track, far from the booths themselves, and I aimed my feet and held my breath and – eventually – washed ashore there. My only company on that narrow beach were the teachers and parent chaperones from a dozen different high schools. A man in a tracksuit looked me up and down, then looked away.

Yeah, I wouldn't have bothered with me, either.

The sidelines offered a better view of the presentation floor: a flotilla of college booths sprawled beneath a complicated sky of catwalks and lighting grids. A banner dangled high above: CENTRAL COAST COLLEGE FAIR – WELCOME CLASS OF 2013.

I spotted Vanessa and Cece as they entered the stream. They split up quickly, Vanessa rising on her toes to scan the booth banners. Cece appeared to be driven by two competing interests: the list in her hands and the bobbing head of the girl she seemed to be following, not inconspicuously. I recognized the girl: she was my seatmate from the bus. Ada something.

"You're not going to map your future from the sidelines," a voice said, and I turned to see the tracksuited man studying me again.

"What?"

"I said you're not going to map your future from the sidelines." He nodded towards the crowded floor, framing the view with two hands, like a cinematographer. "Your future's out there."

Sigh. "Thanks," I said, wondering if I could put some distance between me and this guy. He nodded curtly and wore a satisfied smile, as if proud he'd set me on the right path.

The college fair wasn't explicitly a mandatory event... but it was definitely more than a suggestion. I'd tried arguing with Ms Grace that I had no plans for college. She'd suggested we talk to my brother...and I really didn't want him getting the idea of college in his head, so I caved. And wound up here, where I couldn't be more out of my depth.

Vanessa and Cece, they belonged at a place like this. Those girls couldn't be more unalike – Vanessa's family had money, judging by her bicycle, and she'd probably get to go anywhere she wanted; Cece was more like me, from the kind of family where everyone had calluses on their hands as they passed food around the dinner table – but they were both wickedly smart. Money or not, they'd both be in college soon. Graduate top of their class. Line up six-figure jobs.

It wasn't that way for me. And it wasn't that I wasn't smart. I was smart enough. But that didn't factor into it. Things were different. Because my family needed me. Needed me at *home*. All hands on deck, so to speak.

I let the current carry me around the building, taking in the booths that represented futures completely out of my reach: Harvard, Yale, Princeton. All the California schools: UCSB, UCLA, UC Berk, UC Davis, USC, Stanford, Cal State, San Diego State… Even the schools I'd never heard of were walled-off paths.

Ms Grace thought I didn't care about college. But that wasn't it, either. If things were different… But I had reasons to put college out of my mind right from the start. If she'd asked, I'd have told her why I wasn't going to college. I had a whole list.

1. College costs a hell of a lot of money.

2. College = staggering debt. For, like, *years*.

3. College ≠ guaranteed job. So you get to live with that debt. Forever.

But those are just the practical reasons. The real reasons I can't go to college have names. Rachael. Robin. Mama.

Even Derek. If they didn't need me, if they didn't need every extra digit I could add to my pay cheque, then yeah, things could be different. I'd let myself think about college then. Hell, it wasn't even like I'd have to actually *go*. I could just *imagine* it. I could join in the hallway conversations I heard every day: *What college did you get into? No WAY.* The other kids thrilled at the idea of leaving Orilly. They were all straining at their leashes. They'd all caught a whiff of that impending freedom, the freedom that would land on them with a jolt as soon as they walked the stage at graduation.

Just to feel those things myself – that could almost be enough. A guy could live a lifetime in a moment of feeling like that. Come back to your body feeling like, for just a second, you'd been somewhere else. Been some*one* else. A second of feeling like that could probably float a guy for years.

But college wasn't real. Derek had gone, for a flicker of a moment. He got out, started a life. And then Orilly, like a strong current, dragged him right back.

Orilly's like that.

Well, for some of us.

10

VANESSA

Locating Cornell's booth took *forever*.

It was in the eleventh row of schools. Eleven rows of booth after booth after booth, half of them deceptively tinted burgundy. The arteries of the expo centre's aisles thick with students. I felt like Theseus, struggling through the labyrinth. But at last I'd found my minotaur: row eleven, booth 3,472,041.

Along the way, it had been impossible to miss Cece. She flitted from one school to the next, scooping up brochures and cramming them into her bag, then hurrying after Ada. I found Ada's poise startling. She moved through the crowd with excellent posture, shoulders slim and high and strong, eyes patient and glittering. Cece had very good taste, I had to say, but it was hard to imagine a world in which Ada would ever go for a girl like Cece. Where Ada was practically ready for the red carpet of the world, Cece was already stooped beneath the weight of her bag, lurching around like a mad scientist's henchwoman. Much as I loved Cece,

Ada was simply beyond the girl's reach.

Watching Ada move so confidently through the room made me think of my mother. Mom was Asian American as well, and exuded this sense of *belonging* wherever she went. I didn't have that sense of self-possession, that's for sure. While I'd moped around Aaron's house after we moved in, Mom had dived right into our new town. She'd discovered an unoccupied seat on the city council, run unopposed, and won. Just like that. For a few months there, her name was all over town, on lawn signs and plywood billboards. ELISE BARTLETT FOR CITY COUNCIL.

I wasn't entirely unlike her, at least. Though the mirror reflected my father's face back at me most days, traces of Mom were there, too. My eyes were deep chestnut brown, like Mom's. I'd scored one of her two rather winning dimples. But aside from the dark hair, it seemed her Japanese heritage had simply passed me over. I was a quarter Japanese, but you'd never know it. I still looked mostly like *him*.

And boy, would he ever be disappointed – no, pissed – to see me here, standing at the Cornell booth at last.

Good. He deserved it.

Except the booth was empty. I'd briefly entertained a fantasy of meeting someone important at the booth. An astronomy alum, maybe. They'd spot a glimmer of something that would inspire them to throw a scholarship at me, we'd fall into a stimulating conversation about the Pleiades or something, and—

A clatter, then a shout, from behind me. I turned and spotted the source of the commotion. Someone at another booth had knocked over a rotating display tower; they straightened up, lifting the tower back into place, and I recognized the red hair.

Zach started to gather up the brochures and booklets he'd spilled, but a volunteer waved him off. Zach took a step back, bumped into another girl, who yelped loudly. *That was unnecessary*, I thought. I cursed her from afar. *May you always have rocks in your shoes.*

Zach looked as if he wanted to vanish, which wasn't easy for a flame-headed boy who towered over the other students. But that wasn't all: he also wore an expression of longing. I looked past him, at the booth's banner: THE FLECK INSTITUTE OF ART AND DESIGN. The walls were blanketed with student art and photos of the school's campus.

I barely knew Zach, but it was obvious he belonged at a school like that.

His embarrassment won out, and he shrank into the crowd, putting distance between himself and the art-school booth. I watched him go, then turned back to the empty Cornell booth and picked up an information packet. On impulse, I snaked through the crowd and lifted an application packet from the Fleck table, too.

Cece appeared at my shoulder. "We have to go. I can't stop stalking her. I'm awful."

As we moved towards the exit, I slid my backpack from my shoulder and safely stowed the Cornell and Fleck paperwork inside, two tickets out of this rusty old town.

11

ZACH

A girl-shaped shadow fell over my sketchbook, and I squinted up. The sun leaked around a female silhouette. "Hi," I said, not sure who I was looking at. The girl noticed my blinded state and moved to block the light, revealing a second girl behind her. Vanessa and Cece.

Cece leaned forward, inspecting the exposed page of my sketchbook. I'd been working on an insectile oil rig, its spindly legs rising from the sea, smokestacks jutting from its back, between resting wings. Its head dipped forward, jabbing its slender proboscis into the sea, its body full almost to the bursting point. "I didn't know your drawings were so…political," Cece said appreciatively.

"All art is political," Vanessa said. "Isn't it, Zach?"

Cece blew a raspberry at Vanessa. "I'm going to go, uh…"

Vanessa finished: "…see a girl about a horse?"

I blinked at Vanessa as Cece departed. "See a girl about a horse?"

She laughed. "Who knows."

"Where I come from, that means you've got to pee."

"Maybe she does."

"You meant something else, though."

"She's got a crush," Vanessa said.

I remembered watching Cece inside the expo centre. "Right."

"On your seatmate," Vanessa added.

I pretended not to recall. "Who?"

"Ada."

"I don't remember."

"I don't believe you."

I shrugged.

"The most stunning girl in school sits beside you for nearly two hours, and you just, what, blanked?"

"Happens when I draw. Sometimes, at least. You don't know Ada very well, do you?"

"I've seen her around."

"I've been in a bunch of classes with her since she moved to Orilly," I said. "And I don't think Ada sees herself the way you just described."

"Let me see," Vanessa said, holding out her hand.

"See…what?"

She gestured at the sketchbook. "I didn't see what you were drawing." I opened the book and showed her the page. "Ah," she said. "Yes, you were so fixated on drawing

Transformers that you didn't notice the model who sat beside you."

"It's not a Transformer."

She dropped the good-natured jabs then and smiled. "I know. I saw your other one, on the bus. The sea, biting back at the town. I didn't realize you were such an environmentalist. Cece was right – you *are* political."

I didn't dissuade her of the notion. Better than confessing the truth: I drew the things that scared me. The sea, lurking just offshore, like a lion circling a campsite in the dark. The oil rigs, like war zones our brothers and fathers are drafted into.

"We're all environmentalists," I said weakly. "Or we should be. Right?"

"Oil companies are going to drain the planet," she announced, adopting a politician's tone. "Leave the earth a little shrivelled-up raisin, just drifting around the sun. No wonder the ice caps are melting. The ocean just wants to get bigger. *It's coming for us.*"

"Damn the man," I agreed, perhaps a little weakly. She'd put into words what I put into my art. She had no idea how right she was.

Vanessa laughed, then dipped closer. "Yeah, but Zach," she said, "you live in an oil town. All hail our benevolent overlords. Right?" She shook her head. "I mean, my stepfather works for Bernaco. And I don't know you all that well, but I figure it's a safe bet your dad does, too."

I let that one pass. She didn't know any better.

"My brother," I said. "Not for Bernaco. Just one of the dive outfits." If I had to wager, her stepfather had never set foot on the rigs. Probably he was an executive. Nice shoes. Didn't know the heft of a wrench, like Dad had.

Vanessa nodded, then looked off into the distance. Her gaze settled on something, and her faraway stare melted into an almost giddy expression. Fifty yards away, Cece was happily locked in conversation with Ada.

"I think you just lost your seatmate," I said.

"Right on!" Vanessa shouted, loud enough that both Cece and Ada looked up, startled. Cece's face flushed pink with embarrassment. Vanessa turned back to me. "Isn't she adorable?" Then she pointed at the bench where I sat. "Scoot, mister."

I scooted.

On the bus ride back, Vanessa claimed a window seat and patted the space beside her. We watched as Ada and Cece boarded a moment later. Vanessa shook her head, grinning as the other two girls sat together in the back. "That girl talks a good game," she said, "about not being tied down."

"Cece?"

"The one and only."

"It's just the first month of senior year," I pointed out. "I'd be willing to bet most senior-year hook-ups don't go the distance."

As the bus rumbled home, I kept working the oil-rig sketch, and Vanessa alternated between watching me and the scenery as it slid by. "I love it here," she said.

"In Orilly?" I sketched a little skiff on the water below the rig, like Ahab and his men recoiling from the great white whale.

"Like, this specific part of California. This coast." She drew a deep breath. Wind from the open windows ruffled her hair, carrying the scent of salt and sunlight.

"I just know Orilly."

"You've never lived anywhere else?" I shook my head, still sketching, and she abruptly changed the subject. "Giger. Do you know him?"

"Gee-gur?"

"H. R. Giger. The Swiss artist. Have you seen *Alien*?"

"I, uh, don't see a lot of movies."

"But you know movies exist, right? And you're aware one of them is called *Alien*?"

I wasn't, but I shrugged as if I was.

"I saw it when I was seven. My father showed it to me." She paused as if waiting for a reaction. When I failed to comply, she repeated: "*Seven*, Zach."

"That's…bad?"

"It's, like, seriously R-rated. Like, really gory." She hesitated again, then went on, maybe a bit underwhelmed by my lack of reaction. "My mom was pissed. Because I was—"

"Seven?"

"Right. Anyway – the alien in the movie is based on the designs of this artist. His stuff is really…I don't know how to describe it. Like, mechanical, but also organic. And kind of creepily sexy? But gross, too."

I looked at my drawing, then at her. "And this reminds you of that?" Her turn to shrug now. She seemed suddenly uncomfortable, so I said, "What was your father thinking? Showing you that at—"

"Seven?" She shook her head. "He wanted me to take sides."

"Against…your mom?"

She looked away, watching the hills drift by. "It's funny," she said softly. "I don't think I realized that's what he was doing until just now. I thought he was sharing something he thought was amazing, but he was just trying to get under my mom's skin. Jesus, what a dick."

I kept sketching, waiting for her to continue, but she didn't.

"I've never thought of an oil rig as a creepy-sexy alien," I said finally.

Vanessa tapped a metal tube protruding from the belly of the rig, jutting into the sea. Her meaning was obvious.

She glanced up at me, about to explain, then stopped: "I'm weirding you out."

"Only a little."

She laughed. *Man*, that laugh.

12

VANESSA

Back in Orilly, Zach walked me to the bike rack. Cece drifted off, dreamy-eyed, with Ada, lost in conversation. I fiddled with my bike lock and then turned to him and said, "Want to walk?" He looked uncertain, but only for a moment, and then he nodded.

I pushed my bike in silence, worried the spell of our bus ride home had been broken. Then, to my pleasant surprise, he said, "Do you ever wonder, like, when you're old, what it'll all have meant?"

"You mean, before I die, will I know what I was here for? What my purpose was?"

"Sure," he said. "When you're sixty, or whatever."

"Sixty? Not ninety?"

"All the men I know die young," he said.

I wasn't sure how to respond to that. "What do you think your purpose is?"

He shoved his hands into his pockets as we walked. He had a peculiar way of hunching his shoulders, like a turtle slowly retreating into its shell. "I don't know," he said. "Maybe to have a family. Raise good humans."

"That's all? Be a good dad?"

"That seems like a lot to me. What's more important?"

I considered that. "Yeah," I said, thinking about my father, and about Aaron. "Yeah, okay. I could see that."

"What's yours?"

"To name something," I said without hesitating. "To put my name on something that'll outlast me."

"Ooh. Like the floating garbage island in the ocean?" He chuckled. "Seems like that'll outlast us all."

"Ha," I said. "No. I want to name a star."

He cocked his head at me. "That's ambitious."

"Yeah. Maybe. I mean, most stars are just letter-number pairs, right? Like, the most famous stars have *name* names, and then all the others get catalogue IDs. You know the name of the North Star, right?"

"Polaris?"

"Right, Polaris. But it's also Alpha Ursae Minoris in one catalogue system. And in another, it's, like, HD889... something."

Zach chimed in. "Not to mention the Mayans, who had different names from the Greeks, who had different names from the Romans, who—"

"Zach."

He stopped walking. "What?"

"Have you always been this big of a downer?"

He grinned and looked at his feet. "Yeah, pretty much." We started walking again, and he asked, "So how come you're into stars? How'd that happen?"

"When I was little, someone loaned my father a box of VHS tapes," I said. "All these old movies and things. And I found this set of tapes labelled *Cosmos*. Which was this beautiful old mini-series from the eighties. You've got Dr Carl Sagan in this fabulous turtleneck, and you're on this imaginary spacecraft with him, and...I must have worn those tapes out. My father hated it. Every time he came into the room and saw me watching it, he just turned around and walked back out." Zach was staring at me, and suddenly I felt my neck grow hot. "What?"

"I just like listening to you." He reached for my bike and pushed it awhile for me. When I didn't immediately start talking again, he added, "Don't stop. I *like* listening to you. What was your favourite part?"

"Of *Cosmos*?" I said. I thought about it a moment. "There's this part where he says we're all made of 'starstuff'. I liked that the best. My mom says I wouldn't shut up about it for months, that I had to tell everybody we met, from the grocery store clerk to the librarian."

Zach nodded. "So...if you name a star..."

I saw what he was getting at. "Then one day that star will die. It'll explode, and everything it was made of will scatter across the galaxy, and eventually become a part of something new."

"Like little Vanessas, kind of. On every planet, in every solar system."

"Every planetary system," I corrected. But then I felt a little embarrassed, talking about things so much older and bigger than us, on this cracked sidewalk, in this little dumb town. "Is that stupid?"

"No," he said. He seemed surprised at my question. "No, it's not stupid."

A moment later we reached the corner of Higuera and Marsh. He handed the bike over. "This is, uh, where I leave," he said. "I can't be late. For work."

I said, "Bye, Zach," but instead of leaving, he lingered, just a moment longer. Something weird was going on with his face. Like he was trying to hide a smile.

"Yeah," he said. "Um, bye." The smile zipped to one corner of his mouth despite his best efforts to disguise it. He had a nice smile, when he let it show.

After he'd gone, I climbed on the bike and cycled up the hill to Aaron's house. In the garage, I leaned the bike against the wall and waited for the automatic door to slide shut. Even from here, I could smell dinner.

Enchilada night.

Damn.

If there's one skill Mom never developed, it's food.

Not even food prep, just...food. In general. She'd put pickles where they didn't belong. Season the wrong things with paprika. Serve up something cosy and inviting, then break out the fish sauce, or olives, or something else completely wrong for the dish. Since I was three, she claimed, I had loved at least one of her meals: enchiladas. "You'd toddle into the kitchen and demand *chiladies*," she'd told me a thousand times. "You couldn't pronounce the word. It still cracks me up." And maybe the story is true. But a toddler has no idea that enchiladas aren't usually made with Veg-All.

Inside, Mom and Aaron were conducting the usual post-mortem, analysing the day's battle scars. "Two days of depositions, just *erased*," Aaron complained. "Melanie thinks we should switch to a different stenography service."

"You can always re-record depos," Mom said. She was bent over, peering into the oven, waving one hand dismissively behind her. Satisfied with whatever was happening to the enchiladas, she straightened up and said, "I've got you beat. Cornelius Clarke is out."

"Already?"

"Dodged my calls for three weeks, and today his lawyer notified the council that he's out." *Out* meant another major investor had bailed on Costa Celeste, the resort project the city council kept trying to get off the ground. "Just like that."

I stood on the stairs, watching them. They hadn't noticed me yet.

"You don't seem upset," Aaron observed.

"I mean, Jim called it a week ago. Nobody was surprised. But then, nobody's *happy*, either."

I cleared my throat. "Do I get to play this game?"

"Nessa!" Aaron's face split into a wide grin. "I didn't even hear you come in."

"What game?" Mom asked.

"Bad Day Bingo."

She laughed. "Goodness, Vanessa. I always tell Aaron, you have a flair for the dramatic."

"The two of you are positively *melo*dramatic," I said. "*Oh, my problems. Alas! Oh, however shall I go on?*"

"Did you have a bad day? If not, then—" Mom drew an invisible zipper across her lips. "In the meantime, set the table."

My iPhone hummed. I slipped it out of my pocket.

sorry for ditching you today.

I tapped back a reply.

don't sweat it, yo.

An ellipsis appeared in a bubble as Cece typed back.

but i feel baaad. pizza and a movie?

"Vanessa?" Mom said, looking pointedly at my phone. "The table?"

"Yeah. Yeah, okay." I quickly replied:

mom made enchiladas. :/

I slid the phone back into my pocket.

"So, Vanessa," I said, taking plates out of the cabinet. "How was your day?"

"That's right – college fair!" Aaron remembered. "Well?"

I dealt the plates, then returned to the kitchen for silverware. "Well," I began, "let me see…"

"Was your school there?" Mom asked. *Your school.* She'd made her case against Cornell a hundred times if she'd made it once. I'd practically memorized her talking points.

1. *It's a million miles away.* That one is decidedly not true. The circumference of the earth itself is just under twenty-five thousand miles. Ithaca is a little less than three thousand miles from Orilly. There just aren't enough zeros to substantiate her claim. Point: Vanessa.

2. *You haven't even* considered *anything else.* This one is a dummy argument, a placeholder for what she's not saying, which is: astronomy was my father's mistress, the obsession he shared with me but not with my mother. That I persist in my pursuit of the stars, despite his decision to abandon us, confuses her. But it's my life, not hers. Point: Vanessa.

3. *It's not even the best school you could get into.* "Children always want to run so far away from their parents,"

she chided. But it had nothing to do with *best*. It was the astronomy thing. We both knew that if I'd chosen Oxford, or the University of Dublin, or college on the moon, she'd be completely on board – so long as my major was archaeology or literature or anything that had nothing to do with the stars. Point and match: Vanessa.

"Was it everything you hoped it would be?" Aaron asked. I didn't tell them the Cornell booth had been empty.

"What other schools did you visit?" Mom asked, checking the oven again.

I tried to steer the conversation away, but my attempt backfired. "You should have seen Cece. Her backpack probably weighed as much as she does."

"Your friend's got it right," Aaron said. "I keep telling you, these days, you don't limit yourself to just one school. Backup plan, that's the ticket."

It wasn't worth the argument, and it would definitely be an argument, so I dropped it. I finished setting out the silverware. My phone vibrated again.

oh noooooooo i am so sorry

I stifled a laugh, but before I could reply, a new message appeared:

Then another: 🍕 🍕 🍕

DO NOT EAT THE CHILADIES 💀

"Vanessa. No phones at the table," Mom scolded.

I took two steps backwards, slowly, holding my phone an inch from my face. "What?" I asked loudly. I crossed my eyes, mimed furious text-messaging skills. "Sorry, what? Did you say something? I wasn't listening."

Mom was unamused.

I put my phone away with a sigh and took my seat at the table. Without asking, Mom lifted my plate and spooned an enchilada onto it. *Spooned.* I don't know how to make enchiladas myself, but *spooning* one onto a plate seems like, I don't know, maybe a sign that you're making them wrong. Little orange carrot cubes and cylindrical green beans spilled out of the enchilada-thing.

Aaron tried once more on the college front. "You know, Stanford has astronomy courses. I spent some great years there when I was studying law."

"Courses," I said. "The operative word. They don't offer a degree."

"Oh," he said. But he smiled. "You've looked into it."

Shit. "Just to compare against Cornell," I said.

"Maybe you should think about law," Mom suggested. "Just think about it."

"I don't want to be a lawyer."

"Just think about it, I said."

"Okay." I paused and closed my eyes and counted silently to three. "There."

"Don't be smart."

"I thought the *point* was to be smart."

We'd had this conversation so many times, whipping the topic back and forth like a deflated tennis ball. How hard was it for a parent to let something go? I wanted to ask her, but I knew what she would say. *I don't know, Vanessa. Why don't you ask your father?* And I didn't want to do that to her. Things had been good for her here in Orilly. I wanted to have left all traces of my father behind in Santa Barbara. For her sake as well as my own.

But it was hard when she looked at me and saw his face. Or heard his dreams coming out of my mouth.

Well, I knew how she felt.

"Here's the thing, though," Aaron said, returning deftly to his earlier topic. "We can't lose today's deposition. Today we found out that the whole thing might not have been Bernaco's fault. The whole thing might have been a faulty pipe sleeve." He sighed heavily. "I don't know if I can get that witness to say that again."

A moment later, though, we were back on Cornell. "You know," Mom observed, "Berkeley has an astronomy programme." She saw my face change. "What? If you *have* to study that...*stuff*, at least Berkeley is *close*. I don't have to lose my baby entirely."

One chiladie later, I excused myself, washed and stowed my plate, and went upstairs. In my bedroom, I slumped against the door. Carl Sagan smiled at me from a photo pasted to my bulletin board.

"Help me, Dr Sagan," I groaned. "You're my only hope."

The next several hours passed in a blur. I logged into the Common Application, uploaded my transcripts, my writing samples, completed my profile. When I heard Mom and Aaron go to bed, I glanced up at my phone. Eleven fifteen already. By the time I checked the Early Decision box and clicked Submit Application, it was almost three a.m. I fought a yawn as I sprawled across my bed. My backpack bounced from the jolt, and the art-school application slid out. I'd forgotten to give it to Zach.

My phone buzzed.

did you die of chiladies

Somehow Cece always knew when I was still awake. We texted for a few minutes, our messages as hazy as I felt. I'd almost drifted off when the phone vibrated again.

i cant stop thinking of her

she does roller derby

nobody knows it

how cool is that

she has secrets

she is wonderrrful

I glanced at OSPERT and wondered: If I had enough energy to get out of bed, and I tipped his lens towards the impound lot, would I see Zach's familiar silhouette scaling

the fence? What other secret things was he up to when he
thought nobody was watching?

I typed back:

i know what u mean

And slid into sleep before Cece replied.

13

ZACH

I reclined on the couch with my sketchbook. The house was quiet; the girls and Mama had been asleep for hours. Leah had said Mama had a really good day; they'd even talked. "Well, for a minute or two," she'd said, "and then she was gone again."

With faint lines, I sketched out the shape of a building similar to one I'd seen at the art-college booth earlier that day. The building wasn't the focus of my drawing; the lawn was. Bright green, students splayed out in the shade. Some making art, one reading a book about Basquiat.

I was still awake when Derek's key sounded in the lock. He spotted me on the couch.

"Sorry. I tried to be quiet."

I flipped the sketchbook shut and pushed off the couch. "Hungry?"

He glanced towards the clock on the oven. It was nearly midnight. "I shouldn't," he said. But he had that look.

"Did you eat?" He didn't always look out for himself,

and I added, "I'll scramble some eggs."

There were two left in the carton. I made a note to pick some up from work tomorrow night. We had enough on the benefits card. The times we didn't, sometimes Maddie sent me home with food. She never said a word about it, but I knew she'd seen the card. Now and then I'd find a sack of things – canned food, some produce, maybe day-old bread – under the register where I kept my bag.

"How'd it go?" I asked.

"Certification exam? Got delayed." He took a seat at our little kitchen table. "Madsen was out sick."

"You've been sweating it."

"A little."

Not a little. He'd been studying all hours. Staying late to get more time in the dive pool. Certification would mean more money. He'd qualify for deeper dives, more work. Better pay. He was definitely sweating it.

I cracked the eggs into a bowl and whipped them with a fork. Added a splash of milk to the bowl, and a pat of butter to the skillet. I slid open the small kitchen window; the stove had a ventilation hood, but the fan rattled and would wake the girls. "School called me today," Derek said. "Z, you've got to make sure the girls are on time."

They'd missed the bus because Robin couldn't find her shoe. Leah had driven them. They'd only been five minutes late, but I let it go. "I will."

"And make sure Mama eats. *You* do that. Leah can't do it all."

He was wound particularly tight tonight.

"I will."

"How was she today?" He yawned. There were plum-coloured sacks beneath his eyes. He rubbed his face, exhaled slowly. "I should peek in."

"Let her sleep. Leah said she talked for a couple minutes. She said good night to the girls."

"You talk to her?"

The last doctor had put it most clearly: "I *could* help her," she'd said to us, "but it's as if your mother's standing on the other side of the door. Right? Except she's holding the knob so I can't turn it. She has to want to be helped." It had been this way since the accident. There was a Dad-shaped hole in the middle of everything. The rest of us edged around it, tried to step over it; Mama, though, had just fallen right in. She'd always been somewhat…quiet, but losing Dad turned that melancholy into something with teeth. Derek said once it was like she got swallowed up by her sadness, but I've never thought so. Sometimes I'll sit with her, watch her eyes as she tracks something moving across the room, something I can't see. In those moments, it's as if time had unravelled and permitted her to still see *him*: putting his clothes away in the bureau, carefully shaving at the bathroom mirror. A smile flickered over her lips now and again, as if she still heard his wise-ass remarks.

"No," I answered. "I didn't."

He asked about school. I didn't mention the college fair, the art-school booth. I said it was fine, then served up his eggs and a glass of milk. He'd hung his work shirt over the chair. His name was stencilled on the left breast: D. MAYS III. On the sleeve, a patch bearing the DepthKor logo, a silhouette of a diver holding an underwater torch. It was his only work shirt. I'd wait until he went to bed, then walk down the street to the twenty-four-hour Laundromat.

"Next few exams are harder," he said, returning to the previous topic. "They're deepwater exams. For the easy ones, I'll be gone a week. For the deeper ones—"

"A month. I remember." Dad had been through the certification programme, too.

"Decompression alone is nearly forty-eight hours."

"Plenty of time to reflect on your strong performance," I said. My persistence got to him, at last, and it warmed my insides to see him smile. But it didn't last.

"I hate to put all this on you," he said. I'd heard this before. "You're a senior, you should—"

"Done?" I scooped up his empty plate and glass and went to the sink to wash them. When I was finished, he said, "I just wish I could do better, Z."

"You do fine," I said. "Go to bed."

He did. I stuffed his shirt into a plastic bag with some of

the girls' school clothes and went to the Laundromat. I sketched while I waited, the clothes tumbling, the dryer warm and loud.

In the morning, Derek was gone when I woke. I rattled cereal into a couple of bowls, then rapped on the girls' door. While they ate, I took Mama her oatmeal. I told her about the day ahead and how well her girls were doing in school, and listened for Leah. I put the girls on the bus, then started the long walk to school; as I walked, it began to rain. I waited under the awning of the Shell station on Nipomo Street until it backed off. The girls would be on time, but I wouldn't be. That was okay, though: today Derek would pass his certification, and we would celebrate. That's what we do. Celebrate anything we can, no matter how small.

We have to.

The bell rang as I scanned the library shelves. There were a half dozen books by Carl Sagan there. *Cosmos. Comet. Pale Blue Dot.* I picked up one titled *The Varieties of Scientific Experience: A Personal View of the Search for God* and read the flaps. It was a few years old, but it appeared as if it had never been read. Surely, Vanessa had checked it out. No, that wouldn't be true – anyone with a bicycle like that could afford to buy her own books.

My remaining classes blurred together. My shoulders

ached from lugging all my books around. There hadn't been time to visit my locker until now. I skirted the crowd that jammed up the intersection of A and B wings, then halted when my locker came into view.

Something protruded from the door slats.

On the second day of senior year, someone had pushed chewed-up tobacco through those same slats. And over the summer, a pipe had burst in the ceiling, and water had seeped into what would become my locker. It smelled like a mouldy baseball dugout inside.

But the thing in my locker wasn't tobacco. Or gum, or a used Band-Aid, or any number of things I've found in my lockers over the years. This was the corner of an envelope. I spun the combination dial and opened the door. A packet fell past my fingers. I squatted to retrieve it. The outside of the envelope was blank, except for a lime-green Post-it note.

Your future alma mater? :-)

There was no signature.

I looked around, half expecting to see Ms Grace or another teacher waiting with a thumbs up and an encouraging smile. But there were only kids milling about, none the slightest bit interested in the contents of my envelope.

Which happened to be an application for the Fleck Institute of Art and Design.

14

VANESSA

Zach wheeled the television cart into Mrs Harriman's class. I hadn't seen a working VCR in years; in Santa Barbara, my old school had Blu-ray players and high-def projectors in all the classrooms. This antique, unsurprisingly, didn't work.

"Well, take it back to the AV room," Mrs Harriman said with a sigh. "See if he has another." As Zach wound up the cord, someone behind me murmured, "Maybe send someone without shit for luck."

Mrs Harriman missed it, but Zach hadn't. He didn't look up, but I caught the twitch in his posture, the most subtle flinch. I turned around and studied faces but couldn't tell who'd said it. When I turned back around, Zach had slipped out the door with the television cart, and Ephraim was at my desk with my exam. He placed mine face down on my desk, then kept moving. I turned it over. In neat red pen, Mrs Harriman had written 102, not bad. I'd done the bonus essay question for five extra points…which meant I'd gotten at least one normal question wrong.

I paged through the exam, searching. Yep. Page 2: *Name three physiological signs of stress.* I'd missed it entirely. The answer blank was just that: blank.

Cece flashed her exam at me with a bright smile. *105! Exceptional.* She spotted my grade and mimed a sad face. "What'd you miss?"

I showed her the answer blank.

"Ooh," she said, cringing. Then she ticked off the answers: "Headaches. Muscle tension. Also, I would have accepted 'the crushing disappointment of utter defeat.'"

"And Cece takes the lead," I said.

"Hush. You don't even care."

"I don't."

"Well, I don't, either."

"Liar."

She shrugged. "Fine. I care a little." She leaned close. "Did I tell you about my cousin Eduard? Second smartest in his class for years, behind this girl Clarissa. He couldn't ever beat her. Girl was just stupid smart. But in the eighth grade, she moved away."

"And little Eduard inherited the throne," I finished. "So are you moving away, or am I? I just got here—"

"Hold up," she said. "So Eddie's tops in eighth grade, then ninth, then tenth. All the way to senior year."

"And then she came back, didn't she?"

"*She totally came back*," Cece squeaked. "Can you believe

that? Sailed in like she'd never been gone, and *boom*, Eduard's salutatorian. He said he fired rubber bands at her during her speech."

"Little shit."

"Little bit, yeah."

"Wait," I said. "So am I Clarissa, or am I Eduard? Who are you in this story?"

Cece's eyes popped, and she straightened up in her seat. I turned to see Mrs Harriman, arms folded, staring at us. I hadn't even noticed how quiet the room had gotten.

"Ladies," Mrs Harriman said. She glanced at the clock. "Well, since Mr Mays appears to have been delayed, I might as well introduce our video. We're watching the 1993 film *Philadelphia*, which at its time…"

Mrs Harriman insisted on providing a film's credits each time we watched something. After her set-up – "The film was a landmark issues picture, confronting the subject of AIDS unflinchingly" – she rushed on to the part she loved most: "The film was directed by Jonathan Demme, and stars Tom Hanks and Denzel Washington. You might know these actors from their Academy Award–winning movies *Forrest Gump* and *Glo*—"

"*Training Day*, yo," someone said. "'I'm king of the world.'"

"No, no, man. That's *Titanic*. He said he Godzilla."

"He *said*, 'King Kong ain't got nothin' on me.' You're both wrong."

84

"'King Kong ain't got *shit* on me,'" someone corrected. Mrs Harriman frowned and took a breath, but her retort was interrupted. The classroom door opened, and Zach entered, carrying a VCR. Mrs Harriman looked at the VCR, then back at Zach, then said, "Zach…"

"Boy forgot the damn TV," someone else complained.

Zach blinked, then placed the VCR on Mrs Harriman's desk and walked right back through the door.

Cece poked at her chicken strips. "Somehow these looked a lot better under the heat lamps," she said. "Do these look – I don't know – *aged* to you?"

We were parked at a corner table, near the cafeteria windows. I unwrapped the lunch Aaron had packed for me that morning: a BLT on grilled sourdough, with heirloom tomatoes and balsamic mayo. I handed half to Cece, who pushed her lunch tray aside and took a large bite.

"My god," she said. Juice from the tomato dribbled down her chin. "Your stepfather is better than—" She paused thoughtfully. "Are there even any *good* TV chefs I could name? Pick one."

"So what did you and Ada talk about?" I asked. "On the bus. Like, did Ada know that was a date? That was practically a date."

Cece glared at me. "You shut up. I don't need my *abuela*

to hear gossip and get ideas."

Cece's family was Catholic through and through. I'd met them; they were all sweet. And I didn't think anyone would have *said* so, but there was definitely an expectation Cece would get married someday and manufacture lots of new Catholic babies. Her grandmother was old-school and might not handle a different outcome so well.

"She'll like Ada," I said.

"She *won't*. She'll hate her for corrupting me."

Maybe this was the thing about mothers: they raise you, they tell you you can be anything, but they never tell you they've got an idea already of who you're going to be. You go do your own thing, and they quietly freak out on the inside. In Mom's case, maybe not so quietly.

But my father hadn't been any different. He'd just hidden it well.

The night before he left us for good, he woke me just after midnight. I was thirteen, and it was a school night. But it had been a few years since he'd woken me up for some celestial event, so I climbed out of bed, drowsy, annoyed. On the deck, he pointed towards the Santa Ynez Mountains, a pale ribbon on the horizon. Beyond them, he said, was Vandenberg Air Force Base, and in a few minutes, they'd put an Atlas rocket in the sky, carrying a satellite into orbit.

At some point, I realized he was watching me, not the sky. "Cass."

His voice was different. I asked what was wrong, but he didn't answer. The silence mounted, and eventually, the rocket saved him from answering my question. I spotted it first and pointed at the golden thread unravelling skyward.

"You know," he said, "they named the rocket after—"

"The Greek god of astronomy," I finished. "Forever condemned to hold up the sky."

He watched the rocket. "Most people say he's holding up—"

"The Earth. They're wrong."

I saw it on his face, clear as the moon: he thought he'd taught me everything he was ever going to. I was only going to move away from him now. Like that rocket, on my own trajectory. I wasn't the little girl who adored him any more, and he didn't like that. He muttered something beneath is breath, and though I couldn't understand it, it was... *petulant*.

In the morning, his Jeep was gone. It was still gone that evening. By the following morning it still hadn't returned, and I knew. I'd been wrong, though. In my analogy, I wasn't the rocket at all. The rocket was our family, and my father was the satellite payload we carried with us. He simply detached and drifted away, searching for his own unfamiliar orbit.

I'd always thought Mom was still in touch with him. Not because she hoped she could coax him home again, but because so many things happened next that couldn't have happened without his participation: his house was suddenly in Mom's name, and then there was a FOR SALE sign in the yard, and then Mom moved us into a two-bedroom apartment on Pedregosa. She took me to the bank and opened a savings account and stuffed it with money from the house sale. "Now you don't have to worry about college," she said.

"About *Cornell*," I corrected, even then.

I'd expected things to get harder after that, but they hadn't. In the years after my father left us, Mom did everything with me. We took a surfing class. (We never found our sea legs.) We took a scuba course. (We nearly drowned.) We took a tourist boat and went whale spotting. (I saw a dead jellyfish.) We got through things.

Together.

When I was fifteen, she started dating. Quietly, slowly. She wouldn't bring any of them home to meet me. Until one day I opened the apartment door, and there was Aaron. Mom and I didn't grow apart then, but she was more preoccupied than before. I started babysitting, saved some money, and bought OSPERT. I kept a journal, charted all my backyard discoveries. Over dinner each night I told Mom and Aaron about what I'd found: how sharp the moon was, how bright Mars was. Aaron even looked through the viewfinder a few times. He bought a star chart for my bedroom wall.

We'd tried knitting and yoga, learned how to line dance and make pasta by hand, but Mom never once looked through OSPERT, never once saw the sky through my eyes. By then I knew well enough not to ask.

Cece touched my wrist. "Where'd you go?"

I hadn't heard a word she'd said, I realized. "What?"

"I said she's a *bruiser*." Cece had polished off the sandwich while I was lost in thought. "She doesn't look like it, I know. She showed me this scar on her shoulder, from this epic wipeout last season. And there's a bruise on her thigh shaped like Greenland."

"Her thigh?"

Cece nodded. "Her *thigh*."

"What are we talking about?"

Exasperatedly, she said, "*Roller* derby. Jesus."

Around us, first lunch period was coming to an end, and the second-period crowd was lined up at the doors. A few students were still collecting their food at the cafeteria windows. Zach was there, holding a ticket and an empty tray. I watched him long enough that Cece turned to look, too. Her annoyance faded into sympathy.

"I hate that they make it so obvious," she said. "I was blue-ticket until sixth grade. Kids are cruel enough *before* they know you're poor."

The bell rang, and the second lunch crowd flooded into the room. As I watched, Zach returned his empty tray to the stack, pocketed his ticket, and walked out of the cafeteria. I hadn't touched my half sandwich, either. But it didn't feel like the same thing.

15

ZACH

"You know I'd give them to you if I could, Zach." Maddie brushed back a greying curl and exhaled regretfully. "I just don't have them to give."

"Just a few hours," I said. "You don't have to pay me the overtime. Just the normal—"

"Kiddo, overtime is supposed to pay more. Not less. There are laws."

I opened my mouth, then closed it again. She already knew how things were for us. Saying them aloud wouldn't change anything.

"Thanksgiving is getting close," she added. "And you remember how many turkeys we *didn't* sell last year." She studied my face for a moment, then sighed. "Look. Maybe I can do an extra day or two a month. I know it doesn't add up to much, but—"

"I'll take it." I stood and gripped her hand, too enthusiastically. "Thank you, Maddie." As I turned to leave, something occurred to me, and I stopped. "You've got a lawn, right? I mow lawns every weekend. I could do the little islands in the parking l—"

She stopped me there. "Drought. Remember?"

"Oh. Right." She wasn't wrong. I'd dragged the mower all over town for the last couple of years, and it wasn't as if I hadn't seen all the brown yards. Still, even with water rationing, I got a bite now and then. Usually on the other side of the highway, in the hills. Those lawns were always thick and green.

Back on the floor, I split the stock with Luther, the only other stocker Maddie kept on. He took the dairy cases, and I took the produce pallets. I could hear him chucking jugs of milk onto the cold wire racks from halfway across the store.

My mind drifted as I arranged sheaves of lettuce in the damp produce case. Today was Derek's rescheduled certification. He'd ace the physical part of the exam, I was certain, but I knew he worried about the written bits. Those were still rough on him. But he'd pass. I knew he would. Which meant we'd celebrate. There was still a bit of money on the benefits card. Maybe enough for a small cake from the store bakery. Or at least a box mix, and I could make one myself.

Then I remembered using the last two eggs for Derek the night before. We needed more. Butter and milk were low, too. Bread for the girls' sandwiches. Before long, I'd tallied a whole grocery list in my head. If I got half the things on the list, I'd run through the remainder of the card's monthly allowance.

So maybe no cake.

I stocked the rest of the lettuce, then the carrots and russet potatoes. I'd just started in on the corn bin when I heard my name.

Vanessa stood a few feet away, cradling a plastic bag of artichokes. I saw her look me up and down, and took stock of myself: T-shirt, jeans, old sneakers. Apron streaked with water from the produce sprayers. I wished I had my hoodie; I could tug the hood over my head and vanish. Instead, I felt utterly exposed.

"I didn't know you worked at Maddie's."

"I, uh, didn't know you shopped at Maddie's," I replied. And I'd never expected to see her here. Most of the hillside folks shopped at the organic grocery a few exits further up the 1. And Vanessa definitely seemed like hillside people.

She held up the bag. "Mom has this whole 'shop local' thing."

"Artichokes," I blurted. *Oh god, Zach.*

She looked at the bag, then laughed. "Yes."

She'd caught me up in her tractor beam. I just stood there, not functioning. If she noticed, she was kind enough to hide it.

"So this is the after-school job," she said, nodding and looking around. "Must be nice to contribute to the world, right? Sometimes I think I should get a job. I don't have any skills, though." Her face brightened. "Hey, I could work here!"

I just stared at her.

I could almost see her mentally replay her words. Her face turned red. "I didn't mean that only unskilled people work— shit. That makes me sound so…"

"Elitist?" I offered.

The colour drained out of her face. "That's not what I meant."

"Of course not," I said.

"You probably think I'm thoughtless."

"I mean, it was totally thoughtless," I said. "But it's cool." I tapped my forehead. "See? Just made a mental note: *Vanessa is thoughtless. And elitist.* Good to go. I never forget."

She laughed – but uncertainly. She couldn't tell if I was being serious. I didn't let her swing there too long.

"I'm kidding," I said. "Just messing with you."

Her colour came back. She lowered her head, so subtly I wasn't even sure she knew she'd done it, and let out a sigh of relief. Then she straightened up, wearing a fresh smile. "Did you get my package?"

Package?

"I wasn't sure I had the right locker…"

The envelope. "That was you?"

"I confess, I felt a little like a stalker," she said. "I had to

94

follow you after health class to see which was yours. Which was good, because I'd thought it was, like, the one next to yours." She wrinkled her nose. "Your locker is funked-up, though."

"Tell me about it."

"I, um— It's just –" She faltered, then pressed on: "I saw you stop at that booth at the college fair, and then you left so fast." When I didn't reply, she added, "Well. Anyway. I grabbed one for you. Just in case. I mean, you'd be a shoo-in, don't you think? They'd be lucky to get you."

I could feel the benefits card in my pocket. I thought about the cake I couldn't afford. The pay cheque I turned over entirely to Derek, and how it was never enough. I didn't want to go down this road with Vanessa. It would only lead to heavy places.

"So – artichokes," I said.

"Mom likes them. They're so much work, though. I never know if they're really worth it."

I didn't tell her I'd never had one. "Your mom's here?"

She looked around. "Yeah. Somewhere." She dropped her voice. "We're having a fight, so I took half the grocery list and made my escape." She held up an actual torn list. "I'd even rather be shopping with my stupid dad than with her right now."

Jesus. Every single conversational road slammed right into a shitty dead end. "A fight?"

"Mom would classify it as something significantly less...
well, significant," Vanessa said. "A disagreement. But I
prefer *fight*. It's more visceral."

"Or a brawl," I suggested.

"A tussle," she countered.

"Spat."

"Tiff."

I'd quickly run out of synonyms. "Um – hoedown?"

She laughed out loud. "*That*. I'm keeping that one."

"What's it about?"

A cloud passed over her face, and I realized I'd just
pushed her down an unpleasant conversational path of her
own. "The usual," she said. She almost left it at that, then
added, "I have dreams. She wants me to have different
ones." She changed the subject herself. "You're going to the
game, right?"

I had no idea what she was talking about. "Game?"

"We're playing SLO tonight."

"Football?"

"Yes. Throw ball. Catch ball. Hit people. A regular
hoedown."

"Probably not," I said, imagining the cake I wouldn't be
baking.

"Oh. Well, okay."

"I have a family thing," I said.

"Maybe after your family thing," she said hopefully.

"The games always go late. If you do come, you should look for me."

"Look for you." *Wait. Was she asking me…?*

"I mean, you don't have to."

"Vanessa?" The voice came from the coffee aisle. "Vanessa."

Vanessa's face crumpled. "Sigh," she said, and waved the bag of artichokes. "Putin calls."

That made me laugh, and her face lit up again. With a little wave, she disappeared around the corner, and I turned back to the corn bin. Every time I was near her, I felt like a spaceman on re-entry. So warm I practically glowed. I could almost hear the lettuce wilt in the case beside me.

Football, huh. I imagined the scene: cool metal bleachers. Crisp air. Brown grass, dusted with chalk. Her, sitting beside *me*. Had she really…?

No. I shook it off. Of course she hadn't.

Besides: Eggs. Butter. Derek. Dinner. The girls, their homework. Bedtime. Mama.

With a sigh, I emptied the corn into the bin, then gathered the empty cartons from the pallet and carried them to the baling machine in the back room. I glanced down the coffee aisle as I passed.

Nobody there.

16

VANESSA

I rode to the game with Aaron and Mom. At a stoplight, I saw Mom's hand settle on Aaron's leg. I couldn't see her face, but she wore her smile with her whole body. It was in the bounce of her hair, the uptilt of her shoulders. Aaron leaned towards her, and they kissed.

I couldn't remember any similar moments of affection between Mom and my father. Had my father stifled her? I didn't think so. I remembered all the nights after he left us. How I'd climb in bed with her, how she'd hold me close against her neck as I cried. Her fingers cradling my head, reassuring me. No. She was affectionate.

Just not with assholes.

Not for the first time, I thought that maybe his leaving was exactly what she needed. Now she was with someone who saw that part of her, who echoed it back. Was it what I needed, too? *That* I didn't know. All I knew was how easy it was to hate the man who'd left us.

At the game, Mom and Aaron sat where all the parents

did, on the lower rows of the bleachers. Students claimed the uppermost rows, and that's where I sat with Cece, watching the game. Well, I watched; Cece was fixated on the marching band, where Ada stood in a blue uniform. She was a drummer, but not just any: she was the bass drummer. She made the toy-soldier suit and feathered hat look good and wore the enormous drum as if it weighed nothing. Her shoulders were square, and she moved lightly from one toe to the other, like a runner staying warm. Cece was a melted pat of butter on the bench beside me.

"I can kinda see it," I said. "The roller derby thing."

"What?"

"She looks like she could lay a girl out," I said. I pointed in Ada's direction. Cece frantically grabbed my arm and pushed it down again.

"*Nessa*," she accused.

"I bet she's ripped under that uniform," I said. "I bet she could take out the quarterback without trying."

"Ripped," Cece breathed, staring again.

"Oh, Cece." I tousled her hair playfully. "It's cute seeing you this way."

"I remember when she was the new girl. Freshman year." Cece sighed. "It was like she came from outer space. Just landed perfectly. She didn't do that thing you're supposed to do, where you find one friend and latch on for survival." She looked at me. "You know, like how I was that one friend for you."

"Pfft," I sneered. "You're the one who—"

But Cece was off and running. "She came from this town in Oregon, right on the coast. Anchor something. Bend? Anchor Bend. We all thought she was the prototypical Hot Girl. She'd steal the homecoming king right off the stage, you know?"

"But?"

"She was just in her own world. Perfectly nice if you talked to her, but she didn't *need* you to. Seemed like she didn't *want* you to. Whole time, none of us knew she was cracking skulls on a roller rink in Monterey twice a week." She shook her head. "She's *so* not what I thought she was. Turns out she has a big sister. Just as much of a knockout. She's an extra on some show in LA."

"But Ada doesn't want to be a star, I take it."

"No, actually," Cece said. "She wants to write books. She didn't even want to tell me she writes, but she does. Like, she's working on her first novel. Her first *novel*, Vanessa. She's seven*teen*. She already knows nobody will take her seriously."

"Because of that pretty face."

"Because of that pretty *everything*," Cece corrected. "I mean, authors come in all shapes and sizes, right? Statistically, at least a few have to look like...*her*."

"You should go down there. Wish her a good show."

She whirled on me. "Absolutely *not*."

"Why not?"

"Because, Nessa. Because I'd try to say *Hey, good luck*, and instead I'd probably blurt out *HEY I LIKE YOU IN THAT WAY*, and I'd have to live with it. Forever." She thought about that, then added: "Which probably wouldn't be long."

"That whole time on the bus, you didn't tell her you, like, want to eat her heart and carry her inside you for ever and ever?"

"God, wouldn't *that* be nice." She tucked her knees against her chest. It was getting cold. "No, of course not. I figured she was dumb, right? Because of that stereotype about how models are as dumb as horses. But nope, it turns out she's smarter than all the horses put together. And I'm the dumb one for thinking she wasn't."

"Hey. She told *you* about her book thing. She told *you* about her secret roller derby assassin games. She gave you a secret. *Two*, in fact."

"Yes," Cece replied. "But the only secret I could give in return is the one secret I can't tell her."

"Would it be so bad? I'm just saying."

"And *I'm* just saying: The best thing for all of us is if I keep my mouth shut. Then I'll go to college, and I won't have to leave her behind – that's the best-case scenario – or spend my senior year embarrassed and miserable. Which is the worst and most likely case."

"Your best case needs some work," I suggested. "She could always choose to go away with you. To college. Writing programmes are *everywhere*, aren't they?"

"But then she'd find some beautiful writer to fall for. And that would be that."

"Tell me one writer who wouldn't want to spend her life with a Supreme Court justice," I said. "You're selling yourself *way* short."

"And you're overestimating me."

"Someone's got to."

"I don't think you know how destructive overestimation can be."

"And I don't think *you*—" I stopped. "You know, can we just watch the game? No, scratch that. *I'll* watch the game. And you can just go on staring longingly at Ada Lin's very intelligent ass."

While Cece did that, I watched the field. And the stands, and the parking lot. But Zach – unsurprisingly, I knew – didn't show. He'd *told* me he wouldn't, right after he fumbled that excuse out of nowhere. Look, I got that he was a nervous kid, maybe a bit more introverted than the average high school boy, but "a family thing" was a particularly unimaginative lie.

The dude wasn't into me. Maybe not even in a friendly way. Was a friendly kind of *into* what I even wanted?

I could feel a coastal wind sweep over the field. Cece

huddled against me for warmth, our half spat already almost forgotten. I elbowed her gently. "Sure you want to do that?" She looked confused, so I nodded towards the band pit, where Ada – who had noticed Cece scoot closer to me – turned away quickly.

"Oh, shit," Cece swore. "Shit, shit, balls."

"You know," I said, "when I was little, Mom would make brownies. And I discovered that I could roll them around in my palm until they turned into these little balls. I called them poo balls." I nudged Cece, who wasn't really listening. "But that's not what you meant by – and I quote – 'Shit, shit, balls.'"

"Now I really do have to go talk to her, don't I?"

A sudden cheer erupted from the opposing bleachers. The PA crackled, and our announcer reported that our quarterback had just been sacked. Again. "That's four sacks for San Luis Obispo," he said drily. "Rattlers, we're not even halfway through the first quarter. Let's see if we can start playing football, instead of whatever you boys are doing down there."

The Rattlers didn't improve, and by the third quarter, their fans – their parents, mostly – began streaming out of the stands. Cece's parents called up to her from below. Her father twirled the car keys on one finger. Cece still hadn't talked to Ada.

She grabbed my arm. "Talk to her for me. Tell her I'm not into you."

"Not that I'm not perfectly nice," I said. "A catch, some might say."

Cece shook her head. "Never mind. Don't do it. Don't talk to her. That would be bad."

After she left, I drifted down to the concession booth. Marlena, from my AP English class, worked the window. "Heya, Loch Nessa," she said. "I'm about to shut down. What do you want?"

"Cocoa?"

Marlena turned away, fussing with packets and cups, and I hugged myself against the wind. I didn't even notice Zach arrive. He was suddenly just *there*, at the corner of the concession shed, hands shoved into the pocket of his hoodie, cheeks pink.

"*Gah*," I said, clasping my hands to my heart. "You could *kill* a girl, Zach. *Jesus*."

For a guy who didn't talk or smile terribly much, he sure carried his feelings in plain sight, if you knew how to read them. And I was learning. It was all in his eyes. He half smiled, mostly with those eyes. His lips were thin and chapped.

Marlena put a Styrofoam cup on the window ledge. I screwed my face up and said, "One more? If you could?"

She looked towards Zach, then back at me, and raised one eyebrow wordlessly. But she complied, and when she returned, I reached for my pocket. Marlena said, "I already closed the till. My treat."

"Thanks, Marlie." I scooped up both cups and passed one to Zach. Marlena closed the window, and we started towards the stands.

"You didn't have to do that."

"Dude," I said. "It's like the Arctic tundra out here." I grabbed the sleeve of his hoodie and ruffled it. "And you're wearing *this*."

He nodded, then took a slow sip.

"You got here just in time," I said. "Listen closely – you can probably hear our death rattle. No, wait. That was two quarters ago."

I could feel Mom's and Aaron's inquisitive gaze upon me as Zach followed me up the bleachers. I tried not to look in their direction. When we sat down, I made no pretence of watching the game. Nobody likes to watch a slaughter, anyway.

"So you made it," I said. "Family thing go okay?"

He looked distinctly uncomfortable. I'd hit a nerve.

"Subject change," I said. "See those two people down there? Guy with the scarf?" Below us, Aaron was looping his scarf around Mom's neck. "They're a couple of dorks, but they're okay." Zach looked and nodded, but he didn't say anything. So I cleared my throat, and I said, "I'm sorry I ask so many questions."

"It's okay."

"Can I tell you something?" I asked. "Like, you'll know I'm saying it because I like you, and not because I'm a jerk?" He didn't answer, but he turned towards me, just a little. "Are you okay? You look – I don't know. Like you maybe haven't slept in a while."

I wondered how often anyone asked him things like that. If he was all right. Hungry. Happy. Maybe nobody did, but I hoped that wasn't true.

Finally, he said, "Just...tired."

"Long day at work," I observed.

"I keep trying for more hours."

"How many do you work now?"

"Too few."

This really wasn't going how I'd hoped. Then again, what had I expected?

"Okay," I said. I clapped my hands, like Mom did when she was trying to lift a mood with sheer brute force. "What did you want to be when you were little?"

"What?"

"Fine. I'll start. When I was four, I wanted to be a fire station." He looked at me sceptically. "You heard me right. Not a firefighter. A fire station."

He made an odd coughing sound that I thought might have been *almost* a laugh.

"Mom said I really liked that fire stations have bells. And poles to slide on. And spotted dogs."

He shook his head. "So your life's goal," he said, maybe warming up a little, "was to grow up, somehow turn into a physical *building* that a dog could live in with a bunch of people who slide down poles."

I leaned forward and whispered, "Not *was*. Still is. Don't think I haven't been doing my research."

"Were all Santa Barbara kids that…"

"Moronic? Nope. Just me. Okay. Your turn."

"Four years old," he said. "I don't know if this is specifically from when I was *four*, but—"

"It's all right," I said. "I've got to hear this."

"—but I remember I wanted to be a plant waterer."

I blinked. "A plant waterer."

"Yeah."

"Like, a botanist?"

"Nope. I remember this kid who was allowed to water all the plants in my kindergarten class because he was so responsible. And I just wanted to be him. I wanted to be the plant waterer."

The hometown crowd, sparse as it was now, surged to its feet, stomping and cheering. On the field, a wiry second-string Rattler sprinted madly for the end zone. The Tigers offence raced for him, but for once, our boys remembered how to protect the ball carrier.

I moved a little closer to Zach and felt him look down at me. He didn't move away.

The runner was *fast*. He seemed utterly afraid, and totally surprised, to find himself in his current position.

"*Go!*" I shouted.

This kid wasn't going to get creamed. He was going to score. And while a touchdown wouldn't save the game, a little burst of defiance was good for the soul. As we watched the kid cross the thirty, I looped my arm through Zach's. I swear I felt a shiver run through him; it made me smile to myself. The runner plunged forward, crossing the twenty, the ten – and from nowhere, a Tiger rose up and took him down, hard. So hard the boy's helmet carved a furrow in the field.

The two teams took their positions at the line, except for the runner, who still lay on his back, chest heaving, staring skyward. He clapped both hands against his helmet, then held them out at the sky, the universal sign for ARE YOU KIDDING ME. Tapped out, he let his arms fall to the ground.

Zach just said quietly, "Know how he feels."

As the game ended, we walked slowly down the bleachers. On the field, a bunch of kids tossed around a football while their parents stood around, chatting idly. I turned to Zach, and before I realized what was happening, he flew to the sidelines and snatched a toddler away from the field. Four boys went down in a heap at his feet a moment later, wrestling one another over an escaped ball.

"Did you just—?" I started, but two young parents darted over. The father lifted the girl out of Zach's arms, then swept his wife and child away to the parking lot. The toddler waved at Zach over her father's shoulder. Zach waved back.

"That was ungrateful," I said, when he returned to me. "You just saved their kid from getting splattered."

He shrugged. "They don't know me. It's okay."

I heard a whistle and turned towards the stands. Aaron and Mom were looking in my direction. Aaron mimed a steering wheel: *Are you riding with us?* I replied by walking my fingers through the air. He smiled and gave a friendly wave to Zach, who lifted his hand. Mom stood there a little too long, shifting her gaze from Zach to me and back again.

"They seem nice," Zach said. A hollow bang sounded from above the field, and he flinched.

"Just the sodium lights," I said. The tall lights faded quickly, ticking as they cooled. "Can I walk you home?"

"That's okay," he said. "But I'll walk with you awhile."

"What was the family thing?" I asked. "If I can ask."

He grunted. "It's not a big deal. My brother had a thing. I wanted to do something for him."

"But it didn't work out?"

Another grunt. I could feel him closing up again. I searched for something else to talk about. In the distance, a fog formed in the hills, emphasized by the construction-site lights at Costa Celeste.

"You know," I said, nodding towards the resort, "if that thing ever becomes real, it'll ruin this town."

"Ruin it how?"

"It'll be the start of turning Orilly into a tourist trap. We'll get bead shops, a microbrewery on every corner. Outdoor jazz festivals. Farmers markets that are less about the farm, more about the market."

He considered this. "Seems like Orilly could use that kind of stuff."

"No, listen," I said. "Once, my parents took me on this cruise. I was…eight? The ship was *huge*, basically a floating city. In the middle of the night, I'd stand on the deck and look up. My father always told me you can see the stars best when you're at sea. Except that stupid ship was so bright that it washed out the whole sky."

"Couldn't see anything, huh?"

"Just the moon," I complained. "On the Bortle scale, the ship would be a nine."

"I'm sorry, the *what* scale?"

I explained about Bortle's Dark-Sky Scale, a system of measuring light pollution. "Most big cities are a nine. You can only really see the moon, or maybe a star cluster or two. The darkest sites are a one. There aren't too many of those left. I've never been to one. Supposedly there the sky is so vivid that the Milky Way is not only clearly visible, but it *casts shadows*. Understand?"

He nodded.

"Right now, Orilly's a little like a quiet, dark boat in the middle of the ocean. Maybe between, like, a four or five on the Bortle scale. So at night I can see almost anything I want to see. But throw some luxury hotels and golf courses and nightclubs into the mix—"

"And Orilly becomes a cruise ship." But his tone made me think he disagreed. "I see your point – but that's really just about you. Not about the tourist thing." He kicked at a rock, and it went skittering ahead of us into the dark. "Tourists mean money. Money means people buy more things. That means more business at the market, and I could get more hours. Maybe overtime, even." He nodded towards the glow of the resort. "Heck, I could even get a job there. Caddy for rich people who tip well." He added quietly: "My brother wouldn't have to dive, maybe."

And there it was. I saw just how oblivious I'd been. Below the resort, I could see lights moving on the highway. The same highway that split our town in two, firmly placing us on opposite sides. Orilly was a different place for him altogether. He was right: I was just thinking about how change would annoy me, not how change would *change* things for me.

I didn't like the way it felt to realize this. So I changed the subject. "Was the application hard?"

"Application," he said. "Oh. No. I don't know. I haven't filled it out. I don't know if I will."

"They always seem scarier than they really are. I mean, those essay requirements are the worst. What are we supposed to write about? We're supposed to have all these big opinions, right? But I haven't *lived* enough to have any big opinions."

He laughed at that. "You know just enough to know you don't want the tourist trap in your town."

"Okay," I confessed. "That's fair." His laugh delighted me.

"So you already finished yours, then?"

"Yeah. It stresses me out to put things off. I applied early decision, so now I just…wait."

"Till when?"

"December? I think."

He whistled. "That's fast."

"Hey, how did you even see that little girl? I didn't even notice her."

He shrugged. "I saw her down there during the game. All wandering around in front of the stands. I kept thinking, if that were my kid…I probably wouldn't sit next to the sidelines of a football game. All those clumsy, unpredictable guys running around like appliances gone mad. Not with a little girl that size."

"So you just, what, watched out for her?"

He shrugged. "Sometimes you can see these things coming. I do this thing, I guess. I can't help it. I just think of the worst outcomes of everything."

"Ugh. That's so *dire*."

"Mama used to say I was like her. She always imagined the worst, too. She said it was so she was prepared for it, no matter what happened. But I don't even think that's it. I think I just…"

He trailed off, but I thought I knew what he didn't say.

"You expect it."

"Yeah, almost." He looked at me sideways. "Man, that's so *bad*, isn't it?"

"Maybe? I like your mom's take on it better than yours."

"Yeah, me, too. She was smart. *Is* smart."

"Maybe you can practise seeing the other side of it, though. Not just the bad outcomes. Not just seeing everything through such a dark lens." I brightened. "You ever see *Powers of Ten*?"

"What is that, like some teen-superhero-squad movie?"

I laughed. "Hardly! But now I want to see that."

We'd walked fairly far by now. At a crosswalk, Zach stopped and said, "You live in the hills, don't you?"

"Yeah."

"Can I walk with you the whole way?"

"Do you want to?"

"I want to."

"Yes, please," I said. As we crossed the street, I put my arm through his again. "So," I said, picking up the thread where we'd left it. "*Powers of Ten* is this old experimental

113

movie. I think it was made for IBM, or the government, or something."

"Sounds thrilling."

"It kind of is," I said, "but not in the way you mean. Okay. Like, imagine that you're looking down on two people, okay? They're sitting on a blanket, having a picnic."

"Looking down?"

"Like you're the camera, and you're just a metre above them. Looking right down on them."

"This sounds like a horror movie. Do they know I'm there?"

I stopped walking. "It's a concept thing. It's about size. And how big or small things are." I made a square with my fingers. "See, first you see these people from one metre up. Then the camera moves to ten metres up. You can still see the people, but they're smaller now, and you can see even more of the park around them." I widened the square. "Then it goes to a hundred metres, and you can see that the park is inside a city, right?"

"I get it. Powers of ten. Like, literally. So next is – what, a thousand?"

"A kilometre, yes. And the camera keeps getting further and further, right? Soon you can see the whole city, then the whole county. Then the state. Then North America. Then the whole planet."

"That's cool."

"But it *keeps going*. It goes as far away as a hundred million light-years. It goes so far that the Milky Way is just this speck of dust."

"I can barely convert litres to gallons," Zach confessed. "I don't think I could handle metres to *years*."

"*Light*-years," I corrected. We started walking again. "Okay, now the camera zooms all the way back to where we started. The blanket, the people. But here's where it gets trippy: It *keeps going*. Like, a hundred centimetres. Then ten, then one, and soon you're *inside* the people's bodies. Subatomic. You can see a single atom inside the person."

"So it is a horror movie."

"I think everyone gets something different from it. For me, it's like: the further from home the camera goes, the more you realize how big and empty the universe is. How scary it is. Then it comes back, and it makes me think about how rare and precious all this is. You. Me. How many things had to line up perfectly for any of this to ever happen."

"That's nice," he said, but he appeared unconvinced. "For me, I think the camera would never move. You'd just see the couple, and every bad thing that could happen to them, no matter how ridiculous. Like, she spills the wine. That's bad, right? But also: there's an earthquake, and the ground opens up under them. Or a helicopter falls out of the sky and crashes right where they sit. Or – *worse* – they have to pee, and there are no bathrooms. Because all they can see is the blanket. They're just trying to make the best of their blanket."

"I like how your worst-case scenario is no bathrooms," I said.

"I'm just saying, though. I can't imagine *all* the unknowns. I only imagine the consequences of things I can see." He sighed. "That's why I saw the little girl, I guess. Imagine if I hadn't. Those morons would have crushed her."

"Yeah, but Zach," I insisted, certain he was missing the point. "More knowledge – seeing more – means fewer unknowns. More possibilities."

"No," he said, resolutely. "More knowledge means even more and greater unknowns. I'm saying the knowns are absolutely all I can handle."

17

ZACH

The whole way home, I thought about Vanessa's house. *House* wasn't even the right word. Small manor? An estate? The lawn was manicured and bright, even in the dark. There were orderly hedges, Japanese maples. Had there been a koi pond, I wouldn't have been surprised. As we approached, I saw a glow in the open backyard: two figures sitting close beside a firepit. "They're pretending they're just reclining with a bottle of wine," Vanessa confided, "but really they're watching us." As she said this, one of the figures raised a glass. I waved back, sort of.

At home, Mama's door was open. Leah sat on the corner of Mama's bed. I slipped into the room, and for a flicker of a moment, I thought Mama saw me. But it was just the light. I put my hand on her cheek and kissed her forehead. "Night, Mama." In the hall, Leah whispered, "She heard you. Earlier, when you were home. She was unhappy you didn't come see her. I told her you'd be back. You'd be proud, though. She was lucid almost ten minutes." She gave me a hug, then disappeared into Mama's room once more.

Derek was in the kitchen, tugging his boots off. He nodded towards Mama's closed door. "She all right today?"

I shrugged. Sometimes it seemed we'd lost both our parents on that day, almost four years before. I looked around, trying to remember if the house had been better when Dad was still here. The kitchen linoleum sagged in places. The crack in the living room wall had grown longer. But most noticeable was Derek's presence. If Dad were here…

"How'd it go?" I asked. "The certification exam."

"Malfunction," Derek said.

I felt the air go out of me. Another delay would only mean prolonging the tension I knew he felt. "What kind of malfunction?"

"The kind that meant the test was over," Derek said. Then he grinned and said, "But they bumped the test back a couple hours and got it fixed. It's why I'm late."

"And?"

Though my brother was only twenty-eight, you'd hardly know it from the seams in his face. When he went a few days without shaving – like now – it added five years or more. It wasn't only the job that did this to him. Worry was the sea we both sailed, never land in sight. But although his eyes were tired, they shone. "You're looking at a Level One certified sat diver."

I whooped, then clapped my hands over my mouth.

He laughed as I threw my arms around him, then patted my back: *Time to end the hug, Zach*, he meant. But I didn't, not right away. "Dad would've been proud," I said.

I felt the muscles in his back tighten. "I don't know about that."

"D," I said. I was the big brother now. "He knew all the risks. So do you. You do what you do, and you both do it well." I winced. "*Did* it well."

Through the walls, we heard our neighbour arrive home: a muffled clatter, the abrupt howl of his stereo. Leah came out of Mama's room and stared sharply at the shared wall, then said, "That man is dumb as a bucket of bolts." She shook her head, closed Mama's door. "He's lucky she's asleep, or I'd go put my foot up his ass."

"He might like it," I said, without thinking. They both stared at me.

"With that," Leah said, "I'm done. Don't stay up too late." She kissed my cheek, then turned to Derek. Her fingers lingered on his neck, and then she kissed him and hustled her way through the door.

Derek held up a finger. "Listen."

A muted banging sounded upon our neighbour's door. Derek grinned. "That poor bastard."

A moment later, the raucous music ceased. In the resulting quiet, I heard Leah's car wheeze to life. "You really ought to marry that girl," I observed.

"She deserves better—"

"Don't be stupid. She knows what she wants. And so do you."

He picked up a pile of mail from the couch. As he paged through bill after bill, he said, "Jesus, it's a good thing my hourly goes up." He whacked the mail on one hand as if remembering something. "I was going to say, Z. You can quit working for Maddie. Enjoy your senior year. Before it's gone, you know?"

"Maddie needs me," I said. *And so do you.* We both knew I'd keep the job. Maybe with the extra money we could open a savings account for the first time.

But he wasn't listening. He'd come to a dove-grey envelope in the stack of bills. *OCC&P* was embossed in the corner.

Ah, shit.

"Lawyers call when they have good news," Derek said. "They send mail with the bad." He tossed me the envelope. I opened it and read it aloud:

```
Dear Mrs Mays:
Regarding the incident of December 23,
2008…
```

Derek watched me as I read on. The letter took a lot of words to get to the point. In short: the other divers involved in Dad's accident had all settled their suits against Bernaco. Dad's case was the only one still open.

"Well, none of them *died*," Derek snorted. He started pacing, working his hands through his hair in frustration. "They're all *alive*."

I read on:

New evidence in the matter has come to light. Bernaco Oil has offered convincing evidence that it was the faulty manufacture of a fitting mechanism on the pipe that caused the unfortunate rupture that occurred…

Derek stopped pacing. "They're saying that? What I think they're saying?"

I nodded, not believing it myself. "They're saying some little part broke, that's all. They're saying they're not responsible."

"*Little*." Derek snorted. "Little! It *killed* him."

For the reasonable loss of wages represented by the untimely death of Mr Mays, the defendant offers a settlement of $52,544. While of course the decision to accept or reject the offer rests with you

and your family, it is our strong and
considered recommendation…

When I finished reading, Derek took the letter from me
and crumpled it into a ball. He threw it across the room,
then pulled open the door and stalked into the front yard,
still barefoot. I watched him pace there for a moment,
and then he just walked off into the dark, down the street.

"Some boys throw tantrums," Mama had once said.
"D's a walker."

When he reappeared, he rested his face on the screen
door mesh. "Fifty thousand dollars," he said wearily.
"Somehow it's both a lot of money and none at all."

"They can't just do that."

"They did."

"So – what, we just accept their claim? Just roll over?"

"We fight it, it'll cost us money we don't have," Derek
said. "Even if we won, we'd lose."

I felt helpless. "It isn't fair."

"World doesn't owe us fair."

Fifty thousand dollars. That was about ten grand for
every year Dad had been gone. If I woke up the girls and
said, *Hey, you can have ten thousand dollars, or Dad could
have been at your kindergarten graduation*, they wouldn't
have had to think about it. The lawyers, the oil company –
they didn't care if fifty thousand dollars was *fair*. They knew

people like us didn't have a choice. Money was money.

"Dad wouldn't have just given up," I said.

"Dad's not here. That's not an option." He slumped against the door, defeated. "People like us don't get options, Z."

In the morning, he was gone before I woke. I found a note on the table:

Meeting attorney today. You think about what I said. Quit that job, focus on school. —D.

Derek didn't often leave notes. Same reason he asked me to read things: he'd struggled with words his whole life. Had a harder time reading than the other kids; writing was almost as difficult. He'd never been diagnosed, but more than one teacher had suggested to Mama and Dad that he was dyslexic. But Derek just figured his shit out. It was what Vanessa's counsellor, Mrs Rhyzkov, had meant when she called him *such a determined student*. He graduated a favourite of his teachers and was accepted into Cal Poly.

So the note meant two things: he felt strongly enough about the message to write it down, which was a non-trivial effort for him; and he wanted me to follow his lead, to work hard. At school – not at any job. He wanted me to finish what he'd started.

In homeroom on Monday, Bryn Bell smiled as I hefted

my backpack onto the desk. Inside the cover of my sketchbook was Vanessa's envelope.

Enjoy your senior year, my brother had said.

All those empty boxes on the application form. I didn't even know if I could fill them all in. I felt Bryn watching me as I rummaged for a pen.

"Here." She held out a blue ballpoint.

"Thanks," I said.

Twenty minutes left in homeroom.

I could do a lot of writing in twenty minutes.

18

VANESSA

"I had no idea you were into the occult."

I looked up from *The Demon-Haunted World* to see Zach standing at the top of the staircase. The library's loft was the school's best-kept secret. I usually had it entirely to myself. But of course he would know about it. I forgot, sometimes, that I'd been here just a couple of months. Zach's been here for years.

I closed the book. "It's not about the occult. How'd you know I was up here?"

He leaned forward and inspected the cover. "Ah. That Sagan guy again. It *sounds* like it's about the—"

"It's not. It's about science teaching people to put aside myths." I put the book down. "I've read it, like, four times."

"You read books that many times?"

"Don't you?"

"I guess if I had time," he said. "I don't know. Maybe I'd rather read something new. There are so many books."

"When I was a kid, I made Mom read *Where the Wild*

Things Are so often I think she wanted to run away like Max."

"I used to draw them," he said. "The wild things. I never quite mastered the teeth gnashing, though. Nobody does teeth gnashing like Sendak."

"You should read this." I held the book out to him. "You'd probably be into it."

He reached into his backpack and sheepishly pulled out *The Varieties of Scientific Experience.* "I'm only, like, two pages in."

"I'm happy to be a positive influence," I said. "Next thing I know you'll be naming the stars yourself."

"Booger. Booger the star."

"You're joking. But someday someone's going to do that – or worse – and we're going to have to live with it."

He sat cross-legged beside me and reached back into his bag. "So…" His hand came out again, this time holding the Fleck application I'd given him. "I could use some help with this thing."

"*Moi?*" I asked, hand to my chest. But I took the application and looked over what he'd filled in so far. It was all the basics: name, address, Social Security number. "You have really nice handwriting."

"I've been writing words since I was a kid," he deadpanned. "You don't have to help. I'm just saying."

The following pages of the application were blank,

except for the first section, *Extracurricular Activities*. He'd started writing something there, then stopped almost as quickly.

"Maybe we start here," I said, ignoring what he'd just said. "What are your extracurriculars? You know. Chess club or computer club or debate or whatever."

He chewed his lip. "I don't have any."

"You don't do anything after school?"

"I, uh – I work."

"Right," I said. "I don't know if that counts, though."

"That's – that's all I've got," he said. For such a tall guy, I thought, I'd certainly made him seem very small very quickly. His face turned crimson, and he reached for the application. "This was stupid."

"No, no," I said. "Hey. It's not stupid. Okay? We'll come back to this part." I held the application tightly and scanned down the page. "Next thing it wants is…okay. 'Honours, awards, or distinctions.'"

He hesitated. "I won first prize in a county art thing once."

"That's *perfect*," I exclaimed. *Whoa, Vanessa. Dial it back.* "When was that?"

"Seventh grade? I think."

Oh. Gently, I said, "I think they, uh, probably mean high school things."

His shoulders slumped. "Of course. Right."

"Honour roll counts, anything like that," I prompted. "Citizenship, attendance, all those nitpicky little things."

He reached for the paper again. "I'm wasting your time."

"Zach, it's fine," I said. "Really. I want to help. It's easy stuff – it isn't a big deal."

"Forget it."

He grasped the corner of the paper and wouldn't let go, and I pulled too hard, and just like that, I'd ripped the application in half.

"No!" I squeaked. "Ah, shit. Shit. Zach, I'm sorry, I didn't mean—"

His expression changed, and I recognized it: he'd had the same look on his face at the football game, when our player sprinted the whole length of the field only to eat it just short of the goal line.

"It's okay. We can do it online."

"I don't have internet," he mumbled, scrambling to his feet.

"There are computers right here. Downstairs." But he had adopted the posture of a scared animal, looking for a way out.

"Zach, I'll just print a new one—"

"I'm sorry I wasted your time," he said. He zipped his bag shut, barely listening to me, and before I could get to my feet, he was on the stairs. I went to the railing and looked down. He jogged across the first floor, towards the library doors.

"Zach, come on," I called after him, prompting a sharp stare from the librarian. But he was gone. Just like that.

"Nothing?"

Cece held up empty palms. We were in A wing, near Zach's locker.

"Maybe he ditched," she said.

I'd printed a new application from the Fleck website. Zach's torn copy was in my bag. "God, I feel awful."

"For what? You were trying to help."

"It's like – we go to the same school, but I must seem like I'm from Io."

"Mars," Cece said. "Most people would say Mars."

"Io's way weirder," I said distractedly. "*Cece.* What do I *do*?"

She put her hands on my shoulders. "Recite after me."

"What?"

"Do it."

Sigh. "Fine."

"My name is Vanessa…" she began.

"My name is Vanessa."

"…and I'm a manic pixie dream girl."

I blinked. "I am *not*."

"You can't just *save* him. You know that, right?"

I didn't answer. She wasn't taking this seriously. And I felt like I was going to crack open.

She noticed and put her arms around me. "You like him. I know."

I dropped my head onto her shoulder. "Tell me I'm not horrible."

"You are mostly not horrible," she said. But then, abruptly, she dropped her arms to her sides and stepped away. I almost fell over. When I looked up to ask what the hell that was about, I saw why: Ada was standing there.

"Hi," I said. Cece had gone rigid. Something had to be said, so I put my hand on Cece's shoulder. "Ada," I began. "Cece has a crush."

Ada looked at me. I swear even I felt a little quiver in my heart area. "On me," she said matter-of-factly. "Yes. I know."

Cece's hard swallow was audible. "Wait, what?"

"She knows," I said. "That's a good thing."

Ada ignored me. "Do you like hot dogs?"

Cece definitely was not a hot-dog person, but she nodded. Vigorously.

"There's a food-cart guy. At the roller rink."

Cece tilted her head. "A food-dog hot-cart rink guy."

I flicked her shoulder. "She's asking you *out*, doofus."

Her eyes flew wide. "What?" She looked at me, startled, then at Ada. "What you're what what?"

"I have a match tonight." Ada was utterly calm. "It's not dinner and a movie."

"More like a wrestling match and a beer," I pointed out, but neither of them were listening any more.

"Yes, okay yes," Cece babbled. "Wait how where?"

Ada smiled at Cece, who *wobbled*. I put my hands on her shoulders to steady her. "My dad and I will pick you up," Ada said.

Cece blanched, then looked at me. I knew she was imagining her *abuela* answering the door.

"Pick her up at my house," I said. "We have some homework to do first anyway."

Ada nodded. I watched as she and Cece exchanged numbers, and then Ada glided away. Cece held up her phone and said, "Ada Lin is my *contact*. She is *in my phone*."

"That's not the only place she is," I said. "Cece, you have a *date* tonight."

Her face paled. "I have to learn everything about roller derby." Then she said, "We don't have homework."

"Nope," I said. "You can just come over and save your *abuela*'s questions for another day."

She practically hummed with excitement. I could feel the nervous energy rolling off her.

"Hey," I said. "Focus for a second. Tell me what I'm supposed to do."

"About my date?"

"About Zach."

"Oh. Right," she said. "Well – if it was me, I'd leave him alone."

"But if you were dumb like me?"

She tapped my backpack, where the application was tucked away. "Well, you've got his address now."

Aaron was grilling on the deck, idly twirling a grill fork in one hand and poring over a stack of papers with the other, when I arrived home after astronomy club.

"Something smells fantastic," I said.

"Hey, Nessassary," he said. He saw my reaction to the nickname. "Okay, maybe that one's a stretch. Nessa-lé Crunch?"

"Just…stop." I leaned past him. "What's cooking?"

He lifted the lid of the grill. "Prosciutto-wrapped sea scallops," he said. "And spinach soaked in lemon vinaigrette." He pointed at a glass. "I already started with the chardonnay. Don't tell your mom. Oh, and hey, you didn't tell me Cece was coming over."

"She's coming over. For just a second."

"Yeah, *that* was weird. I told her you'd be home soon, but she just wanted to wait inside for her ride. Her ride to where? She didn't tell me anything. And then a car showed up, and now I feel like an accomplice."

"She has a date," I said. "That's all."

"So I *am* an accomplice."

"With a very nice person."

"Yeah, okay," he said. "You hungry?"

My stomach was rumbling, but I had things to do. "Maybe later," I said. "I have to visit a friend tonight."

"Well, it can't be Cece. Unless you're chaperoning, in which case, you're *way* late. So it must be the red-headed boy. The one from the game?"

"Where's Mom?" I really didn't want to talk about boys with Aaron.

"Council private session," he said. "The wild excitement of local politics." There had been a few sessions like that lately. "Hey, any word from the League of Ivy?"

"My answer is the same today as yesterday," I said, elbowing him. "I'm sure they're reviewing my application at this exact moment."

He looked at his watch. "At this exact moment, I'm sure they're not. I hope they're not."

"All's quiet till December. That's when early-decision verdicts come back."

"You know, I can still grease some wheels at—"

"I don't want to go to Stanford. But thanks."

"Listen, it's not that your devotion to Cornell isn't admirable," he said, "but astronomy and Stanford are practically synonymous. You know? And if Cornell doesn't work out…"

"If Cornell doesn't work out, I'll flee into the hills with OSPERT on my back," I said. "I can scratch out a living. Tan animal hides. Trade them for food."

"Animals *are* food, in case you've forgotten."

"Do scallops have hides? Maybe I'll hunt wild scallops in the mountains. Clothe myself in their…skins. Shells? Husks."

"You're not leaving without a plate," Aaron said. "Heck, take one for your handsome friend."

"Don't forget cups with lids."

"For?"

"Duh. The wine."

"Ha," he said flatly. "Be home at a reasonable hour."

I loaded the food into my bike basket, then sailed along the highway underpass towards Zach's house. As soon as I'd read his address on the application, I knew why he hadn't let me walk him home from the football game. He didn't want me to see where he lived. As I rode, the sidewalks became rutted with grass, then disappeared altogether. Zach's street was unpaved, and my Kestrel struggled on the loose gravel.

His house was small and subdivided. The exterior was bleached stucco. A window was reinforced with peeling duct tape. Chained to the water meter was a rusted gas-powered mower. In one of the two driveways was a beat-up pickup truck. There was a DepthKor parking sticker on the windshield.

I hoped Zach wouldn't be angry with me for showing up. I knocked before I could talk myself out of it. But the door was opened by a taller, wider version of Zach. Same thick red hair, same faceted green eyes. This was the man who'd nearly collided with me in the administrative office.

He looked first annoyed, then confused, by my presence. "Help you?"

"No," I blurted. "What?"

Good one, Vanessa.

"Can I help you?" he repeated more slowly.

In a stupid rush, I said, "I'm a friend of Zach's I brought him dinner he forgot something at school and I brought that too."

He chuckled, amused by my discomfort. "You bring all your friends dinner?"

I held out the containers. "It's, um, scallops wrapped in prosciutto. And spinach."

"Prosciutto."

"It's, like, really thin ham?"

"I know what prosciutto is. Come in."

He held the door, and I walked inside. Behind me, he stepped outside and lifted my Kestrel with one big hand and carried it through the door. He leaned it against the sofa. "Everything disappears around here," he said. "'Specially really nice things."

"Oh," I said.

"You know Z's at work, right?"

I didn't know that. I *should* have known that.

He directed me to the kitchen. "Boy works too hard," he said. "I tell him quit his job, focus on school, what does he do? Gets more hours. He never listens." The oven, which had to be at least forty years old, groaned as he opened it. "You can put those in here. They'll keep." He watched as I deposited one container on the oven rack, then nodded towards the second one. "You were going to eat with him?"

Yes. "No." I held the container out. "I brought extra."

"Prosciutto, huh," he said. He peered into the container. "And greens?"

"Spinach. And, um, lemon vinaigrette."

While he admired the food, I looked around. Everything in the house was from another time altogether: Formica countertops, goldenrod wallpaper, avocado-coloured appliances. The living room was wood-panelled, except where it wasn't. The sofa, heavily frayed. Stacked neatly on one cushion were a blanket and pillow. I could hear murmurs from somewhere else in the house; did Zach have siblings?

"Um – I'm Vanessa, Mr Mays," I said, turning back to the man.

He laughed. "Oh, I'm not his *dad*, though I do feel that old already. No, Z's my little brother. I'm Derek." He fished a fork out of a drawer and sat down with my dinner. "This

was real nice of you. Listen, you're welcome to stay, but—"
He looked towards the oven, where I saw an old analogue
clock. "Zach's closing. He won't be home for a while."

"Oh. I have to go, anyway." I remembered the real reason
I'd come and fished the envelope out of my backpack. "Zach
left this at school."

"What's this?"

"From the college fair," I said.

"What college fair?" He opened the envelope and peeked
inside.

"In SLO?" All my sentences turned into nervous
questions. "There were, like, a hundred colleges? We all
had to go?"

His face warmed over. "Z didn't tell me about that." He
held the door for me as I rolled my bike out of the house.
"I'll tell him you came. He'll appreciate it. Be safe."

So Zach hadn't told his brother anything about the fair.
That probably meant Zach had forged the consent form,
too. I had the feeling I'd just made a mistake.

My stomach grumbled, and with a sigh, I straddled the
bike and pedalled home.

19

ZACH

Once or twice a month, Maddie scheduled me to close the market with her. By eleven, the store was tidy and dark, and I waited on the sidewalk as she set the alarm and locked the doors. She scanned the empty parking lot when she turned around. "Waiting for your brother?"

"No." He was probably asleep, or nearly there. His promotion came with an earlier shift.

"Want a lift?"

"I'll walk."

"It's cold. It's *late*." When I shook my head, she said, "What's that take you, forty minutes? It's a long way."

Closer to an hour, I thought. And I still had homework. Saying yes would be easier, but I shook my head.

"Well, if you're sure. Night, Zach."

Her pickup rattled away, and I kicked along the road homeward, listening to the static of the waves. The moon was high and clear, and draped the coast in blue lace. The sight would be almost beautiful if it didn't conjure such ominous memories. The sea always brought me to the first time we thought we'd lost Dad. Summer 2008. The storm nobody had seen coming. We didn't know we'd lose him for real before the year was up.

Dad had passed his Level IV certification in July. The big money, he said. Things were good. Then a storm spun up over the Pacific; it lasted three days, generated waves some claimed were thirty feet high. However tall they might have been, they were powerful. They did a number on the oil platforms. Split some pipes, started a few fires. Dad was right in the middle of it. He'd been trapped in a ventilation shaft; they pulled him out unconscious, soot-stained, and barely breathing. But he survived. Three weeks on medical leave, and he went right back into the water.

Such a little storm, in the big scheme of things, and it had almost killed him. Seriously? But now and then I wished he'd been hurt worse. If he had, maybe he wouldn't be dead now.

His promotion had come with a raise *and* a bonus, and shortly after he returned to duty, he took us to Gio's for lobster rolls. We rarely ate out, so Mama knew something was up. "What did you do?"

He pointed his lobster roll towards the marina, at a boat with a faded marlin painted on the side. "We're a boat family now," he said.

"What do we know about boats?" Mama protested.

"We'll learn! Put out some crab pots. Fish a little, take tourists out." He hesitated. "When it's fixed."

"Uh-huh. There it is," Mama said. "And are there even crabs out there? Do you even know?"

Summer and fall were spent at the marina, helping Dad with the boat. Dad tried to put me and Derek to work underwater, scraping barnacles from the hull, but I wouldn't do it. All I could think of was that storm, those waves. I wanted nothing to do with the water. So Derek scraped, and Dad tried to show me how the engine worked. How it *would* work, rather, when it was repaired.

By fall, though, Dad was pulling longer stretches, at deeper sites, and the boat got less attention. Dad was sleeping in a submersible habitat for weeks at a time. He was Aquaman with a tool belt. When he came home, he told stories of giant sea turtles that nipped at his flippers or wolf eels that circled just out of reach, flashing crooked incisors. "And sharks, yep," he added. "Bull sharks, the meanest ones."

His longest rotation came up a week before Christmas. We agreed to postpone the holiday until he returned in early January. He kissed us goodbye, Mama dropped him at work, and we never saw him again. The damned sea had tried for him once; this time, it took him.

And with him went all sense of order in our lives, at least for a while.

As I walked, the moon slid behind the hills, and a field of stars winked into view. "They're so far away that, to us, they never really change," Vanessa had told me. "They don't surprise you. They're always right there, even during the day, when you can't see them." Stars, she'd explained, have order. Predictability, permanence. They made life seem small, manageable; I understood why she liked to look at them.

I liked looking at them, too, I guessed. It beat looking at the ocean, which stubbornly refused to give back my father's body.

I ankled into a pothole then and went down heavy and hard.

The quiet rush of the sea sounded like laughter.

I withdrew the unfamiliar container from the oven, then dished the contents into a pan and started heating them. As I waited, I spotted the college application on the table. *Well, then.* That explained the food. There was only one way that application would have found its way here. I looked around, as if Vanessa might pop out from behind the sofa. She didn't, but my gaze fell upon my blanket and pillow there.

Well, now she knew how we lived. How *I* live.

I felt my body flush with shame, and something else. Irritation. Usually I get to set my own rules about who I bring home and when. Which is nobody and never. That Vanessa had come on her own – what was I, her personal charity case? Operation Get Zach to School.

A college application was a breeze for her. She had all the things I didn't: extracurriculars, awards, recommendations. Money. We didn't have those things. No, we came home with split knuckles, with stains on our skin. Came home to notices stapled to the door. Nothing good ever gets stapled to a door.

The smell of the food filled the kitchen, and despite my annoyance, my stomach growled. It was late; I was tired. There was still homework. The thought of good food, for once, beat back the anger, a little. Anger was...easy. Live like we do, anger's always just a breath away. "A crutch," Dad had said, all those years ago when I acted out at school. "Sometimes it finds you. Sometimes you can't resist it. But you don't keep it close at hand. It's the lazy man's tool."

Maybe Vanessa didn't want to bother me at work. Maybe she didn't know I wasn't home. Maybe she was just trying to be thoughtful. *Thoughtful.* She thought I was college material. And though I knew I wasn't, maybe that was... nice.

But I didn't have time to prove this out to her, or anyone.

It was a quarter to one by the time I finished the food and my homework. The application lay there, staring at me. I turned it over and found another lime-green Post-it:

ZACH

I'm sorry ♡

My eyes locked on that hand-drawn heart.

Maybe I wasn't her charity case. Maybe she saw what I couldn't: That I really *did* want this. That I really was good enough.

That I deserved it.

Impulsively, I began to fill in the blanks as honestly as possible. Extracurricular activities: *I work a job to help support my family.* Awards: *None.* Emboldened, I flew through the pages, and then I arrived at:

Please attach one or more examples of your art. If too large, please attach photocopies and/or photographs.

Carefully, I removed my most recent illustration from the sketchbook: the fogged-over bay, my father's boat – finally seaworthy – only partially visible in the mist, the subtle silhouette of a man at the wheel.

In essay form, describe the motivation behind your work. What statement does your work make on your behalf?

I stared at the page for a long time before I picked up my pen.

I wrote about Orilly, about the single, predetermined

path for people like us. I wrote about how Derek had almost escaped. How he hoped I might succeed where he hadn't. *Above the water or below…* My pen flew across the page: Dad's boat, his accident, the sketchbooks he'd left me. How empty our home was without him. How empty I was. *He was my father, and I loved him.*

I dropped the pen. I knew right then I'd never send this application, why I'd walked away from Vanessa in the library. It had nothing to do with my lack of honours or extracurriculars, or even our lack of money.

If I left for school, I'd only make this home emptier. My family needed me; leaving would only hurt them. They needed me, and I needed them – more than I needed to prove anything to Vanessa or anybody else.

I slid everything back into Vanessa's envelope and dropped it into the trash can. Quietly, I washed the dishes and Vanessa's container. I unfolded my blanket on the couch and tried to sleep. In a few hours, everything would begin again. It had always been this way. It always would be.

And that was okay.

I woke into darkness, slick with sweat, my heart hammering.

Derek said my name, and I rolled over on the sofa and pulled myself up. He was at the kitchen table, lacing his boots by the faint light of the oven lamp.

"You okay?" he asked. "Bad dream?"

I nodded.

"Same," he said. With a nod at the clock, he said, "It's three. I couldn't get back to sleep, might as well go in early."

"What was your dream?" I asked. My mouth felt clotted with dust.

"Same as it ever is," he said. He didn't describe the dream again, but I knew it by heart. He dreamed of the explosion that killed Dad, except Derek was there, unable to save anyone. "Yours?"

Water rising in the house, ankle deep, then waist deep. I slogged through it, shouting. The roof buckled; water poured in. I couldn't find the girls or Mama or Derek. The house filled up, and I swam out through the hole in the ceiling of my old bedroom. I'd surfaced in the path of a ship and pinwheeled backwards. Dad's boat, steaming past under its own power for the first time. A stocky figure at the wheel, backlit by a red sun. I'd shouted for him, but he never turned back.

"Yeah," Derek said, and that was all he had to offer. He crumpled a paper napkin and aimed for the trash can. The sigh told me he'd missed. "You go back to sleep," he whispered, and as I lay down once more, I heard him pick up the wadded napkin and put it in the trash.

20

VANESSA

"You're sworn to secrecy. I have to tell you everything."

Cece took a step backwards. "I'm…not sure I want to know everything."

"Not like that." I filled her in on everything that had happened. "– and he's been ignoring me. For *weeks*, Cece. He literally ducked into the restroom this morning to avoid me."

"Maybe he had to pee."

"Cece."

"Okay, fine. Maybe he had to do number two."

"*Cece.*"

"Nessa, you're overthinking it."

"He didn't come out."

Cece clapped her hands to her face. "Oh. My. Glob. What if he's *still in there*?" She dropped the act. "So he came out after you left. So?"

"That's exactly what he did."

"Which you know," she said, "because you hid. Of course you did."

"He peeked his head out, he didn't see me, and *then* he came out."

"So you're stalking him now."

"No. Yes. Just to see if he was avoiding me."

"And?"

"He's *avoiding* me." I needed her help, and she was being obtuse. "I don't even know what I did wrong. Tell me what I did wrong."

"Oh, you privileged pixie," she clucked. "You do so know." She patted my cheek, rather condescendingly. I swatted her hand away. She went on: "Remember in middle school when all the girls were wearing those fuzzy boots everywhere?"

"Uggs?" I hadn't thought about those in ages. I still had two or three pairs packed away in Aaron's garage. "Ugh. Yes. Mom has this photo of me at Disneyland. It was ninety-five degrees, and there I was in capri pants and Uggs."

"Okay, okay, stop," Cece said. "You're just proving my point. You lived in SB then. Do you know how many people in Orilly wore them? Like, *two*. You know what we called them? *Ugglies*."

I didn't like this. Usually Cece went all mama bear when I was distraught. This wasn't that.

"When you can't afford the popular shit, you mock it," she said. "While you were showing your boots off to Cinderella, I was trying not to tell my dad I'd outgrown the sneakers he bought me two years before."

She was actually kind of mad.

"Cece, I—"

"Just…don't. What are you doing with your face? Is that *pity*? No, fuck that, just stop. We're fine. Right now, I get Zach a hell of a lot more than I get you." Her eyes blazed like a welding torch; I wilted in that stare. "He's *mortified*, Vanessa. You shined a light on all the bare spots in his life."

She was right. "Cece, I—"

"I *warned* you," she interrupted. "This isn't some teen movie. He's not your project. You be your own damn self, and let him be his." She saw me try to speak again and put a hand up. "We're *fine*. But I'm gonna need a few minutes of not watching you try to fix the rest of us."

She walked away and took my heart with her. First Zach, now Cece. All the people I cared about had reversed polarity; where we once clicked, now I was forcing them away.

Every single thing I ever needed, I'd had.

Except maybe a father. But now it seemed clear: maybe it was my fault he'd left, too.

What was *wrong* with me?

PART TWO

NOVEMBER 2012

21

ZACH

Days of dread. Dread, dread, dread.

Most dreaded things, at present:

1. School, for two reasons:

   A. Every minute spent in class was another dollar lost. No – less than that, but still.

   B. Vanessa had become more and more difficult to avoid. She was getting sneaky.

2. Work. Tonight I'd ask Maddie for more hours.

   Again. And she'd say no. Again.

Every time I asked her, I could feel her *like* me a little less. Because she'd have to say no, and I knew she didn't like saying no. Didn't want to. And that meant Maddie probably dreaded seeing me, too.

When Derek was a kid, Dad was around. Derek played football, basketball, even attempted track. He didn't work a job. He gave school every ounce of commitment he had.

Then Dad died, and none of that mattered.

We had an unspoken agreement to keep these things

hidden from the girls. But they were smart. They knew things were hard. They were also young, though, and beginning to ask for things. Nothing frivolous, just reasonable things. Robin wanted to join a book club for young scientists; Rachael wanted to play softball. We wanted to give them everything.

A few nights before, I'd come home from work to see our neighbour stuffing boxes into his car. When I'd asked where he was going, he pointed at his front door, twenty feet from our own. Taped there was a sheet of paper. I didn't have to read it to know what it was. "Landlord is throwing my ass out," he'd said. "Between you and me, I think he's going to sell the place. I bet you bunch are next."

I didn't trust anyone who jacked their stereo up to eleven knowing there were children sleeping next door. But what if he was right? We'd have to find a new place to live, and there weren't a lot of options. We'd need first month's rent, last month's rent, a security deposit. Where was that supposed to come from? That, on top of the girls and their book club and sports things. On top of the water bill, groceries. Derek's truck was running on bald tyres and needed a new alternator.

Maybe the neighbour got the boot because he didn't pay his rent. But we weren't exactly ideal tenants. We'd missed a month here and there; it's why I kept asking Maddie for hours. To catch us up. To climb back to the surface, out of this hole. But we were living on the edge of a cliff. One bad turn of luck, and it could push us over.

But there was a solution.

I did the math. If I stopped hauling the mower around town and took a second job instead, on the weekend, and pulled full shifts both days…I could double what I earned from Maddie. That extra money could mean a full pantry. It was the book club subscription fee; it was cleats and a glove for Rachael. It meant I could leave Maddie alone. It meant the landlord's back rent would be paid, and maybe he'd even fix the roof. (I doubted it, though. The neighbour had been right. Our landlord was a walking shit show.)

In this scenario, everybody won.

Except you, Derek would have said.

In the spring, I'd graduate. After that, I could work full-time *and* keep my part-time hours at the market. Even if both jobs paid minimum wage only, I'd bring home enough money to cover *rent*. Rent, *and* all the bills. That meant we could get ahead. It meant money in that savings account. Meant a computer for the girls, internet for their homework. Home care for Mama.

The bell rang, and class emptied. I waited, watching the clock. When the late bell rang a few minutes later, I slipped into the empty hallway. No Vanessa in sight. But as I jogged to class, I glanced down each wing as I passed and realized I was *hoping* to see her there.

Then why are you avoiding her?

I don't know. Because.

That's no reason. You want to see her.

I do.

So?

I can't.

Idiot. You're just going to hide for the next seven months?

If I have to.

You don't *have to.*

Right now I need to.

But why?

Because.

She was everything I couldn't permit myself to want. She had it all, and I didn't. Anything she didn't have, she could get, and I couldn't. It wasn't about her any more. It was about me. I wanted her to have anything she desired – that was true. But I couldn't watch her get it. Not without some small piece of me raging against the unfairness of it.

Still: I was lying to myself if I thought it wasn't about her. Because it was, at least a little. Before Vanessa, I'd kept to myself. Most people avoided me, citing my diseased luck. But not her. She made me laugh. Hell, even if we were just friends, that would be enough. Wouldn't it?

It wouldn't.

It would.

No. You're doing that thing. Pre-emptively throwing something away so it won't hurt when it rejects you.

It's not that way. She likes me, too.

Not like that. Don't be stupid.

Did it matter what I wanted? After graduation, I'd get that full-time job. But Vanessa would fly away east. She had the good rockets, the ones that would take her anywhere. And me: I was like the manager of a ball club. *This is a rebuilding year,* I'd tell her. *I have to invest in the future.* And the future wasn't me or what I wanted. It was the girls and what they deserved.

You're still thinking about her.

I am.

Stop it.

I asked Maddie for more hours. Instead of saying no, she closed her office door. "Zach," she said, her tone changed. "Is your brother responsible? You're carrying an awful heavy load for a kid your age."

I'd gotten my answer. I stood up. "I'm really sorry. I don't mean to be a problem."

"Zach, you aren't a problem," she said. "Sit. Please."

I didn't want to. But I did. I couldn't look at her.

"I'm sympathetic," she said. "In this town, nothing surprises me. I'm just asking: is there something else going on?"

"No," I said as firmly as I could manage. I could feel my jaw quiver and tried to hide it. "I just need to help. I'm just trying to *help*."

On the floor, I dipped my head when I passed the registers. Pat, the sole cashier, watched me curiously. My eyes had started to burn, and I turned down the canned-food aisle. I made it halfway before the tears came, hot with shame.

22

VANESSA

The windows of Maddie's Market were spritzed with fake snow and Christmas messages. I watched as the store went dark. I could see Zach inside, peeling off his apron, and a few minutes later he emerged with two other people. An older man broke away, waved, and headed for an ancient, dented Ford Festiva. The other was his boss, Maddie. She asked if he wanted a ride; Zach declined; Maddie pointed at the cloud cover. Then they both saw me.

"*Oh*," Maddie said. "I see."

"Good night, Maddie," Zach said. After she left, he looked one way, then the other, as if searching for an escape route.

"You've been dodging me," I said.

He didn't answer. He squinted up at the clouds, then raised his hood. For the first time, I spotted the Bernaco Oil logo on the hoodie. Bernaco – not DepthKor, like the sticker on his brother's truck.

"And Cece's all wrapped up with Ada these days," I added.

"Which leaves me all alone." He still didn't respond. "Not that I'm not fine being alone. But, you know. A girl likes to know her friends are still her friends."

He scraped the heel of one shoe against the kerb.

Okay. The more direct approach, then. "Cece says I embarrassed you."

Zach shoved his hands into his pockets, then started walking homeward. Well, that answered that, I guessed. I watched him go, and at the end of the parking lot he paused and looked back. "You coming?"

I hurried after him.

"Your brother was nice," I said. "Your house is cosy."

"Cosy. That's a real estate-agent word."

"What's a real estate-agent word?"

"A pretty lie. Mama was in real estate once, for about five minutes when I was in middle school. They dress up the words to make a place sound better than it is. *Cosy* means it's cramped. They say *alluring* a lot, because nobody can prove it *isn't*."

"I had no idea that was a thing."

"*Nestled.* That's another."

"Shame on them for corrupting all the nice words."

A hint of a smile. I didn't want to take advantage of him, and it occurred to me, as we walked, that he might think I was inviting myself to his house. Again. "I have to be home soon. Is it okay if I walk with you first?"

"It's a free country." The smile was gone, if it had ever really been there.

"Boy," I said. "I really did a number on you."

He looked at me. "You didn't do anything."

"Cece said—"

"Everybody has things they're ashamed of." He shrugged. "So what? It's not your job to tell me what they are. You probably have those things, too. I could make you feel bad without even knowing I'd done it."

I said, "My teeth."

"What?"

"I don't like my teeth."

His brow wrinkled. "Your teeth are perfect."

I stopped walking and bared my smile. "See this one?" I touched my left canine. "Baby tooth."

"Huh. I never noticed."

"It just never came out."

"Does it hurt?"

"Nope."

"What about your adult tooth?"

"I've had X-rays. There isn't one."

"So if your baby tooth comes out…"

"Then I get my first denture," I said. "Can you call a single tooth a denture?"

"An impostor."

I laughed. "Speaking of X-rays: have you ever seen a

child's mouth? It's *horrifying*. All these cute, small teeth, and then stacked up above them are all these gnarly grown-up teeth. They look like little shark people, or something out of a horror flick."

We waited at an intersection for the light to turn. When it did, Zach took my hand – without thinking – as if it were the most natural thing. As if our hands just belonged together. My chest filled up with warmth. When we reached the other side, he noticed my strange expression.

"What's wrong?"

"You're, um, holding my hand."

He looked aghast and dropped my hand as if it were a hot coal.

"No, I – I liked it. You just surprised me." He looked unconvinced, so I reached for his hand and threaded my fingers through his. "I *want* to hold your hand."

He swallowed. "Okay," he croaked.

"I'm sorry, you know," I said. "For the library. I…I like you. You can't have missed that." He didn't look at me, and I just rambled on. "It seems cliché to say we're from two worlds. But – I just like you."

My face was hot. I wanted to crack a joke about something, anything. But I couldn't think of anything funny.

I wanted to kiss him.

I counted the steps until he said something. Forty-four. That seemed like a lot.

Finally, he said: "Cece and me, we grew up here. We aren't really friends – not really, I guess – but we're the *same*." He shook his head. "I don't know. We *were* the same. Maybe her family's doing better. Sometimes, though, I think we exist only to work."

"Um," I said. "I was wrong. Work does count on college applications. It kind of counts for a lot, actually."

"It doesn't matter."

"Zach—" I stopped, remembering Cece's tirade. I let him speak.

"I don't think my dad ever had a dream. Every man in our family just…worked. Worked until…" He left that thought incomplete. "I don't know *how* to—" He pushed his hand through his hair. "I'm sorry. I'm not used to talking."

I squeezed his hand. *You can talk to me.*

One hundred steps until he spoke again. He *had* things to say. He'd just never said them to anyone. So I let the quiet ride for as long as he needed. When he did speak, it just came tumbling out.

"My mama's sick," he said, worry like a current beneath his words. "They don't know what's wrong. She just lies there, most days, staring at nothing. I don't even know if she hears me."

I didn't mean to interrupt, but I had to ask. I had a bad feeling. "And your dad?"

He didn't look at me. "Everybody knows. I figured you

did, too." Twenty-eight steps. "He's gone." Twenty-two steps. "You know about the rest. The bad-luck thing. People treat me like I've got malaria. Or they're too cheerful, or too delicate."

"I don't believe in luck."

"Easy to say. Easy to say when it doesn't *hunt* you." With a long exhale, he said, "You know, last week I got hit by a car?"

"Zach! Jesus!" Startled, I whacked his arm. "Why wouldn't you *tell* me that?"

"I just did." He rubbed his shoulder. "Maybe because I knew you'd beat me up?"

"You got hit by a *car*? What the hell!"

He just shrugged, as if it were nothing. "I was on cart duty. This old guy just backed up, right into me. I figured he saw me, but...I closed my eyes when I fell down. I could feel exhaust on my head. I opened my eyes, and I was just ... underneath the car. Not under the tyres. He backed up right over me."

"What did you do?"

"Well, he drove away."

"And *then*?"

"And then I pushed the carts inside."

I whacked him again. "You didn't tell Maddie? You didn't file a report with—"

"You know what else? I'm one credit short for graduation."

He ignored my consternation. "I've taken all the same classes everyone else has. I haven't failed anything. But there I am, one credit short. I might not graduate." His hand was cold in mine. "I feel like I'm losing ground. Like something's chasing me. And I know I can't outrun it."

"Zach…"

"You, though… Maybe you're a bit of opposite luck." He gave me such a sad smile that I wanted to throw my arms around him. So I did, or tried to. One second he was there, and then he wasn't. Instead, he was sprawled on the asphalt, staring up at me, bewildered. "Or…not."

"How did that— Did *I* do that?"

He put out his hand. "Help me up."

I did, then brushed grit from his hoodie. He started walking as if nothing had happened.

"Years ago," he said, in a low, confessional tone, "I told Mama nothing ever went on in our town. I said I wanted something to happen, even if it was terrible, just to break the monotony." There was no trace of humour on his face. "Afterwards, I told Derek it was all my fault. If I hadn't wished that…"

He trailed off, but I understood. He'd always talked about his father in the past tense. This, I knew, was something we shared. "My father left us, too," I said. "I thought it was my fault. But it's not. And it's not yours, either."

His gaze was fixed on the distance, on the ocean. I was

supposed to peel away, to go home. We were close to his house by now. But his fingers were knobby and slender, and his thumb lightly traced the back of my hand. His eyes were cavernous. I knew that feeling.

"Zach," I said softly. I stopped walking. I didn't know what to say. "I just…"

Something lovely happened then. He reached out and took my other hand, and it was as if he completed some invisible circuit. I rose onto my toes, and I kissed him. His eyes flew open in surprise. I curled my fingers behind his neck, just touching his hair, then tilted his face downward, until our foreheads touched. He shuddered. I didn't say anything, and neither did he. I wondered if anyone had been this close to him. I didn't think so.

I felt like the first woman on Io.

23

ZACH

On the evening Derek was supposed to return from his latest week-long shift, I'd been scheduled to close the market again. Instead, Maddie sent me home at five. We'd had slow weeks before, but I'd never seen her look so grave. I walked home, thinking about the math I'd done. If I lost the market job, the whole equation would change.

At home, Leah met me at the door. "You need to see your mama."

My heart rate spiked – but Leah was smiling. She handed me Mama's oatmeal, then closed the bedroom door behind me. The room was dusky pink. Mama was sitting upright.

"Z." Her voice was soft, a little hoarse. Like she hadn't used it in a while. She patted the bed beside her, and I sat, cradling the bowl. "Z, I was thinking about you."

I smoothed her hair back. "I know, Mama. I could tell." She smiled, and it was like taking a swallow of air after a year spent underwater. Before we lost Dad, it wouldn't matter if the house was collapsing around us; Mama would smile, and we'd know that things would be okay.

"I want to ask you something," she rasped. I gave her water from the bottle beside her bed. "About your father."

My neck grew hot. I put my hand on hers. Should I stop her? I didn't want to see her upset. But I said, "Ask me what, Mama?"

"Down there," she began. "In the dark. Do you – do you think he thought about us?"

My eyes brimmed. There was no mistaking her meaning. She wasn't asking if he put us out of his mind while he was on the job. She was asking if he thought of us *then*.

In that heartbeat of a moment before he died.

Before I could formulate an answer, her hand relaxed beneath mine. I could see her sinking, right in front of me, a woman drowning. Her eyes turned to glass, and then she was gone. But I knew where she went. Down there, into the deep. Where he had been. Searching those same deep waters for my father. She only came up now and then for us, for moments like this one.

We were her oxygen.

"Yes, Mama," I said, knowing she wouldn't hear. "I know he did."

I spooned oatmeal, then lightly touched her chin with the back of my finger. Her lips parted unconsciously, and I fed her, wondering how long it might be before she surfaced again.

* * *

While the girls ate dinner, I looked over their homework. They were only nine years old, and their math assignments left me reeling. Later, when they were tucked in, I reached for *A Swiftly Tilting Planet*.

"Nope," Robin said. "We finished it."

"We got tired of waiting," Rachael confessed.

"Oh." I closed the book.

"It's not like we don't *want* you to read—"

I wasn't upset. "You don't *need* me to read," I said. "How about this? New bedtime routine: twenty minutes to read to yourselves, then sleep. Fair?"

As they burrowed in, each with her own book, I kissed them good night. When I emerged, Leah was at the table, writing out a note for Derek. She whispered, "They're asleep?"

"Reading," I said. "I'll give them a half hour."

She gestured at the note. "He's still not home, and I've got an early shift."

"Yeah." I sat at the table opposite her. "Hey – can I ask you something?"

She scribbled her name and a heart, then pushed the note aside. "Shoot."

"You ever have a hard time making a big decision?"

"You thinking about something big?"

I shrugged.

"College, maybe?" There was a twinkle in her eye. Like she knew something I didn't.

"Maybe. I don't think it's for me, though."

"No?"

"I can't see it."

"In another life I think I became a professor," she said. "I always thought I'd be great at college. Sleeping in the dorms. Up at the crack of dawn for philosophy or something. Crash sessions in the library."

"You went to nursing school."

"No," she said, with a sigh. "I'm a home health-care aide. It's not the same thing." She patted the table. "Anyway, that's me, not you. Do you *want* to go?"

"I don't know. I can't—"

"—see it," she finished. "That's the second time you've said that. See what?"

I glanced past her, towards the bedrooms. "Leaving them."

Leah nodded, took this in. "If it were me – and it's not, but if it were – I'd think a bit further ahead. Ask myself: when I'm thirty, what kind of life do I want to have?"

"It's not that I don't want to go."

"Think of it this way," she said. "Those girls? They need good examples. Best example you can be? Put yourself first, at least on this one."

"I...don't know how."

"I know." Leah looked sympathetic. Then she turned and looked towards the girls' room, too. The house was quiet enough we could hear the sound of pages turning. "When *they're* grown, they need to know they can get out. And if you stay…what will you have? What'll you do?"

We both knew the answer to that.

All paths in Orilly pointed to the sea.

"I think you should talk to your brother," she said, standing. She pulled my head against her hip, patted my hair. "You're a good kid, Zach. A good man. You'll do the right thing."

In the weeks following Vanessa – and that *kiss* – everything was different. Each morning, Vanessa waited outside our house, and we talked until the bus came to carry Robin and Rachael away. As I walked to school, Vanessa pushed the Kestrel alongside. We found each other between classes; we had lunch side by side, with Cece and Ada. We spent hours in the library loft – Vanessa charging through *The Demon-Haunted World* and then *Contact*, me slowly turning pages of *The Varieties of Scientific Experience*.

I never told Vanessa my birthday was coming, so it was a surprise when she appeared at our door that evening. Robin opened it with a knowing smile. "Z," she sang. "Your *girl*friend's heeeere."

I herded Robin away from the door. "I didn't tell her to say that."

But Vanessa stage-whispered, loud enough for Robin to hear, "But I did."

"Vanessa!" Derek called out. "We're grilling cheese sammiches!"

Vanessa held aloft a plastic container. "I come bearing dessert."

"Z got a caaaake, Z got a *girl* cake," Robin sang. Rachael swatted her with a spatula.

"I didn't tell you about my birthday," I whispered to Vanessa.

"Yeah, but you forget," she said. "I know everything about you." She recited my Social Security number. "I saw your application, remember? I promise not to steal your identity…again."

Before I could think of a clever retort, Vanessa said, "I need to use the ladies' room," and Rachael crowed, "I'll show her where, me, me," and snatched Vanessa's hand. As my sister yanked her away, Vanessa lightly touched my fingertips with her own, and my heart swelled hot, like a furnace.

24

VANESSA

After dinner, Derek insisted Zach give me the tour. I'd only ever seen the kitchen and living room. I knew there wasn't much more, and that Zach wouldn't want to. But he said, "C'mon," and led me down a short hallway. The baseboards looked as if they'd been chewed; decade-old water stains decorated the ceiling. But all I saw were the dozens of framed photos on the walls. One, tinted red with age, drew my attention.

I tapped the photo of a cheerful baby wearing a football onesie. "That's not you. Derek?" Zach nodded, and I said, "You're practically twins, though. How many years between you?"

"Ten." He shrugged. "I don't think they planned for me. And the girls—" He paused, glanced towards the other room. "They definitely weren't."

"Well, they're perfect."

"Yeah. They saved the best for last."

The whole Mays family history played out on that wall.

I fell in love with one image in particular. In it, Zach's parents stood in front of stained-glass windows. Zach's mother held him close to her chest, and he gaped at something out of frame.

"You're so tiny!"

"Derek took that one."

"You look just like your mother. She's beautiful."

He wound a red curl around his finger. "The hair was all Dad, though."

In the same photo, his father was broad-shouldered, barrel-chested, with a brushy red moustache and thick sideburns. "He's a brawler," I observed.

"He had presence," Zach concurred.

Zach wasn't upset by the photos, I noticed. That was my first hint that I'd made a grievous error that day I kissed him. Zach's father wasn't like mine; he hadn't abandoned his family. Zach clearly loved the man.

No, Zach's father was *dead*. I felt like such an asshole.

Zach didn't seem to notice. He showed me a few more photos, then pointed at the end of the hall, where a door stood ajar. Inside, I could see the corner of a mattress on the floor. An alarm clock was plugged in right next to it. Hanging from the ceiling, above a plastic tub, was a wet suit.

"Derek's room," he said.

The next door was inaccessible, masked behind a sheet of clear plastic. Blue tape held the plastic in place. I looked at Zach, but he averted his eyes and walked past that room. Instead, he pushed open the door nearest us. "And this is the girls'."

This room could have been teleported in from some other, nicer house, miles from Orilly. The walls were pale yellow. Where the rest of the house was filled with second-hand furniture, everything here seemed reasonably new. Each of the twin beds was made up in colourful sheets – one printed with Disney characters, the other with *Star Wars* battles.

"Robin's into the usual girl stuff," Zach said, gesturing towards the bed decorated with Mulan and Ariel and Tiana. "But Rachael's hero is this Jedi girl. Ah…Ah-something, I forget."

"Ahsoka," I said. "She's badass." He looked surprised. "What? I like *Star Wars*."

He pulled the door shut. All the light in this house, I saw, was contained in that bedroom. I didn't need to ask to know that Zach and Derek had scraped to afford that bedroom set. I wondered if the girls knew how much their brothers loved them.

Zach skipped the next door, heading back to the party. "Hey," I protested. "No fair not showing me your room."

Before he could stop me, I turned the knob of the door he'd tried to leave unopened. But right away, I knew I'd fucked up. If all the light in the house was in the girls' room, this room was its direct opposite. It was stuffy and dim. I saw prescription bottles, a glass of water – and someone lying quite still in a bed. Her eyes were open.

Zach reached past me and sharply closed the door again. "I—" I stammered. "I'm sorry, I shouldn't—"

Zach's face spun through a series of complex emotions, and he opened his mouth but changed his mind. He turned and left me standing in the hallway. A moment later, I heard the front door bang shut.

I wanted to just hide in the bathroom. When I emerged from the hallway, the rest of Zach's family stood gathered around the cake, which now blazed with candles. They looked from me to the front door and back again, their smiles collapsed.

"I just—" But there weren't words. "I'm really sorry."

I went through the door, calling Zach's name. He hadn't gone far. He stood outside, hands shoved in his pockets, staring at his feet. His breath fogged around him. When I arrived, he started walking, and I did, too. But an icy wall had formed between us. I could see him – but I couldn't reach him.

Under other circumstances, I could have appreciated the view. The sky had shifted violet, and sparse Christmas lights twinkled on a few houses. The sea breeze had claws.

I apologized again, but he said nothing. I walked alongside him, feeling like such a shit. He'd *told* me about his mother. And I'd been to the house before. I knew *someone* slept on the sofa; I'd seen the blanket, the pillow. I'd just forgotten, and now I'd hurt him. Again.

Abruptly, he turned left at Ynez; my momentum carried me a few steps in the wrong direction, then I doubled back and caught up. By the time he left the sidewalk and started across a barren lot, a gibbous moon had risen. The light stretched Zach's shadow like a compass needle, steering us towards his destination.

I knew where he was taking me.

I'd watched him infiltrate the impound lot often enough to know his routine. While he plodded towards the fence, I pushed ahead and started to climb, as I'd seen him do. I navigated the spiny bits at the top, then dropped to the other side. Zach stared at me through the chain-link.

"What?" I asked. "I know a guy who does this all the time." He climbed over. From below, I heard him curse when he reached the top. When he landed, he fingered a rip in his jeans.

"You have to go over bow-legged," I said. "Or that happens."

He frowned, and I knew he'd figured it out. "You're a spy. You and that telescope."

"Well, now we're in this together. Accomplices."

"You never thought about reporting me?" he grumbled. He started walking towards the boat.

"I never saw any crime."

"We're trespassing."

"Oh, *tres*passing." I shrugged. "You say trespassing. I say adventuring."

"If we get caught—" he began, but I stopped him.

"Would you knock it off?" I said. "Let me apologize to you, dammit."

He fell silent, watching me.

"Well – I'm sorry."

He stared at me. "Okay."

"Okay," I said.

"Let's go inside, then," he said. "Before someone really *does* report us."

He clambered up the boat ladder, but I stayed at the bottom. "From now on, I'm a vampire," I said. "I don't enter unless you explicitly invite me. I've already made that mistake once tonight."

He *almost* smiled. "Fine," he said. Without offering an invitation, he disappeared into the wheelhouse. A moment later, honeyed light washed onto the deck. Then he leaned back out. "Coming?"

It was too cold to debate the semantics of what constituted an invitation. I climbed the ladder. My feet made *thunk-thunk* sounds on the deck. "It's hollow," I said, surprised.

"Yeah. It's a boat," he said.

He turned towards the wheelhouse, but I stopped him.

"I'm sorry. I thought it was your room. It was thoughtless. I was thoughtless."

Zach shifted uncomfortably. "The ceiling in my old room turned to mush. There was a storm. It leaked. And then it caved in, right on top of me while I was asleep." He looked up, saw the horror on my face. "I mean, it was, like, *months* ago. A year, maybe?"

That explained the quarantined room in his house. "Landlord keeps promising to fix it," he finished. "But he never does. I'd do it myself, if we had the money."

Which of course should have been obvious. That it wasn't only made me feel guiltier. "I'm sorry," I said. I needed better words. All of mine sounded hollow. Breakable.

Inside the wheelhouse, a sailor's lantern threw shadows against the walls, each of which had been draped in blankets to mask Zach's presence. Pinned to the blankets were dozens upon dozens of sketches. Zach sat in the captain's chair, but I studied the drawings. I tapped one, of a boat pushing out to sea.

"This boat?" I asked.

The boat featured in many of the drawings: bobbing in its marina slip, surrounded by the faintest outlines of other vessels; chasing the sun towards the horizon; anchored in deep waters while two figures worked the nets. Often the same figure stood at the wheel, and I recognized Zach's father immediately: the loose lines of his head and neck, the tighter lines of his brow and boxer's nose, the whorl of charcoal that formed his steady, dark eyes. The hint of a smile in his lips. I saw Zach there, in those features.

My first impression upon entering the wheelhouse had been of a museum, but it wasn't that at all.

The boat was a shrine to Zach's father.

"Dad never took her to sea," Zach said. He cleared his throat, as if he didn't trust his voice. "I wanted him to have that."

I turned towards him. His eyes were damp in the light.

"After Dad died, the slip fee was too expensive. The boat didn't run, so we couldn't charter it. Derek put a FOR SALE sign on it, but nobody bit. We fell behind on the slip fees, and it wound up here."

"Do you ever think of getting it back?"

"Only every *fucking* day." He wiped his eyes with his palms. "I'm sorry. This time of year always wrecks me." The urge to go to him was powerful, but he wanted to talk. Needed to. So I was quiet, and he started to tell me the story. "I was like Mama. I didn't want him to have the boat. Not after that storm. Not after what happened on the rig. It was like we both knew it. The sea wanted him, and here he wanted to *tempt* it." He cleared his throat. "And now look at me. I practically *live* here. At least it's landlocked, I guess."

I waited patiently, quietly.

"He was a saturation diver," he said. "Spent weeks in a little metal bubble, a thousand feet down. We didn't see him much near the end. Because of his job."

His voice broke then, and my resolve faltered. I sat on his lap and drew him close. His cheeks were damp against my neck. I stroked his hair.

"But we didn't know it was the end. We loved his long jobs," he said, and chuckled bitterly. "Because he always came home with these insane stories about sea monsters."

"What happened?" I asked softly.

"Some part gave out. Or something broke," he said. "We still don't really know. Just – there was an explosion."

A chill washed over me. What he was describing…I already knew. I'd seen all the signs and somehow missed them: the DepthKor logo on Derek's truck. The diving gear in Derek's room. The Bernaco logo on what I was now certain was Zach's father's hoodie. This time of year had to be hell. Zach's birthday, Christmas, both of them defiled by the awful anniversary of his father's death.

Zach had some of the details wrong: the habitat was only about 650 feet down. A pipe sleeve split, the pipe ruptured, something ignited, and the whole habitat went up like a submersible *Hindenburg*. I'd seen photos of the salvage among Aaron's papers, spread over the kitchen table as he worked. The divers' habitat looked like a ragged soup can, torn open and twisted. There had been four divers, three working outside the habitat, one asleep inside. The three outside suffered critical injuries: broken bones, collapsed lungs. Decompression sickness and its myriad complications.

The fourth diver hadn't survived. They'd never even found his body. Just his dive compass, flung with such force that it had embedded itself in another diver's air tank.

There had been lawsuits. Aaron, as Bernaco's lead counsel, knew them intimately. When the Mays family's suit – the only one still not settled – landed in court, Zach would sit on one side of the courtroom. And my stepfather would lead the case against them.

I'd gone stiff, and Zach had noticed. Confused, he asked, "What is it?"

I tried to smile. But I wanted to throw up.

25

ZACH

She looked like she wanted to bolt. I'd scared her. Said too much, been too vulnerable.

I led her to the deck, and we shared a blanket, draped around our shoulders. "I'm changing the subject," I said.

"I don't think you're supposed to *say* that."

"Like you've never said it. Subject change: you're stuck on a desert island, and you—"

"How'd I get there?"

I thought about this. "You've been on a cruise ship. Real extravagant. Bonbons and virgin appletinis. But the boat sank. And you swam to the nearest bit of land."

"And it's a *desert* island? Why are they always deserted?"

"Because…being stranded is supposed to suck? I don't know."

"Fine." She blew hair out of her eyes. "And what's the question?"

"You can bring only one book."

"My book got drenched. Now it's ruined."

"You lay all the pages in the sun to dry," I said.

"The wind scattered them into the sea."

"The tide turns, and they wash right back up," I insisted. "And you dry them. Again. And you put a rock on each one so it won't blow away."

"What books did I have with me on the boat?"

"Between you and all the other tourists, every book ever printed was on the boat."

"*Every* book?"

"Every last one." The subject change had worked.

"Even the weird ones bound in human skin?"

I made a face. "If you say so."

"I'm just saying, if I brought one of those, at least I'd have a food source."

"Subject change has failed," I declared. "I quit, on grounds of I'm gonna be sick."

She swung her legs over the edge of the deck and rested her head on my shoulder. I could smell her shampoo, feel the warmth radiating from her skin. "You know," she said. "I missed my father, too. But in a totally different way."

"Different how?"

"Different as in I hated him. *Hate*. Present tense. So… okay, maybe not really the same. More like: I lived through the aftermath. I was never *not* aware of what he'd done to my mom, or to me. To us."

"Why did he leave?"

"I still don't know." She sighed. "You know, for a long time, I blamed myself. Mom said it was normal, but then she said he didn't *have* to leave. He *chose* to."

"Your mom sounds killer."

"She is. We were on our own a long time. She wasn't just my mom. She was, like, my best friend. Sometimes she still got all up in my face, and we had disagreements. Sometimes she was my nemesis, too. But if this were a video game, she'd have been my sidekick, not one of the bosses you have to fight. Not even the weakest one, and definitely not the big, evil ones."

"That's your dad," I ventured.

"That's my *father*," she corrected. "He's *not* my fucking dad."

She pressed her hand against my chest, eased me onto my back. Just like that, we were lying side by side on the deck. She was *so close*. She lifted my arm and put it around her, then laid her head on my chest.

"Um," I said.

She peered up at me. "Why, Zachary, your face is as red as your hair."

"Shut up."

She laughed, and after a moment, she said, "This is nice."

"What is?"

"This. Being with you, on this boat. Under these stars."

"You like the stars."

"Mostly. Now and then they remind me of *him*, and I hate that I love them. He almost ruined the most important thing in the world for me." She sighed. "They make me feel small. I used to like to feel small. But then *he* made me feel small, too, and all I wanted after that was to be as big as I could."

"The stars made me feel small, sometimes. Like I didn't matter."

"Oh, we matter," she said. Her voice became distant, a little reverent. "We're *exceptional*. Cosmic accidents. Even if we aren't totally alone in the universe, we might as well be. We're unthinkably far from anything else. We're on our own. Nobody's going to save us."

"From what?"

"From ourselves."

"Oh." Hesitantly, I touched her hair; she didn't stop me. In fact, it seemed as if she pushed her head upward, ever so gently, against my hand. "Do…you feel alone?"

She didn't answer right away. "Sometimes. Maybe. Not right now." Then she added, "I think the stars are what you put into them. An optimist looks at them and feels excitement; they're only full of possibility. But to a sad person, they can be hypothermic."

I liked listening to her, and I didn't want to interrupt her flow, but I had to. "Hypothermic?"

"You know. Like they just make you feel cold and small

and alone. But you know what I think?" she went on. "We're never really alone. Sometimes I can't sleep, you know? And I like to imagine that no matter how lost or different or lonely I feel, there's always at least one other person who feels the same way at the same moment. Someone's always awake somewhere else in the world."

"Like me." All those nights I'd come to this very spot. Not realizing she was awake, too.

She sat up. "Dude. Have you seen—"

"Did you just call me 'dude'?"

"*Dude*," she repeated. "Have you ever seen—"

"I really don't think you should call me 'dude'."

She ignored me. "—the greatest photograph ever taken?"

"The one with the little girl in the yellow coat, running away from—"

"Ha. Not a *meme*, you jackass. The ultra-deep field photograph."

"I don't know what that is."

"For kicks, NASA pointed the Hubble— You know what the Hubble is, right?"

"Yes, I know what the Hubble is."

"Okay. Well, NASA—"

"I chewed it when I was little. Hubble-Bubble."

She thumped me in the chest. "They pointed the telescope at this one small corner of the sky. Just a couple stars there, right? And they left it there for a few months and assembled a sort of picture of what it saw. And they zoomed in on the picture, over and over and over, and every time, the picture revealed thousands upon thousands upon thousands more—"

"Bananas," I suggested.

"*Galaxies.* Some were so old they were around just a few hundred million years after the big bang. They still might be, but we won't know for a really long time."

"Wow," I said, filling my voice with awe. "Vanessa, you're a...a *nerd.*"

She punched me this time. "Shut up."

"Also, you punch me a lot. I'm not sure how I feel—"

She swung again, but I grabbed her hand and let her momentum pull her close to me. Suddenly her face was near enough that the fog of her breath enveloped us both. She fell quiet, and in that moment I felt every vibrating nerve, every ridge of her fingerprints, like a pattern of glowing coils upon my skin. Her face was in shadow, and the moon turned her hair translucent. I raised my hand to her cheek, expecting cold skin. But it was superheated, flushed beneath my touch. I brushed my thumb over her lower lip; I couldn't imagine a more intimate thing to have done.

"I, uh – should get home," she said. Softly. Shakily.

I didn't want to let go. But I heard myself reply, just as quietly, "Okay."

She pushed against me and got to her knees, then her feet, and helped me up. Her breath came quick and ragged. I knew how she felt; my heart kicked against my ribs in just the same way.

"New subject," Vanessa said. Her hand was warm in mine as we walked back. "If you could have lived in any era, when would you have been born?"

"You mean, like, do I secretly wish I was a pioneer or something?"

"Yeah. Like, sometimes I think I was born too late. Doesn't everybody?"

"Because you wish you were born in the Bronze Age?"

"You know what I mean."

"I don't know. I mean, this era sucks, don't get me wrong. But it might also be the best our family's ever had it. Which isn't saying much. And that's pretty sad. My great-grandparents came here from…I forget. Cullen? Cullentown? Somewhere in Ireland. We're Irish, or at least a little bit."

She eyed my hair. "Never would've guessed."

"Do you wish *you* lived in a different era?"

"I would've been born in the seventies," she said. "But not before. I'd rather not be burned at the stake just because I know how the solar system works."

"The seventies," I repeated. "Not to see *Star Wars* opening day, I'm guessing."

"You know about *Voyager*, right?"

"Satellite," I said. "Right?" She made a face, and I corrected myself: "Okay. Not a satellite."

"It was a *probe*. Though I'll grant you, it does look a bit like a backyard satellite dish with legs. But that was the seventies for you."

"If you were born in the seventies, you'd still be too young to work on *Voyager*."

"Oh, no. I was born at the perfect time for a *Voyager* junkie," she said. "We'll be hearing about its discoveries for our whole lives. You know it's supposed to exit the heliosphere soon?"

"The...what?"

She let go of my hand, formed a circle with hers. "Pretend there's a huge bubble around the solar system, right? We'll never go outside that bubble. At least not in our lifetimes." She was glowing. "But *Voyager* will. We have no idea what it'll see. And – it's got this thing on board, the—"

"Golden Record," I finished.

She stopped walking. "You already know all this."

"Are there people who don't?"

"You'd be surprised."

"I just know what it is," I said. "Not what you were going to say."

"Well – okay. So Carl Sagan worked on the project, right? He fell in love while he worked on it. With this brilliant woman named Annie. That's a whole other story. A beautiful one, but not my point. My point: *Voyager* is going places we might never go. It's taking our story with it. How is that not romantic?" She studied my face. "You really do know all this already."

"Not the falling in love part. I just like to hear you gush about stuff."

"My father was like that," she said. "Gushy about space things. Except he *hated* Carl Sagan. And everything he stood for."

"Well, he's not here, is he."

"Thank *god*," she said, and we started walking again. She looped her arm through mine. "I'd be born back then because he taught astronomy at Cornell. I could have studied under him."

"Your father," I said.

"*Sagan*."

"Oh. Science guy, right?"

She took another playful swing at me, and I tickled her, and we staggered onto someone's lawn, laughing. After I caught my breath, I said, "So you wish you could have learned from him. Like, actually sat in a classroom with him. That's why Cornell."

"*Yes*. Exactly that. That's exactly what I dream of."

"So you'd learn, like, everything you *don't* already know—"

"There's a lot I don't know."

"—from a substitute father figure."

"*Ye*—" She took a hard step back. "That wasn't nice."

"I didn't mean it *meanly*." I reached for her hand, but she pulled it away. "No, see, I just meant…Shit. No, okay. You're right. That was mean. It could *only* have been mean. I'm sorry."

Vanessa bit her lip. I could see her working over her options: stay or go. In the end, she stayed…but something had changed. Her mood had darkened.

Fuck. Dammit.

She walked a few paces behind me for the next block, and then she said, in a much smaller voice, "You're not wrong, though."

I turned back to face her.

"I'd never thought of it…that way."

I wasn't even certain she was talking to me.

"I legitimately *hate* him," she said. "I hate him for poisoning the stars. I can't look at them without thinking of him, even just in the back of my mind, you know? And I hate him for *this*," she said, circling her face with her index finger. "You know my mom is part Japanese?"

I remembered the night at the football game. Her mother's face mostly hidden away behind that scarf.

"Not that you'd know by looking at me." She was angry now, but not at me. Angry at someone who wasn't even here. I knew how that felt. That kind of anger always just beneath the surface, never predictable. Just coming out when you didn't want it to. Like now. She raged on: "I have her hair, see? But *plenty* of white girls have dark hair. The rest of me, all *this* –" that finger around her face again – "it's him. His eyes, his mouth. He had a stupid baby tooth, too. All these fucking reminders of him, and almost nothing from my mom. *She's* the one who stayed. He was the one who didn't even *want*…"

She trailed off, stopped walking.

I reached for her hand, and this time she let me. "I'd go all the way back," I said. "If I could."

She looked at me, still lost in her frustration. "What?"

"If I could have been born sometime else. I'd go right back to the beginning."

She blinked, not understanding. "To the…big bang? I mean…you'd just die. Instantly."

"No," I said. "To *my* all-the-way-back."

She saw it then. "Your dad."

"I wouldn't be born in a different era," I said. "I'd keep this one. I'd relive every single day, if I could, right up until the day he left us for that last shift. Then I'd go back again. Start again."

"A time loop."

191

"Over and over again. Forever."

"There would be consequences," she said. "Everything you want to do with your life, it wouldn't matter. College, if you want that. Raising the girls. You'd cut it all off every time you rewound to the beginning. Time would lose meaning each time you reset."

"Yeah," I said. "But…"

"But your dad."

"Yeah."

She put her head on my shoulder, and I draped my arm around her shoulders. When we arrived home again, I could see Derek through the window, washing dishes. Leah sat on the counter beside him. As I watched, my brother leaned towards her, rested his head on her shoulder. The water kept running. I was torn between admiring the sweetness of the moment and rapping on the window to tell him to shut the water off.

Vanessa stopped me before we reached the door.

"What?"

"We're bound to screw this up," she said. I knew what she meant: the way she'd blundered into Mama's room, the stupid comment I'd made about father figures. "But promise me something."

"What?"

"That you won't just quit." She drew a deep breath, as if it had taken effort to say that. "Like, tell me when I screw up.

And I'll tell you. But don't just…quit." She hesitated, then added, "It's dumb, but I don't think I'd handle that very well."

I caught movement in my peripheral vision, a glimpse of Derek disappearing from the window. He knew we were back, but the front door remained shut.

"I promise." I pulled her in tight and rested my cheek against her hair. She sighed, and I said, "You know, if I could go back – all the way back, like that – then this never would have happened."

Her cheeks were pink. She rose onto her toes and pressed her lips to the tip of my nose. Her dark eyes danced. Softly, she said, "Happy birthday…dude."

26

VANESSA

"Nope. No, nuh-uh, nope," Cece protested. "I don't do dream talk. Not since you told me the one about how your skin was a candy shell and you licked it all off."

"Cece," I pleaded.

"Nope. Dreams are fascinating – when they're your *own*. I don't need to hear more of your freaky, existential nightmares."

"This one really *means* something," I countered. I gave her my best pouty eyes. "Please."

She delivered one of the epic sighs of human history. With a pointed glance at her wrist, she said flatly, "Two minutes."

"It's about Zach," I started.

"Nope, nope, no way. Forget the two minutes. I do *not* want any part of this."

"It's not one of *those* dreams."

"I do not need to know you're even *having* those dreams."

"I don't," I said. "Well, except—"

"*NOPE*," she said, turning away.

"He turned into a bird," I blurted out.

She stopped. "If you humped a bird in your dream, I can't get down with that."

"No," I said.

She frowned. "Two minutes."

"So I'm on this pitch-black road. It's the dead of night. It could have been anywhere. There weren't any landmarks. I could have been in Tunisia, or in Nebraska, or—"

"The surface of Io?"

"Cece," I said. "Io is *covered* with volcanoes. If I was on Io, I'd have known it. And just after knowing it, I'd have died. Hey, fun fact: from the surface of Io, Jupiter would appear, like, forty times bigger than Earth's moon. In fact, you—"

"Get to the point," Cece interjected. "Or I'm done."

"Fine. I remember looking up – you know, to see if I could navigate by stars – and the street was perfectly aligned with the arm of the Milky Way. Like if I'd kept walking, eventually the road would have just merged with—"

Cece touched her forehead and waved one hand. Eyes closed, she intoned, "You'll inherit a prime piece of real estate. It'll be – wait, it's coming, it's coming – somewhere in the vicinity of Ursa Minor, on the planet Betelgeuse."

"Betelgeuse is a star. And it's in the vicinity of *Orion*, not Ursa Minor."

"As if that matters one iota to this conversation."

"*Cece*."

"Fine. Continue."

"Zach was there. He didn't see me. I ran towards him, but just when I thought I would reach him, he unfolded these huge wings. Like, albatross-sized. And he just flew off."

"Which direction?"

"I don't know. Does it matter?"

"Maybe."

"Southwards. I mean, maybe. I watched until he was gone, and then I woke up."

"Were you sad? When you woke up?"

"I don't think so," I said. "No."

"It was a premonition," she said. "You saw the future."

"Zach doesn't have wings."

"No," she said. "But where's that school you tried to push him into?"

The skin on my neck tingled. "San Diego," I said.

"See? South."

"*Cece*." I grabbed her face and kissed her forehead. Ada was approaching, and I gave her an abbreviated wave as I flew past.

"Yeah, you're *welcome*," Cece called after me. "Madame Cecily says come again. And bring money next time."

* * *

"I think I'd rather have giant bird wings," Zach said. "Besides, I never would've pegged you for a dream theorist. Not my Vanessa, Queen of Reason and Logic, Empress Scientist of the Milky Way Gala—" He stopped, reading my face. "What?"

"*Your* Vanessa," I said.

He blushed furiously. "I just – um – I—"

I laughed and hip-checked him. "I thought it was sweet."

His face returned to its usual colour, and his voice dropped. "Look," he said gently – but there was a firmness that hadn't been there before. "College sounds like fun. I'd probably like it. But…" He looked away, as if searching for the words. "Not everybody gets that dream. Or needs it. All the things I'd miss? I can't leave all that. My family needs me. It's not like with you."

All I wanted to do was shake him. He was *so* wrong.

"You disagree," he said. "It's okay, I can tell. You think I'm selling myself short, or something. Maybe you think my family's just this anchor, holding me down."

"No," I said. "Zach, that's not—"

"But I don't think you know what it means to *need* an anchor. If I didn't have them…" He hesitated. "If I didn't have them, I wouldn't want what was left of me. They *define* me. And that's not a bad thing. It's the best thing. It's…the only thing."

From where Zach stood, we were fundamentally

different. We were two people, running side by side, for a moment in time. But whereas my course had a finish line, a destination, Zach's was just an infinite loop. He wouldn't ever be allowed to stop running.

He left me for work a few minutes later, and I biked home, unable to shake the feeling he was right. We *were* two different people. The only reason I would ever fly in circles, I thought, would be to build momentum, to slingshot myself to something greater. And that's what Cornell was. Cornell wasn't my endgame; Cornell was the trajectory, the loop. When I burst free, I'd be going somewhere that mattered.

He flew in circles because he was tied down. And not by his family, like he thought *I* thought. But by circumstance. What would happen to us when I flew away? What would happen to him?

I parked the Kestrel in the garage, hung my helmet on the handlebars. Before I went into the house, I hesitated. Something was off. Something wasn't…right. And when I opened the door, I could hear it. The sound of Mom and Aaron fighting.

I'd *never* heard that sound before. Their disagreements could have been used as a syllabus in conflict-resolution classes. *We don't have to agree,* one of them would say. *I respect your point of view, and it doesn't make me love you any less,* the other would reply.

But not today.

VANESSA

I waited inside, at the bottom of the stairs, listening. I'd always been afraid a day like this might come. Now that it had, it could mean only one thing: The bloom was off the rose. Aaron had finally found something about Mom to dislike; Mom had found a hint of my father in Aaron. The marriage had an expiration date now, and when it arrived, Mom and I would be alone again, wounded and searching for somewhere safe to land.

But we'd done it before. If it came to that, we'd do it again.

When I reached the top of the stairs, they looked like raccoons caught raiding the trash. "What's going on?"

Mom's eyes were red, I saw in the instant she met my gaze. Then she looked away.

Aaron was red-faced, sweating. He looked at me, then turned back to my mother. "Elise, you have to tell her," he said.

"Tell me what?" I asked.

"Ask her," Aaron said quietly. "Ask what she did."

Mom held my gaze, but I could see that it took considerable effort. Her jaw twitched ever so slightly.

"What's he talking about?" I asked. "Mom, what did you do?"

Her lips parted, but it took a moment for her to say the words. She closed her eyes. "It's gone," she said, finally. She shook her head. "It's all gone, Vanessa."

"What is?" I asked.

Mom didn't answer. She whirled about, slid past Aaron, and disappeared quickly down the hall. A moment later, I heard the bedroom door click shut.

I looked at Aaron. "What did she do?"

"I'm so sorry, kiddo," he said. "I didn't know."

"Didn't know *what*?"

"Our savings," he said. "Your…college money. It's all gone."

The room tilted. My stomach slid sideways.

Cornell spun away from me in that moment; the news slingshotted me in the opposite direction. I was supposed to find out in a few weeks if I'd gotten in. Years of hoping, planning – and at that last minute…this?

Slowly, waveringly, he told me the story. Over the past several months, Mom had drained both accounts dry. Every penny had gone into Costa Celeste, the lead balloon that she and the rest of the council kept trying to pump full of air.

"It was our savings first," he said. "When that was gone, she took the rest." He choked up. If I hadn't realized before how much Aaron cared for me, it was on full display now. "Everything that was yours."

I had to sit down. Aaron pulled out a chair for me, then sat beside me.

"It wasn't just her," he went on. "Everyone did it. The whole council. Investors kept dropping out, and the council decided – off the record – to self-fund the project." He ran a hand through his hair. "So damned stupid. They thought if they could just open the doors, then overnight the town would drown in tourist money. They'd get it all back, and more."

"Stop," I said. It was getting hard to breathe.

"I bet tonight there are conversations happening all over town just like this one. All those empty bank accounts, all those cashed-out pensions, second mortgages. And all for that damned—"

"*Stop.*"

He went to the kitchen and poured a glass of water for me. I took a long swallow, and he said, "Better?"

"No."

"I knew she'd put aside college money for you," he said with a sigh. "After the divorce. I just figured she'd put it into an education fund. Something protected. Not just a savings account."

"In her fucking name," I swore. I looked up at him. "She – she really took it *all*?"

His eyes were wet. "Yes." He took a deep breath, and I could see him trying to make sense of it himself. "She thought she was doing the right thing," he said. "I'm sure they all did. I'm mad as hell, and more than a little hurt, for both of us, but she—"

"Don't," I said. "Don't do that." My ears were ringing. "I was *going* somewhere. Now I'm not."

"Hey. There are still scholarships," Aaron said. "Financial aid. I promise this isn't the end, no matter what it sounds like. And…" He paused and put a hand on my shoulder. "I know you don't want to consider it, but there are a hundred schools that would take you in a heartbeat. Like *that*." He snapped his fingers. "We'll figure this out. I promise."

"I don't want a school to *take* me," I said, fighting tears. "I want to go to the one I *love*."

His mouth opened, closed. "I'm sorry, kiddo. Don't give up. Not yet."

I could hardly hear him. The ringing in my ears became a roar, and I ran to my room and shut the door and sagged against it. Beside my desk was a bookcase stuffed with books by Carl Sagan; on the walls, posters and news clippings. I fought a sudden urge to tear everything down, to hurl his books through the window, onto the lawn.

Cornell had been a dream; now it was a mirage. Worse, it meant my father had been right: my hero was dead. And now so was my future.

Everything that had mattered an hour ago no longer did. My application, the imminent early decision…

How naive and stupid I'd been.

PART THREE

FEBRUARY 2013

27

ZACH

"Four waters," I said, delivering four glasses to the table. When I straightened up, Jill, the morning-shift manager, beckoned to me.

"Yes, ma'am," I said.

"Maybe you got a field promotion," she said, "but didn't I hire you as a busboy?"

"Yes, ma'am."

"And yet I see you serving."

"Yes, ma'am. It's just, the customer asked me, and—"

"You're wearing the apron of a busboy, are you not?"

Sigh. "Yes, ma'am."

She shielded her eyes, looked both directions. "Do you see any of the servers wearing that apron?"

"No, ma'am."

"So you do know the difference."

"I do, ma'am."

Jill nodded towards a table in the corner, where a party of four was pulling on their jackets, abandoning half-finished stacks of pancakes and cold, Play-Doh-yellow eggs. "Then do your job, please."

"Yes, ma'am."

Maddie, of course, had severely trimmed my hours after Christmas. She had me there Tuesdays and Fridays after school, in four-hour shifts. She'd released two other stock boys and Pat, the cashier. Pat, as it turned out, worked as a line cook at Dot's Diner in his off hours. He'd hooked me up with this job. Jill was happy to fill my empty schedule with hours. When I wasn't at Maddie's, I was here. When I wasn't here, I was at school or collapsing onto the sofa at home. What I wasn't doing was spending any time with Vanessa.

Something had gone sideways with us. She didn't wait on the sidewalk for me and the girls any more. She'd started ducking me at school. No more walks from class to class, no more free periods spent reading in the loft. I sat down to lunch with Cece and Ada, and Vanessa simply didn't appear. In health class, she wouldn't look at me. If I saw her in the halls, she vanished before I could reach her.

Each day I expected to find a note in my locker slats: *For a time, we occupied the same orbit. But every orbit decays. It's time for me to move on.* But the note never came, and I kept replaying her words on the night of my birthday: *Don't just quit. Tell me if I screw up, but don't just quit on us.*

Well, I hadn't. And yet here we were.

I'd expected this at graduation. She'd leave town,

ascending like a rocket. But we hadn't even made it to January. She was still here – I could see her – but she wasn't, not really. After a few weeks, I'd handled all the uncertainty I could bear. I lingered in the hallway outside her AP calculus class. I'd prepared a whole speech in my head: romantic and forceful – in a romantic kind of way? – but I didn't get to deliver it.

"Zach?"

Cece and Ada appeared in the hallway. The end-of-class bell hadn't rung yet. I'd scammed a hall pass from my teacher, but I didn't know what the two of them were doing out here.

"Hi," I said.

Cece looked at me, then the door to Vanessa's class. "So," she said. "You're – what? Stalking her now?"

I felt dewy with sweat. "I'm not."

"Precisely what a stalker would say," Ada supplied. She removed a tiny notebook from her pocket and jotted something down. "What else would a stalker say?"

"I'm not," I repeated, mouth dry. "Not a stalker."

Ada kept writing. "Uh-huh."

"Look," Cece said, perhaps realizing she'd put me on the defensive. "You're not. Bad joke. But you should probably go before the—" The bell sounded, and up and down the hall, doors opened, leaking teenagers. Cece sighed. "Before that happens."

I could see Vanessa inside the AP calc room, at Mrs Ashworth's desk. Cece noticed, too, and shook her head.

"Just...don't," she said. She sounded resigned.

Ada touched Cece's hand. "I have creative writing. Find me after?" She trailed her fingers over Cece's collarbone as she departed, and Cece turned to watch her leave.

"Do you have any idea what's going on?" I asked. "She just fell right off the planet."

"It's her business," Cece said, a little too firmly. She watched until Ada was gone, then, with a sigh, she admitted, "Honestly, she barely talks to me now, either. Something's up, but I don't know what."

A flash of movement drew my eye. Vanessa stood frozen in the classroom doorway, thumbs hooked beneath her backpack straps. She was wearing a huge pair of noise-cancelling headphones. She stared at Cece, then me.

"Nessa," Cece started, taking a step away from me.

Vanessa held my gaze for a moment longer, and I tried to read her face. But I couldn't. I didn't say anything; my speech withered in my head, forgotten. Then she turned sharply and walked away.

Cece shot me a severe glance – *You see?* – and gave chase, calling Vanessa's name. I stayed rooted where I was. Kids bumped past, threw me annoyed looks, but all I could think was: *This is a lesson. You've learned a lesson.* Thing is, I already knew this one. It wasn't new: *Lock yourself up tight. Nobody gets a piece of you.* In other words, save it all for the people who deserve my care, my time. For my family.

I'd hammered that lesson into my skull after Dad's death. It earned me a reputation for being the loner, for being difficult. The whole "bad luck" thing underscored that narrative, and that was okay by me. Life hands you lessons like this all the time. I've found it's better to take them than resist.

But Vanessa had taught me the opposite: that it was okay to be vulnerable, to let yourself be seen. Until now, I never thought I'd have to lock myself away from her, too.

After that, the days went hazy, and I moved through them as if they were fog. Without Vanessa taking up space in my day, in my head, I gave those hours over to the diner, and to Maddie, when she needed me. I trudged home near midnight most nights. I signed my pay over to Derek. He didn't like that I was working more, but he didn't lecture me about it, either. He did his part; I did mine. If I wasn't asleep, I was at work or at school. I'd done the math; between those two things, I knew where my time was best spent.

I was running out of space for school.

28

VANESSA

I peered over the top of the stairs and sighed with relief when I saw that the loft was empty. No Zach. No anybody else. I threw my backpack down and sank into one of the fat beanbag chairs. I'd scoured the shelves for something to read, anything to take my mind off how sour things had turned. Nothing about space. Nothing by Dr Sagan.

I stared at the cover of the novel in my lap, and everything within me threatened to revolt. The book was popular among my fellow students. A *Times* bestseller. From the first sentence, the author corrupted the English language. Cece would have cringed to see me reading it. "Porn for narcissists," she'd called it once.

It was perfect.

I removed the headphones. Down *there*, they served as my own bubble-making device, sealing me away from the rest of the world. But here, in the library, I didn't need them. The loft was my bubble. No one ever came up here. And anyway, my ears ached.

Forty pages later, I heard footsteps on the loft stairs. I sank deeper into the chair, willing myself to vanish. Then Cece's face rose into view.

"Hi," she said. She'd caught me without the headphones; I couldn't pretend I hadn't heard her. She noticed the book, but withheld comment. "You're hiding from Zach," she went on. "I didn't think you'd run from me. But maybe you're hiding from all of us."

I didn't say anything, and she dropped into a cross-legged position beside me.

"Not going to talk to me?" She scanned my face. I saw a range of emotions flicker across her features. One of them was anger. "Fine," she said. "Don't talk to me. But I'm here because I give a damn."

She unzipped her backpack and removed a blue folder. "Mrs Harriman handed back our exams," she said. She held up a stapled packet. "Here's mine. See?"

A large red *101 – Woot!*, circled and tagged with a smiley face.

Then she held up another. "And this is yours, which she gave to me because you skipped class for the second day in a row. That's a twenty-two, Vanessa. Do you know why?" She fanned through the pages. "Because you chose A for every multiple choice, and you skipped every written one."

I didn't say anything.

"Oh, I'm glad that's fine with you," she went on, her eyes

diamond hard. "If you'd actually *tried* and failed, maybe I'd be more worried. I'd really worry something was wrong. But I'm glad to know you're just sabotaging yourself. For what? Is this fun for you?"

I went back to my book.

"I knew this kid once," she said. "Liked to play those city-simulation games. He'd build these elaborate, complicated cities. Lay pipelines, install power lines, construct intricate highway systems. Took him weeks to get everything just right. But then there was nothing left to do, you know? So you know what he did?" She paused, waiting, but I didn't say a word. "There were these disaster buttons. He'd send a tornado ripping through the city. Or drop a meteor on it. I asked him why, after he'd worked so hard, and you know what he said? He said once you mastered something, the only thing left was to burn it all down." She paused. "Like you're doing now."

"If I wanted to kick your ass at this stupid valedictorian thing," I snapped, "I'd have done it already. Believe me. You're not that smart."

She stared at me, fuming – and more than a little hurt. "You don't even understand."

"Oh, let's hear it. Call me more names. Am I the manic dream girl today? Or the entitled fucking pixie?"

"It's worse," she said, lowering her voice. She leaned closer. "You're lying to yourself. And you know you are.

Stop pretending you aren't."

I pulled my headphones up and flicked the noise-cancelling switch, drowning her in white noise. It was as if someone had pulled the plug on Cece's microphone. The muscle in her cheek twitched; her eyes were rimmed with tears. She threw my test down, then snatched up her bag and stormed away.

When she was gone, I wiped my eyes with my sleeve and hurled the novel across the loft.

I ditched the rest of the day. Instead of biking home, I kept going. Orilly's one selling point: bike paths. I followed the bike trail that ran parallel to the southbound highway. The sun was high at my left shoulder; the wind whipped at my face. The path sloped downward as I coasted; the bike accelerated, and the yellow grass and cracked asphalt blurred as they flew past.

In December, as I'd expected, an email had arrived from Cornell: I'd been wait-listed. I wouldn't know until March if I'd gotten in. And now it didn't matter anyway. I didn't even want to know what Cornell decided. There were only two possibilities here:

1. Cornell could accept me. I'd be too broke to accept *them*, so the news would only be more heartbreaking than if they'd just rejected me.

2. They could reject me. My dream would be crushed, but, more than that, I'd have made an enormous stink about Mom's betrayal – only for it to never have mattered anyway.

Everything had gone so wrong. Mom had torn Cornell out of my hands. I'd torched things with my best friends. Now I was stacking dynamite around my academic record. None of it mattered. It all cut deeply – I felt like I was watching myself bleed out – but I was too numb to feel any of it.

You're lying to yourself, Cece had said. *Stop pretending you aren't.* The words chased me down the trail. I couldn't make sense of them. What was she talking about? The real hell of it was that Cece – as usual – was right. But I didn't know how I knew that. I didn't know what she was trying to say – only that it *felt* true.

Which made me feel like shit.

As I rode, I tried to sort it out. Lying to myself about Cornell? No. That was off the table. *College* was off the table.

Wasn't it?

Cece wasn't the only one who had called me out on this. Aaron had, too. Gently, in his way. They were both right. It didn't matter if I didn't graduate top of my class; my GPA would still get me through a hundred different doors. Aaron's and Mom's savings were gone – but their credit was aces, and I knew Mom's guilt would drive her to take out a sizable loan if I asked. There were scholarships, financial aid; I was young, strong. A million kids before me had worked their way through college; there was no reason I was any better than them.

All these things were true. All of them meant I was *still* better off than lots of other people. Better off than Zach, who clung to the barest thread of hope that he might someday do something to get out of Orilly. The barest thread, and here I was holding a braided rope.

My eyes burned as I steered headlong into the wind. I imagined running the Kestrel right off the trail, leaping off, watching it dash against the rocks. I wanted to smash something.

I was still angry.

Only now I didn't know why.

By late afternoon, I'd reached Big Sur. My thighs burned, and I coasted down to Pfeiffer Beach. A few lonely people walked along the shoreline, one of them waving a metal detector slowly over the sand. Dogs barked, chasing sandpipers. I climbed off my bike and lay it against a rock, then wandered down to the water. Just offshore, there's a massive rock formation with a gap right in the centre. The sun sank perfectly through that gap, and the beach fell into shadow except for that golden bridge of light.

I came across a trio of signs screwed to metal posts in the sand. The usual warnings about swimming and rip currents, even one about a shark attack that had occurred thirteen years before. The third sign warned about unseen waves. It was clearly referring to the 2008 storm, the awful way it had wrecked this coastline. The light leaked out of the sky, making the words difficult to read.

Around me the beach was dotted with debris, and I surveyed the wreckage as I walked. A fibreglass boat protruded from the sand, warped and beaten in by rocks and surf. Most of it had been buried. There were other signs of that storm: timbers jutting skyward, their white paint abraded away. I recognized them as the legs of a lifeguard tower, but they were snapped in two. The structure atop them had long since disappeared, probably broken apart by those giant waves. I patted the timbers, and to my surprise, they wavered. The sea had done this. Split timbers as thick as my body. Driven a boat so deep into the sand it couldn't be unearthed.

I lay on the sand as the sky changed from pink to violet to deep blue, and then, at last, it was dark. I wrapped my arms around myself, willing away the cold. I couldn't see the moon, but the stars revealed themselves like stage performers entering a scene. Among them I spotted the pink pixel that was Venus; it only made me think of *him*. Worse, the whole sky was now a permanent reminder of everything my mother had taken from me. The thing I loved most, forever stained by my parents and their selfishness.

I used my iPhone's flashlight to pick my way back over the sand and rocks to my bike, but the Kestrel wasn't there any more. It was the last indignity I could stomach today; my vision blurred, and I turned and hurled my phone into the dark. I heard it skitter across the sand, the flashlight stabbing upward into the darkness. I felt as if I'd been jolted by a live wire; a hundred thousand volts crawled through my veins like manic bugs.

"*Fuck*," I muttered, and the word was magic. Everything drained out of me, and I trudged across the sand, towards my lonely phone. I picked it up, shook off the sand, then swiped through my contacts until I found Aaron's name.

Thirty minutes later, he appeared at the side of the highway, and I climbed into the passenger seat, exhausted. "Your mother and I were so worried," he said, and what I meant to say was *I'm fine*, but instead I fell against his shoulder and burst into tears.

29

ZACH

Here's the thing about grand, unanswerable questions: you can live with the not knowing. Are we alone in the universe? What would it be like to live forever? Why did my dad have to die so young? Deep inside, people understand they'll never learn the truth. Questions like those might keep you up all night every so often – but they don't derail everything.

It's the pesky little questions, the ones that have real answers that you can't quite get to, that'll send the whole train right off the tracks.

I'd made up my mind to drop out of high school. Senior year, just months before graduation. It wasn't the right decision for anybody else. Just for me.

But I couldn't do it without answering the question of what the hell had happened to me and Vanessa.

It had been years since I'd passed notes in class. My third-grade teacher, Mr Summers, had caught me passing around illustrations of Ninja Turtles to my classmates. I'd labelled them with little price tags: fifty cents a pop. I'd only been caught when a line of paying customers formed at my desk.

I slinked into health ed just before the late bell rang. As I passed Vanessa's desk, I dropped a folded note into her lap and kept moving. I'd written it hastily in the hallway:

CAN WE TALK? PLEASE.

Mrs Harriman paced at the front of the room, kicking off the day's topic. "Has anyone ever had a family member who suffered from addiction?" she began, searching for hands. "No one? That's good. Well, let's discuss what to look for."

I couldn't tell if Vanessa had opened the note. For all I knew, she'd shoved it in her pocket for later. But as Mrs Harriman droned on, Miguel Garza flipped my note over his shoulder. I caught it, then tucked it beneath my book. When our teacher's back was turned, I unfolded it.

library.

At the board, Mrs Harriman chipped out the stages of substance abuse with pink chalk: *Stage one – experimentation; Stage two – regular use; Stage three…*

After class, I maintained my distance and followed Vanessa to the library. She never once looked back or slowed her pace. It was weird to tag along behind her. I couldn't help feeling like an overly attached puppy.

Inside the library, she climbed the loft steps. When I reached the top, she was standing there, waiting, a book clasped against her chest, her headphones around her neck. I felt my heart compress within my chest, as if all the air had been vacuumed out.

She was impatient, her tone curt. "Well?"

It threw me off. "Hi," I said. "Cool. How are you?"

"Zach. What do you want?"

All business. No: trying to *appear* all business. But I'd spent enough time looking into those eyes to read the signs; they flicked subtly down and to the left, and she rocked lightly from heel to toe. As if she were using all her energy, struggling to maintain this composed state.

"Well?" she said again.

"I saw Cece and Ada," I said. "At the diner. They had milkshakes." She didn't reply, just stood there. "It was old-school. Cece seems really happy. Ada, too, actually."

"Zach. I have to go."

I took a step back, opening her path to the stairs. She didn't move.

"Look," I said. "Something's up."

She looked away.

"I don't know what it is. You don't have to tell me. It's just – I'm right *here*, you know? I haven't gone—"

"Zach," she said. Her jaw tensed; I couldn't tell if she was pissed or on the verge of tears. "Shit happened. Okay? I'm dealing."

"Are you okay?"

She turned away from me. "Fine. It's not your fault." She was quiet, and then she added: "Or your problem. Okay?"

"You don't have to tell me," I repeated.

She sighed, and her shoulders slumped. Softly, she said, "I can't go to Cornell."

Damn. I knew what that meant to her. I wanted to go to her, but I stayed where I was.

"Can't?" I asked.

"I'm not going."

"Did something—"

"*I don't want to talk about it.*"

"Hey," I said, quickly. "That's fine. We don't have to. Are you okay?"

"I'm fine." Her words clipped. "I said that already."

I hesitated. I couldn't help myself; none of this made sense. "It couldn't have been your grades—"

"*Zach.*"

"I'm just trying to understand," I said. But I'd lied, saying we didn't have to talk about it. We didn't *have* to, but clearly I was the idiot who was going to try to force the issue. "The Vanessa I know wouldn't give up on this. So…it's got to be something big."

"Stop."

"Is it your family? Did something happen?" I moved close, put my hand on her shoulder.

She whirled around. "I'm not your damn property," she snarled.

From below the loft, I heard a shushing sound.

But her outburst had dissolved something in me. I couldn't keep my mouth shut. "What happened?" I repeated. "One minute you were kissing me, then you were just *gone*. Where did you go?" She didn't answer, and suddenly I was annoyed. "All this time, you've tried to get me to think about my future. But now – what? Same thing doesn't apply to you?" I took a step closer. "Am I wrong? Tell me I'm wrong."

She shook her head and backpedalled. "I said stop."

"You *want* Cornell. It's your *dream*."

Dimly, I heard a bell ring, announcing the start of the next period.

"Just – *stop*." Vanessa was wound so tightly her teeth were practically chattering. "Please. Knock it off."

I couldn't, though. Until this moment, I hadn't let myself feel the hurt of being shut out. She'd done exactly what she'd asked me not to do. I hadn't realized she was the kind of person who could do that to someone else. To *me*.

"You have no idea," I said. "No idea what someone like me would do for even a *shred* of the chances you have." I rocked back on my heels, adrenaline spitting through my veins. "Must be nice, Vanessa. Must be *so* nice. To just throw things away. Just throw a dream away like it didn't mean anything. Just throw away *people*."

Her eyes flashed, like I'd lit something in her, too. "Don't put that on me," she hissed. "You *do* have chances, you – you *dick*. You just won't let yourself take them! Life's so hard for you? *Do the work, Zach.* Nobody gives you anything? *Take* it." She put a finger on my chest, tapped hard. "But *no*. You get off on it. On the suffering. Don't you? Don't say you don't. You make it your thing, you pretend you're all *noble*, but you're doing the same thing, Zach. You just throw it all away, all that possibility, and for what? Huh? For your f—"

She choked on the word, and the fight went right out of her as she realized what she'd almost said. But I heard it. Heard it even though she didn't say it.

Throwing it all away.

For your family.

My teeth were razors in my mouth. I didn't stop to think about how we'd gotten here, how we'd gone from a passed note to attacking each other in the library. I just spat back. "I would give *everything*," I snapped, "do *anything*, for any *one* of them. Unlike *you*."

Another shush, sharper now, from below. Footsteps on the loft stairs. A voice: "Excuse me."

Vanessa covered her face with her hands. "I didn't mean that," she moaned. "Zach, no. No, I didn't mean that."

"My dad told me once, when someone shows you who they really are, *believe* them." She took a step towards me, arms out. I backed away, looking her up and down. "I'm glad I know now."

"*Zach.*"

"Excuse me," came the voice again. The librarian, Mrs Barrett, appeared on the stairs, breathing hard. "You're being very loud. And the bell has rung. I suggest you move along to your classes."

"I'm going," I said.

"Zach, wait," Vanessa pleaded. "Zach, it wasn't up to me. It was my *mother*, she— I didn't – she—"

"Miss Drake," interrupted Mrs Barrett. "The bell has rung. Let's break this up. Now, please."

"You just don't get it," I said. "You have so *much*. I don't care what happened. It's hard? No problem. You'll just quit. Do the work? That's *all* I do. But not you. Right? Have you *ever*—"

"*Mr Mays*," Mrs Barrett stormed. "Move it along *now*, or I'll ask you to join me in the principal's office."

"Nah," I said, backing down the stairs. "That's cool. I quit."

Vanessa's eyes flew open. "*Zach*—"

I turned and took the steps two at a time, without looking back. Mrs Barrett repeated Vanessa's name twice more, and then I pushed through the library door, into the annex. At the end of the hall, I walked right past the administrative office, out the door, into the afternoon sunlight. Nobody stopped me. Nobody followed.

I'd needed more space.

Now I had all the space in the world.

30

VANESSA

February became March.

I couldn't stop being mad at Mom.

Cece wouldn't speak to me.

Zach *hated* me.

I missed him.

Things couldn't get worse.

It was difficult to celebrate when the news arrived:

Voyager has left the building, folks

by Twylight Guy | March 4, 2013 • 4:11 p.m.

Un. be. lievable. <u>Unbelievable!</u> Guys, it's <u>legit</u>, it has happened: <u>Voyager 1</u> has officially departed the solar system. According to the big scientists, ol' V'ger passed through the heliosphere sometime around August, last year. Our spindly little friend has eclipsed

our wildest dreams; it's the farthest man-made object
from our little blue home...

It was good news, to be sure, but I hated that it made me
think of my father. Had he seen the news? I'd wondered
about him so many times over the years. Not only why he
left us, but what had become of him. He'd simply never
been in touch. I told Mom once I didn't care to know what
he did with himself, but she suggested I was wrong. "When
you're older, maybe you'll be curious," she'd said. "You
might even want to find him." Over my grumbling, she'd
added gently, "And when you find those answers, I'll be
right here."

That day might come – but it hadn't yet. I was content to
invent stories about him, chief among them the notion that
he had another family now. A new daughter, perhaps, one
who didn't yet know all his secrets. For my father, knowledge
and power were inextricably linked to some false notion of
love. When he no longer held the upper hand, that's when
he withdrew his affection, his kindness.

Though she was a fiction, this new daughter broke my
heart. *One day*, I wanted to tell her, *you'll know everything he
knows. And you'll find out what happens when he has nothing
left to teach you.*

Voyager was gone, carrying with it a record of everything
we were: our voices, our feelings, the pulse of our brain

waves, the thrum of our hearts, beating into the dark. What had my father taken with him of me? Of my mother? Little more than memories, I suspected. Ephemeral things, memories. Easy enough to put out of one's mind.

Voyager was gone, and there was no bringing it back.

Just like *him*.

I followed my nose into the kitchen. It was late; I'd fallen asleep without meaning to. Aaron was bent over the countertop, chopping scallions; on the stove behind him, a deep pot of steel-cut oats bubbled. He'd set out his other ingredients: two brown eggs, a wedge of Gruyère, a sriracha bottle. I knew before I reached the doorway that I'd find him, and not Mom. Since her...*betrayal*, life around our house had changed. We hadn't shared dinner in ages. Aaron kept long hours at the office, and Mom stayed mostly out of sight. Too ashamed, I hoped, to face us.

My stomach rumbled, loudly enough to give me away. Aaron looked up and grinned. "I thought you were asleep already."

I shrugged, then indicated the food: "Can I get in on this?"

His eyes flicked past me uncertainly, and I turned, following his gaze to find my mother, sitting uneasily at the dining table, in shadow.

"Oh," I said.

"There's enough for three," Aaron said. "I'll get another egg."

"No. That's fine," I said. "I'm good."

I turned to leave, but Mom stopped me with a word: "Vanessa."

I paused in the doorway, my back to her.

"I will eat in another room," she volunteered quietly. "We don't have to talk."

I hesitated, then said – coldly, flatly – "Yeah. Could you?"

Without a word, my mother pushed back from the table. I turned away as she passed by.

"I'll bring it to you," Aaron called after her. Down the hall, the bedroom door closed softly. He sighed, then turned towards me.

"Is this the part where you defend her?" I asked, folding my arms.

"No," he said. He bent into the refrigerator to find a third egg. When he popped up again, he admitted, "Hell, we've barely started talking again. But – you know, Vanessa, you'll learn this more as you get older—"

"Here we go." I rolled my eyes.

"—but people make mistakes."

Trite, Aaron. "That's too soft a word."

"It is," he agreed. "And yet it's exactly the right word."

"Mistakes aren't calculated," I said. "What she did…"

"Don't confuse *mistake* with *accident*," he said.

"Semantics. Lawyerspeak."

"Husbandspeak."

"But not fatherspeak," I said. Inwardly, I winced. I couldn't believe I'd said it – but I didn't take it back, either. Aaron turned away and cracked the eggs into a skillet. Without acknowledging my words, he pushed the wedge of cheese towards me.

"Shred," he said. "Please."

As I grated the cheese into a bowl, I skimmed the newspaper. He'd left the *Chronicle* on the counter. According to it, the world was in disarray. The president of Venezuela had cancer. The United Nations was doubling down on sanctions against North Korea. A map depicted seismic activity in the Sea of Japan.

"Anything interesting?" he asked. He stirred the scallions into the oats, then filled three bowls. I passed the cheese to him and kept reading.

"Seven earthquakes in Japan in the last seven days," I summarized. "They say none are particularly significant when taken individually, but together, 'scientists believe they may suggest an imminent, larger event'."

"Oh, I hope that isn't true," Aaron said. "They've been through enough. Did I ever tell you about the story I heard, after that big quake in 2011? Saddest thing I'd heard in a long time."

That Aaron wore his heart on his sleeve, I knew, was one reason Mom had fallen for him. I hoisted myself onto the counter, watching as he drizzled sriracha over each bowl.

"What was it?"

"Story of an old man in this little town," he said. "Otsuchi, I think it was called. Quiet old man. Not prone to emotional displays. But he'd lost his cousin to the tsunami." He passed me a bowl of oats and a spoon. "Take it to your mom?"

I glared at him.

"Had to try," he said. "You keep that one. I'll be back." Another bowl in hand, he disappeared down the hall. As I waited for him to return, I punctured my egg yolk, then stirred it into the oatmeal. When he came back, he said, "Where was I?"

Through a mouthful, I mumbled, "Grumpy old man."

"That's right. Nobody ever saw him laugh or cry. Well, after the tsunami, he went out to his garden, or what was left of it, and right in the middle of it, he built a telephone booth." He blew on a spoonful. After a bite, he continued. "He put a telephone inside, but he didn't connect it to anything. Just a telephone."

"Why?"

"When he felt sad about his lost family, he would go into the booth and pick up the phone."

I wrinkled my nose. "I don't understand."

"Something happened when he did. He talked to his cousin."

"*God.* That's so tragic."

"All the things he could never say aloud, he said into the phone." Another bite. "It was cathartic, I imagine. Well, word got around. People told stories about the old man with the telephone that could talk to the dead. They called it the wind telephone.

"One day, the old man looked outside, and there was a stranger in his garden. Another old man, just staring at the telephone booth. He was there for a very long time, just standing there. Finally, he went inside, and he picked up the phone – and he just began sobbing. Before long, strangers from all over the country came to the phone booth."

Aaron poured a glass of water for each of us, and we ate in silence for a few minutes.

"What was it like here?" I asked him. "In 2011."

"People were terrified," he said. "The tsunami was supposed to hit us hard. And we all remembered how bad that storm had been, just a few years earlier. News said we should find high ground, so we did. Then...nothing happened."

I thought about the debris I'd seen on the beach in Big Sur. Even the swells from a storm like that one, so minor compared to a tsunami, had been immensely powerful.

Aaron blew on another spoonful. "Imagine," he said. "Finding oil in a place like this. The sea's just lurking out there, waiting to teach us a lesson."

"Yeah," I said. "But we're pretty high up." I thought about Zach and his family, practically sitting ducks down there at sea level. "We're...lucky."

Aaron shook his head sadly. "In Japan, they lost *everything*. Can you imagine? Being so adrift, so desperate for one last moment with the people you've lost, that you confess your sins on a disconnected telephone in an old man's garden? Makes you think, you know?"

My cheeks flushed hot, and I looked away.

He kissed my forehead lightly. "Night, kiddo."

Here's the thing about *Voyager*: eventually, it'll run out of power. It'll stop transmitting and sail through the dark, just a lonely artefact flung into the night by its makers. We won't be able to reach it, the gulf between us as wide as death. None of us who lived now – or any of our generations to come, likely – would ever know if *Voyager* found life somewhere in the vast dark. We would never hear from it again.

With a heavy sigh, I peered through OSPERT's viewfinder. Though the sky was clouded over, I wasn't looking for celestial bodies. I was searching for life. Just one.

I brought the firelight of the oil platforms into view. In the dark they appeared just as Zach had drawn them: loathsome, insectile. Steel monstrosities, gutting the planet. Our town depended on them – but that didn't make them benevolent.

I watched someone walk a dog on the beach, flashlight bobbing, then scanned the town until I found the market. The lights were out, the lot empty. I moved to the impound lot, but I didn't see Zach. Even if he were on the boat, I wouldn't have known. The blankets he'd hung over the wheelhouse windows would have hidden him away.

With a sigh, I gave up looking for him and just whiled away time observing our little town's drowsy activities: someone pumping gas beneath the lights of the Chevron sign, someone mopping the floors in the all-night McDonald's. The diner was alive, truckers and retirees stopping in for their evening— Wait. Was that—? I sharpened OSPERT's focus. On the sidewalk outside Dot's, Zach was removing a checked apron. He folded it, pinned it between his knees, tugged on his hoodie. He worked at Dot's now?

I hadn't seen him since the day he'd walked out of the library. In health ed each day, I waited, hoping it was all just an outburst, that he would come through the door and take his place at the back of the class.

But he'd really quit.

He tore open a white envelope and removed a slip of paper. A pay cheque? It brought a big smile to his face, and he folded it and stuffed it into his pocket. My heart ached, watching him stroll contentedly across the lot.

You can't just save him, Cece had said.

She was right, I knew. Cece was always right. But that didn't make it hurt any less.

At the edge of the parking lot, he paused. There were no street lamps where he stood, and in the dark, he tipped his head upwards. Curious, I moved to the window and looked up. The clouds had parted above Orilly, ever so slightly, and a watery moon shone through, just for the briefest moment. And in that moment, I felt…calm. We weren't speaking, and our paths had firmly diverged, but the same sky connected us.

When I peered through the scope again, Zach had walked out of view. I resisted the urge to turn OSPERT and follow him home. Instead, I closed the drapes and sank onto my bed. Had our paths really diverged? In ten years, in twenty, would Zach still be working at diners and grocery stores? Would I be any different? *Voyager*, that little bucket of bolts, had conquered the sun's gravity, had left our entire solar system in its rear-view mirror.

Surely I could do the same with Orilly.

Couldn't I?

31

ZACH

"You're late," Derek said when I came in.

He sat at the kitchen table, his back to the door. I dropped my backpack and apron onto the couch, then joined him. He studied me over a glass of milk.

"You're late a lot of nights."

"Yeah."

"I noticed that, you see." He wiped milk away from the moustache he'd grown practically overnight. "You're tired, too. More than usual. I noticed that, too."

"Same as you," I said.

"I noticed Leah's here more, longer. Here when you're not. She's tired, too, you know."

That was true as well. Some nights she practically slept upright in Mama's room, in the chair beside the window. I felt bad about it, but what was I supposed to do?

I took the pay cheque from my pocket and pushed it across the table.

"What's that?"

"Money," I said. "Same as it always is."

He took the envelope but didn't open it. "It never bothers you, Z? All this money you earn, just handing it all over?"

"What else would I do with it?" As he opened the envelope, I took his dishes to the sink and started scrubbing them.

Behind me, he said, "Z, what is this?"

I looked at his reflection in the kitchen window. "What's what?"

"You get a raise?"

My spine stiffened.

"No," he said, flipping the payslip to the earnings statement. The stub I'd forgotten to remove. "No, these hours here. They're not paying you more, Z, you're *working* more." He started to assemble the facts out loud. "Working more. Coming home late. Tired all the damn time, making everyone else damn tired." The chair scraped the floor as he stood up in a rush. "Z, don't *tell* me you quit. I better not hear that."

"Okay," I said. Lightly, trying to lift the moment. "I won't."

If it hadn't been so late, if Mama and the girls weren't asleep, I think he might have thrown something at me. Instead, he gripped the back of the chair so hard I saw the moulded plastic flex. Then, with a grunt of frustration, he wheeled and stormed through the front door. The screen clattered shut. I could hear him outside, pacing on the gravel.

Quietly, I put away the dishes, then sat down at the table. The house filled the silence well enough on its own: air rattling in the pipes, the faint groan of the settling foundation. My brother didn't return for several minutes, and when he did, he didn't sit down. He stood at the edge of the kitchen, the front door open behind him. I could hear the surf in the distance, like faint radio static.

"God damn it," he swore. He ran his hands through his hair, and then he did sink into the chair again. "God *damn* it, Zach."

Derek looked exhausted, but it was more than that. The expression he wore was one of defeat. I'd seen both of those looks on my parents' faces. In our house, exhaustion and defeat often went hand in hand.

"It's better this way," I ventured. "You know it is."

He'd buried his face in his hands, elbows splayed wide on the table. He said something, but I couldn't understand it.

"I don't know what you said."

His hands parted, and he peered at me with wet, red eyes. "I said I won't let you."

"It's done, D. I already—"

He shook his head. "I can't believe you would..." He trailed off, then tried again. "After what happened to me..."

"What are you talking about?"

"*This*, Z." Derek spread his arms wide, indicating our home, everything in it. "This."

Dad had dropped out of school in the tenth grade. Took a job, started helping his family. When he died, Derek had quit college and come home. He didn't complain, didn't protest; nobody asked him to make the right decision. It had cost him things. Cost him a life.

"You're their hero," I said, nodding towards the girls' bedroom. "Mama's. Mine."

But it was the wrong thing to say.

"Nothing *heroic* about it." His face flashed with anger – and something else I'd never seen before. "Not a *damned* thing. You think there's ever a day I wake up and I don't hate you? All of you? Every day, just a little bit? And hate myself for feeling it?"

Shame.

My brother *was* my hero. Did he think I'd never felt guilt? He'd gotten out. He'd *made* it. It was us who dragged him back. All of us. When Dad died, we all lost something. And then we'd taken something more from Derek.

"D," I said. "You're human, that's all. You're—"

"Like I could change a damn thing," he swore, as if I hadn't spoken. "Put food on the table. Keep you kids in school." I wanted to protest at that, being lumped in with the twins. But he charged ahead. "I can't fix anything. Can't stop any of...*this*...from happening to you, too. Heroic? Z, I'm just hanging *on*."

I opened my mouth, but he wasn't finished.

"And what did you do?" he demanded, dragging his hands down his face. He was on the verge of tears. "What did you *do*, Z?"

"It's going to be fine," I said. "I'm working full-time. We can save a lot of money. Start to get ahead."

"Everything I do, and you're still on the same damn road," he moaned. He turned away from me. "You just don't get it."

I saw it then. I couldn't believe I'd missed it; Derek was so much like our father that I shouldn't have been so blind. For Derek, it wasn't about how I could help shoulder the load. He didn't care about the load; he'd already accepted that it was his to carry.

My quitting school meant he was carrying it for nothing.

He felt like a failure.

"Derek," I said, but then his whole posture changed, as if he'd had an epiphany. He walked away, without speaking, and disappeared into his bedroom at the end of the hall. When he returned, he had a piece of mail in his hands. Triumphantly, he dropped it on the table in front of me.

"I know I did one thing right, Z. Did one thing about as right as a man can do."

The envelope lay face down. It had already been opened.

"What is that?" I said, my voice flat.

"Open it."

The envelope was good paper, not the usual utility-bill stuff. There was visible grain, and the opened flap bore a torn seal with a scripted *F* printed on it.

I looked up. I knew what that was. "What did you do?"

"I did the right thing," he said. "But too late now, I see."

I turned the envelope over. FLECK INSTITUTE OF ART & DESIGN, the return address announced. SAN DIEGO, CA. Printed in the centre was my name, our address.

"D," I said, weakly.

There was just one folded sheet of paper inside. I knew without reading what it would say.

"You got in," Derek said, quietly. "Your ass got *in*."

My vision blurred, and I wiped my eyes. "How?"

And he reminded me of the morning we'd both woken early. The bad dreams. The wadded-up napkin he'd shot towards the trash can. I remembered, then. He'd missed. I'd gone back to sleep, and he'd put the napkin in the can. And he'd found my application.

"That sweet girl brought it for you," he said. "I don't understand how your brain works, Z. You filled it out, then you just threw it away. But you'd done the hard part. So I did the rest."

"We can't afford it," I protested.

"Financial aid," he returned. "What else you got? Huh?

Let's hear. Vanessa? The girl brought it to you – she's already *in* your corner. You call her up, she hops a bus to come visit. Done. What else?"

Don't make me go, I didn't say. *Let me stay. This is where I belong. I'll take care of everyone.*

He was waiting for an answer, though, so I told him the truth.

"Mama. The girls. *You.*"

"No," he said, unmoved. "We're not your leash. Don't you put that on them. Not on me."

"I just— I *can't*," I wept. "Not when you need me."

Not when I need you.

Derek came around the table. Close to my ear he said, "You think you have to stay. I know. You think you have to be a hero. But you *don't*, Z. So here's how it's going to be. You listen to me. Want to take care of us? Do right by those girls? *Go.* Show them how. Want to do right by Mama? Make her *feel* that pride. Give her a reason to come back to us."

I buried my face in his shoulder and cried.

"You want to do right by me?" he asked, his voice tight. "*Give* me this. Show me I didn't come home for nothing." He wrapped his arms around me. I could smell the sweat of his day, that harsh blend of grease and salt. "You understand, Z? You give me this."

* * *

The man who answered Vanessa's door had a kind, easy face. Waves of brown hair gone grey at the temples. Ruddy cheeks, eyes warm beneath a knit of slightly unruly eyebrows. He wore an open-collared shirt that revealed a fading tan line. Jeans, socked feet.

"Help you?" he asked.

Vanessa was the only person I needed to tell. About what Derek had done, about where I was going. I hadn't seen her since that day in the loft. Was she pissed at me? Maybe. Had she given up on me? If I were her, I would've. But I had a lot to say, if she would let me.

"I, uh..." I'd expected Vanessa.

The man clapped his hands, pointed at me. "Hey, you're the football-game boy," he said. Then he laughed. "Sorry. You have a name, of course."

"I'm, um – I'm Zachary," I answered.

"Pleasure, Zachary." He turned and shouted Vanessa's name into the depths of the house. Through the open door I saw expensive furniture, an enormous flat-screen television mounted on a wall, a fireplace. "It's really nice to finally meet you," he said, offering me his hand. As I took it, he said, "I'm Nessa's stepfather. Aaron. Aaron Bartlett."

The world shattered. I recoiled from his hand and stumbled down the steps. My mind reeled. *Aaron Bartlett.* I knew that name. Knew it far too well.

"Hey," Mr Bartlett said, his voice tinged with concern.

"You're— Zachary, son, are you all right?"

From somewhere in the recesses of the house, I heard Vanessa call back, asking who was at the door. The sound of her voice, the dissonance of this moment, turned my knees to water. My heart was a piston in my chest.

All those letters with the Bernaco Oil emblem. All the legal documents, the filings and depositions, all the rejections and disavowals, they'd all arrived with a single name attached.

AARON BARTLETT
Lead Counsel
Bernaco Oil

Sincerely, Aaron Bartlett. Warmly, Aaron Bartlett. And later, as our lawyers pressed back, the letters had lost their feint towards kindness. *Regards, Aaron Bartlett. Awaiting your reply, Aaron Bartlett.* And ultimately, just: *Aaron Bartlett.*

The most recent letter ran through my head, text and subtext blurring into a hateful, shouted speech.

Bernaco has offered—

Your father was just a statistic—

A joke—

Don't bother us with this—

Here, a few dollars for your pain—

Jesus Christ. We were the Montagues and Capulets. Two

warring houses, a goddamned literary cliché. We'd never been just Zach and Vanessa. We were Romeo and Juliet.

I staggered down the sidewalk, backing away from Vanessa's stepfather, from his mask of concern. My hands clenched and released, forming fists so tightly my knuckles throbbed.

What are you going to do, Zach?

What will you do, hit me?

Go ahead. Hit me. DO IT.

Here I am—

You've been waiting for this—

Put your fist through my teeth—

Do it for your family—

"Zachary," Mr Bartlett repeated, and the world rushed back in. I tripped and fell from the final step, sprawling hard on the pebbled sidewalk. I'd cut my hand – I saw blood – but the pain hadn't registered yet.

"Zachary, son, are you okay?"

"Zach? Zach—" Vanessa's voice cut through the static, repeating my name, but I couldn't see her. It was as if there were a storm raging behind my eyes, crowding out every other input. Things made *sense* now, and nothing made any sense at all.

Everything swam. I shoved myself to my feet. All I wanted to do was run.

32

VANESSA

Zach loped down the sidewalk, seemingly in a haze.

Immediately, I realized what had just happened. I couldn't let him leave. I could fix this. But Aaron half blocked the door as I approached.

"Vanessa, what is going *on*—"

"That's Zach *Mays*, Aaron; his name is *Mays*." Aaron's face paled at that, and he moved aside. I took the steps two at a time, pursuing Zach down the sidewalk. "Zach!"

He wobbled like a man struck by lightning. I shouted his name twice more, but I wasn't sure he really heard me. I caught up with him easily, four houses down the block, and took his hand. The palm was slick with blood.

"Zach," I pleaded. "Zach, just *stop*. You're bleeding. Stop."

He did and stood unsteadily. I wondered if he was in shock; maybe he was. His eyes were unfocused, swimming with tears.

I put my hands on his face and tilted his gaze towards me.

"*Zach*," I said. "Look at me. Come on."

After a moment, his gaze sharpened. He looked into my eyes, and all I saw was pain. I said his name again, and he laughed. He *laughed*, and it was bitter, and broken, and awful.

"You see?" he asked. "You see, I knew it. They were right. I'm cursed."

"Zach—"

"All that shit about bad luck," he went on. "I let them say it. It wasn't real. It was just a joke. What did it matter?" He blinked at me, and his eyes spilled over. "But it's *true*, Vanessa. All this time it's been *true*."

"Zach, he just works there. He doesn't make the decisions – he does what he's told. None of it was Aaron's doing, nothing is—"

"You were the only friend I had," he said, and his face crumpled in my hands. Before I could tell him how wrong he was, that he mattered, that I loved him, he tugged free of my grasp. He backed away, not looking at me, and in that moment, all his fears were confirmed.

It began to rain.

Zach tipped his face heavenward. Rain slicked his hair, trickled down his face in ribbons. When he looked at me, his eyes were filled with sad amusement. "See?"

I stood dry, just a few feet away, the boundary of the sudden storm between us. It was everything he'd said.

It was a curse. He was in the thick of it, and I was on the outside.

"I'm glad," he said. "That you don't know what this is like." He laughed again, but there was no humour in it; it hardly sounded like a laugh at all. It was a guttural sound, one of acceptance. He was exactly what he feared: the butt of some grand, cosmic joke. One that everyone else was in on, including me.

"Zach," I said, stepping towards him.

"No," he said, backing away more. "Wouldn't want you to get wet."

He left me standing there, on the sidewalk, dry as a bone.

Outside, the storm unfurled, the rain finally enveloping the house. Too exhausted to cry, I lay on my bed, listening to it. The sound took me into sleep, and when I opened my eyes, the rain was gone, and the walls were Creamsicle orange. The sun was coming up. I'd slept for twelve hours.

My phone vibrated. A voicemail from Aaron. He wanted to talk, when I was ready. He was confused, worried. He loved me. Mom loved me. He hoped I wasn't angry. He understood if I was. I put the phone down, and it vibrated again.

"Damn it, Aaron," I muttered.

But it wasn't my stepfather. It was a Facebook

notification. A friend request. I tapped the red badge – and dropped my phone.

It was from Jonathan Drake. My father.

Irrationally, I worried my mother might burst into the room, as if psychically alerted to my father's presence. Her worst fears, confirmed: I was in secret communication with my father; all this time it was *him* I wished I were with, not her.

But my bedroom door remained shut.

I picked up my phone, carefully, as if it were scorching hot. My father's profile photo wasn't his face, but a Volkswagen emblem. The large, wide photo behind it showed bare feet in sharp close-up, framed against spongy tundra. But that was all I could see. A message on the page read *Become Jonathan's friend to see what he shares with people on Facebook.*

A private profile.

Not knowing what lay behind that barrier was agony. What had brought him out of the woodwork? Why now? I didn't want to be his *friend*. I felt my heart detach and sink into my gut, thudding and echoing in a sea of nausea. *What did he want?*

There was only one way to find out.

I bit my tongue – and accepted the request.

The page reloaded.

My god. There is so much here.

My father was a blogger now. Much of his Facebook wall was links to the many, many posts he'd published on a site he called *Farewell, Andromeda*. The most recent entry was titled "The stars look very different today".

Oh, brother.

The title of every entry, even the name of the blog, were tributes to old songs and albums he'd loved. Traces of who he'd been when I knew him. If in all this time he hadn't changed, would that be a good thing? Or the worst thing?

I searched for anything more revealing than his blog. I refused to read the entries. I didn't want his words in my head. On the ABOUT page, everything was blank. Birth date. Family members. Relationship status. All blank.

With trepidation, I tapped PHOTOS. What unspooled before me was a repository to rival the Library of Congress. Dozens of albums, precisely named and dated, stuffed with hundreds of photos each. *Yukon, October 4–7, 2012. Big Sky Country, February 11–21, 2011.*

DIY Star Bus.

I tapped that one.

The first photograph depicted a rusted old Volkswagen bus parked on a gravel driveway before a small cabin. The vehicle was utter junk: sidewalls split and fraying and flat, windows grimed over, cracked, or missing. The body was pitted and scarred.

The caption read:

Three hundred bucks at auction, and I had to tow her home. She doesn't know it yet – but she's going to be my *Niña*, my *Pinta*, my *Santa Maria*. We'll sail the starry meadows together.

Gag.

I studied the cabin behind the bus. So that was where my father lived now. Red shutters, a red door, huddled beneath an enormous evergreen. Where was this?

The photo had more than two *hundred* comments, including one from someone named Georgina Paraholt, who wrote: *You've adopted lots of strays over the years, Jonny, but this one's a real beaut.*

Jonny? Strays?

The next few photos were close-ups of the battered van. Shattered headlights, a chewed-up tailpipe, rotted carpeting. But I happened across one that gave me pause: a selfie, taken on a sunny day. In this one, my father laughed, holding an electric drill with his free hand. Behind him, the van rested on blocks, a patient awaiting surgery. But I couldn't take my eyes off my father. The man I knew had valued order, and it had shown in his often tight expression, his restrained wardrobe. *This* man, however…

His hair was longer than I recalled and lightened by the sun. His hairline had hardly moved. He wore a scruffy beard over a deep tan. The crinkles around his eyes had deepened, but the combination of all these things only made him look more youthful. A man unencumbered.

This was my father? This blissed-out cabin dweller in hemp necklaces and beads? Who wrote swooning love letters to the universe on a website and restored junkyard vans?

Beneath the photo:

Day one of Operation Stargazer! Lots and lots of work ahead for this beautiful baby.

The first comment belonged, again, to Georgina: *My sexy mountain goat!*

Ugh.

Over the course of seventy photos, the Volkswagen transformed. Whitewall tyres appeared. The interior was gutted and power washed. The old transmission was lifted out, a rebuilt one plugged in. I'd known my father to be handy, but now he documented a construction project in the van's belly: he fashioned the wooden bones of a living space, with a bed-frame, cabinets, hidden compartments, a bookshelf, a sink. The windows were replaced, the body sanded and painted. Curtains were hung, cabinets were stocked. The grand accomplishment was the skylight he installed in the roof, complete with a removable panel.

The final photo: the finished Volkswagen, parked on a

rocky plain. A shadowy range of mountains crawled across the horizon, purple in the day's fading light. A campfire, a column of smoke twisting skyward. The faint pricks of stars just visible above. And there, protruding through the skylight panel, the barrel body of a remarkable telescope, aimed skyward.

I was wrong. She's not my *Santa Maria*. She's my wandering Star Bus, my magical Hubble-on-wheels.

I'll keep the cabin warm and waiting, Georgina wrote, *while you and your lady wander the earth*. Oh, how I hated her. I tapped her name and saw in her profile picture a laughing woman with her eyes tightly shut, lazy blond hair looped up with a string. She was beautiful and probably a decade older than Mom. She wasn't alone, either: part of my father's bearded face, teeth bared in silent laughter, pressed against her cheek. The next photo was hauntingly intimate, taken from the inside of a tent. The flap was open, pines stretching away into the distance. In the foreground, tangled together, were two pairs of bare legs. Beads around her ankles, tattoos of the sun and moon upon the top of each foot. The other legs, I was certain, belonged to my father.

That's enough. I wanted no part of this world. For the first time, I felt grateful that my astronomy career wouldn't make it off the launch pad. My father still clearly pined for the stars. I wanted no part of a world in which I had to share the skies with him.

I returned to his page, intent on rescinding this new "friendship". The page loaded slowly, and when it finally did, I saw a fresh red badge pinned to the MESSAGES icon.

Fuck.

So. Back to school.

Derek worked his magic. The entire administrative staff adored him. School had been harder for him than other kids, so he'd just worked harder, endearing himself to a whole bunch of teachers along the way. They did what they could to help him, and, by extension, me. Ms Grace arranged for me to make up the missing credit after school. At Derek's insistence, I quit both of my jobs and spent every spare hour bent over my books, trying to gain back lost ground. By late April, I'd salvaged my GPA. It wasn't anything special – but at least it wasn't a charred heap of fail.

I'd become well practised at the art of avoiding Vanessa. She wasn't happy with the arrangement, I knew; she tried catching my eye frequently, and once a note wound its way back to me during our shared health class. I left the note on my desk, unopened, when class ended. Was I angry at her? I didn't know. What I did know was that I couldn't figure a way to let her actions slide. All along, she'd known about her stepfather. Known what he and his employer meant to my family. And she'd kept that from me. What had she thought would happen?

When I told Derek, he was surprisingly unruffled. In fact, he took Vanessa's side. "The girl loved you, Z," he said. "And come on. You're both kids. You don't know how to handle the hard stuff yet." I protested, but he shut me down. "You get a few years behind you. You'll see what I mean."

"The daughter of my enemy is my enemy," I said. Then, frustrated by the bemusement on his face, I exiled myself to the bathroom since I didn't have a bedroom door to slam. I turned the sink on to drown out my brother's laughter – but only for a moment. Water costs money.

I glared at my own reflection in the mirror, trying to remember the last time I'd been so angry. *He just does what he's told*, Vanessa had said, but that didn't change anything. She might as well have said it wasn't personal. But how could it *not* be personal? Our dad was *gone*.

The spring after Dad's death. My first week back at school.

That was the last time I'd been this angry.

My classmates had kept their distance, as if tragedy were contagious. During exams, I'd catch my teachers studying me intently. *Are you okay?* they asked with their eyes. They'd pull me aside after class: *If you need to talk…*

Bobby Longdale witnessed one such exchange with a

teacher and made a sign with Magic Marker. He held it up during class for everyone to see:

IS WIDDLE ZACHAWY OKAY?
DOES WIDDLE ZACHAWY NEED TO TALK?

Nervous laughter, stifled giggles, from our classmates. Encouraged, he scribbled another one and held it up, too.

DOES WIDDLE ZACHAWY MISS HIS DADDY?

Until that day, I hadn't really known what it meant to see red. Had I gotten across the room before Mr Ballard looped his arms around my chest, I think I might have broken Bobby's jaw. Instead, Bobby went to the principal's office, and I spent the day with the nurse, lying quietly on a cot in the dark. I felt as if I were a kid again, replaying the events of that long-ago day when Bobby had poured milk on my artwork, and I'd wallpapered him with lasagne. Remembering that day brought back Dad's gentle lecture about love and anger.

That anger, I sometimes thought, had maybe never really left. It was always there, simmering under a thick skin of regret. And I thought if I just allowed myself to really *feel* it, maybe things wouldn't be so hard. Maybe I just needed to let it out. But at who? At the names on the law-firm letterhead? At Vanessa's stepfather? At Derek, for not being Dad?

At Dad, for being gone?

Suddenly I was just tired. Tired of being angry, of feeling like a victim. Holding this lit fuse inside me that only ever scorched *me*. For a moment, I saw what Derek had meant. The accident wasn't Aaron Bartlett's fault. If it hadn't been him writing those letters, it would have been someone else. Vanessa wasn't a player in this story. What was she *supposed* to say to me? And when? That night on the boat, when we were so close? When I'd told her about Dad?

That's real sad, she could have said. *Um – by the way, I live with the man who's twisting the knife. Oops! Sorry!*

Derek was right. It wasn't her fault. But it still hurt to look at her.

So at school I held my tongue. When I recalled the fleeting intimacy between us, I pushed it from my mind. I carved a narrative, like a mantra: *We're finished. We're done.* I was finished with her, and she with me. That was it. I had other things to look forward to. Like college, where maybe things would be different. Where maybe *I* could be different.

So I threw myself into the work of graduating. It didn't matter how much money Derek thought he could set aside. It would never make a dent in tuition. So each night, after homework, he and I filled out applications for grants and financial aid. April tumbled into May; prom came and went, and I didn't go. By year's end, I really wasn't mad at Vanessa any more. There were no more notes; she didn't try to catch my eye in the hall. She'd accepted it, too. And I stopped thinking about her.

Until the day I saw her mother on the front page of the local paper in a group photograph. The headline loomed large above her face:

CITY COUNCIL CONTROVERSY
Council members gamble on resort, go bust

So that was what Vanessa had meant. *It wasn't up to me.* The writer of the piece described it as "a folly of magnificent proportions" and quoted the anonymous spouse of another council member, who said, "I want to kill him, and then I want to divorce him, and then I want to kill him again."

Even with how things had turned out between us, I felt awful about our argument, about not being there for her. But I turned to my mantra. We were finished; her happiness had never been my responsibility, and being there for her – well, that wasn't on me, either. Not any more. *Remember what you get for letting someone in*, I reminded myself. *It feels good for a little while. It hurts for a hell of a lot longer.*

I'd had enough of hurting. So I left her alone.

* * *

And just like that, my senior year ended. No more homework or spending my days in class. With a couple months before I departed, I considered returning to Dot's. I could ask for my job back. Might as well work as much as I could before I left, stow as much as I could in the family account.

I mean, that was one option.

Another one kept tickling me, lodged somewhere in a corner of my mind.

When the girls had gone to bed, Derek and I celebrated quietly. He opened a bottle of beer, then passed another to me. "To doing things right," he said, raising the bottle.

"Doing it right," I agreed.

We sat on old lawn chairs in the strip of grass that passed for our backyard. Mama's window was open, the *whir* and rattle of her electric fan audible on the breeze. A trawler clanged somewhere in the bay.

While Derek slid down in his chair, heaving a gust of relief, I propped my sketchbook on one knee, idly sketching by the light of the kitchen window behind me. I could hear him swallow, smack his lips lightly.

"I've been thinking," I began slowly.

"Uh-oh."

"I've been thinking that I should leave…sooner."

Derek rolled his head onto his shoulder, searching my eyes with his own. He drummed his fingertips on his bottle. "Like how 'sooner' you thinking?"

"I've been thinking about, like...tomorrow."

He frowned. "Why so fast?"

"It's like this," I said, straightening up, putting the sketchbook aside. "I leave tomorrow. I get down there with, what, a couple months till the semester begins? I have some time to get to know the town. Get my sea legs."

"Start to make it your own," Derek mused. He wasn't disagreeing; it sounded as if he were just ordering his thoughts, rearranging them to get himself on board with the idea. "Get a head start on the other kids."

"Know my way around from day one," I pointed out. "No getting lost in the halls. None of that."

"They even open the dorms that early?" He cocked his head at me, then pointed the bottle my way. "I don't know why I ask. You wouldn't have planned all this in secret without doing your research."

"It's called pre-semester work," I said. "They give you work on campus, like groundskeeping or cafeteria prep or whatever, and in exchange you get your pick of the dorm rooms, and you get to live there rent-free until classes start."

"So you get some money in your pocket, or just a bed?"

"They pay, a little."

He sighed, sounding resigned. "You leave tomorrow, I don't get to see you walk at graduation."

"That's the thing. And I feel bad about it. I feel like you should see me do it. Like you've earned that much."

"Z, come now." But he thought it over, and then he said, "You're ready to get started, aren't you?"

I nodded. "I think I am."

"Well, I suppose they can mail your diploma," he said finally. "I kinda like the thought of it," he went on. "All those kids on the stage, prancing and posing in their robes, and meanwhile you're down the road ahead of them."

"I mean, it's not a competition—"

He waved his beer at me. "Yes, yes, I know, I know. Still." He drained the bottle, then went inside for another. When he returned, he said, "You sort things out with the girl? With Vanessa?"

I stared at my feet, which seemed like answer enough. "That part of the reason you want to leave early?"

I shrugged.

"You know," Derek said, sinking back into his chair, "me and Leah, we tried keeping it together when I went away to school. It didn't work out. You throw a young guy into a school with a bunch of interesting strangers, things just happen. Home seems awful far away."

"It's not that," I said, and it wasn't. I didn't like the idea of bumping into her at graduation, or around town all summer. Whatever had been there just wasn't any more. Which made us no better or worse than your average high school fling. We weren't special.

"Something else, then?" Derek asked. He studied me,

then sighed. "You always were good at putting that load on yourself, Z. Even when nobody else put it there, you'd do it on your own."

"I'm excited. I wasn't, but now I am. Except..." I hesitated. "Except I don't know if I can—"

"Don't," he interrupted. Then he handed me his beer. "Hold this. Hold up." Once again, he disappeared into the house. When he came back, a moment later, he was holding an envelope.

"What, you want me to mail the bills before I go? One last errand?"

That made him laugh. His voice had gone rich and low recently, and I wondered if the deeper saturation dives were somehow responsible. Maybe the higher pressure, the gas mixtures he had to breathe, did a number on his vocal cords. I tried to recall if Dad's voice had dropped like that, but Dad had always sounded like a foghorn, sonorous and deep.

"This'll ease you a bit," Derek said, passing me the envelope. The envelope was marked with his employer's logo. I glanced at him, then opened it to find his pay cheque. This wasn't anything new; we'd sat at the table together many nights, tallying our earnings for the week. Partners of a sort, each of us throwing ballast out of the boat, trying to keep the family afloat.

"Go on."

I pulled out the pay stub and nearly choked when I saw the number there.

He howled. "Your *face*, Z. Oh, god, your *face*."

I coughed, hammering my chest with one fist. My eyes watered. "This real?"

He took his dive card from his shirt pocket and handed it to me. It was crisp and new, printed on stiff, shiny stock. I spotted the new certification immediately.

"You qualified," I said, struck stupid.

"Just Level Two."

"You didn't tell me."

"I didn't want to jinx it," he said. "Now you know."

I turned the card over in my hands. As an air diver, he'd been at sixty-foot depths for the past year. They'd started sending him deep enough to require a gas mixture in his tanks. Level II, though, that was where you started to get into the real depths. Eventually, if Derek kept ranking up, he'd wind up working underwater for weeks on end, living in a little tin can.

"So how deep do they let you go now?" I asked. "Hundred?"

He shook his head.

"One-twenty?" I waited, but he just looked smug. "One *fifty*?"

"One-eighty," he said. "And boy, that's where you start seeing Dad's weird-ass sea monster shit." He took the dive card back, then said, "My point, Z: clear your damn head. This is good money. Maybe I can hire someone to help with Mama and the girls. Even send you a little scratch sometimes."

We sipped our beers. The moon floated above as though tethered to our lawn chairs.

After a while, I said, "He'd be proud, you know. He'd throw you a party."

Derek knocked his bottle against mine. "Wouldn't be a *good* party," he said.

I laughed, remembering how inept Dad had been at pulling things together. "That time we went to the beach, and we both swam in our underwear because he forgot to bring anything resembling swim trunks," I said.

"He'd be proud of you, too," Derek said. "First college boy in the family. Well," he said, reconsidering, "first to graduate, at least."

"Fancy-ass *painting* college," I said.

"Still college, though."

"Still college," I agreed.

In the morning, Derek told me he'd gotten his orders. Six days on the rig. I felt uncomfortable leaving home while he'd be away, but Leah reassured me that she'd be staying there with the girls, and with Mama.

Mama.

I didn't tell her I was going away. I sat beside her, hoping she might swim up from that fog to see me. But she lay still, eyes only slightly open. She didn't make a sound when I rested my hand upon her cheek, when I smoothed her hair. I told her I loved her, then kissed her cheek, as I always did.

In the driveway, Derek put his arms around Leah. "You're sure you're good?" he asked her. "I'll bring the girls back in a few hours, but then I'm due at the rig, and—"

"We're good," Leah said. "We're always good." Then she turned to me. "Z, be good to the ladies you meet. And don't blush, now. Your whole head turns red."

As Derek steered onto the highway, I half turned in my seat. Orilly receded behind us. I could see the hilltop neighbourhood where Vanessa lived, and I wondered if she was looking at us through her telescope. I waved, just in case. There would be time to kill on the bus ride south. Maybe I'd write a letter. Maybe I wouldn't.

The cheapest Greyhound station was in San Luis Obispo. Along the way, I taught Robin and Rachael to play punch buggy. Two miles outside of Orilly, Robin spotted an orange Beetle and belted Rachael hard enough to make her cry. I explained the rules of moderation, and Rachael anxiously awaited the next Volkswagen sighting so she could slug back.

It quickly became clear that there just weren't enough Beetles on the road to play the game, so we agreed to expand the roster of vehicles. We were thirty miles out of Orilly by then.

"PT Cruisers," Derek suggested. "Those things *look* about as dumb as Beetles."

"Beetles are cool," Rachael protested.

"Hummers," Robin said. "They're *kind* of rare, but not too rare."

"Hey, do bug vans count?" Derek asked. He pointed at the opposite side of the highway, where a Volkswagen bus, robin's egg blue, puttered north, towards Orilly.

"Sure," I said. "Why not?"

My brother slugged me in the shoulder. "Punch buggy, then."

We had an hour to kill in SLO, so Derek treated us all to burritos at Chili Peppers. Afterwards, we walked to Meadow Park and watched a pickup game of volleyball in the sandpits.

When it was time, I wrapped the girls in a shared hug, kissed their cheeks, offered advice. Derek locked me in a tight grip next, pounded his hand on my back. "Do me proud," he said.

I wished I had something comforting or eloquent to say, but I didn't trust myself to speak. I just waved goodbye as the bus pulled away. I kneeled on the seat, watching until they receded into silhouettes against the glow of the Greyhound station, glad they couldn't see my eyes.

34

VANESSA

I'd never met my father's parents, and he'd never talked about them. Mom would only say, vaguely, that they'd had a poor relationship. After my father had left, when Mom was certain he wasn't coming back, we began boxing his things into cartons that she stacked in the garage. For what purpose, I didn't know; he certainly never returned for them. As we worked, I happened across an unfamiliar key and showed it to her. "Goodness," she said, and led me to the small closet beneath our staircase. From a crawl space I hadn't known existed, she lugged a fireproof safe into the open.

Inside the safe were artefacts from another life, another time: a scarred Zippo lighter; a dented sheriff's deputy badge; a Southwest Football Officials Association card, softened with age. The name stamped on the card was PHILIP EMERSON DRAKE.

"Your grandfather," Mom said.

In a folder stuffed with yellowed documents, we found a marriage certificate in the names of Philip E. Drake and

Haley Rose Sanders and a decree of divorce from the California courts, dated twenty-one years before.

"Your father never liked to talk about it," Mom said, but she recounted a story he'd shared, reluctantly, about a family vacation. A road trip through the Midwest. My grandfather abandoned his family at a highway rest stop. "Nobody knew he was gone for half an hour, when he didn't return from the bathroom," Mom explained. "Your father was ten. And he never saw your grandfather again."

I understood that day that what my father had done to us was, perhaps, inevitable. That I might never see *him* again. Was it his fault that he had a coward's blood, that he was too weak to rise above his own genetic predispositions? I promised myself I would never do what he did, not to anyone.

That was before I shoved Cece away. Before I lied to Zach about who I was.

So.

I didn't answer his Facebook message. I didn't tell Mom about it, or Aaron. I thought that if I ignored my father, he might just go away. He'd already proved quite capable of doing just that.

I know you're probably angry, he'd written. *Confused, even. There are things I'd like to say, but not like this.* There were plenty of other words, too, but they all faded into one another. I didn't want to read them.

He would know, of course, that I'd seen the message. Facebook would tell him so. But I wouldn't write back. I wouldn't give him the satisfaction. Instead, I hoped he would stare at the screen for hours, waiting for my reply. For weeks. Forever. He deserved exactly that.

So I didn't reply. I unfriended him.

Facebook was unbiased, at least. It made it easy to pretend nothing had happened. With the tap of a button, he was out of my life again. Gone, banished to his cabin in the woods, where he belonged.

Until the day I arrived home to find a Volkswagen bus parked in our driveway, and my father leaning against it.

Dot's was nearly abandoned, to my chagrin. I'd hoped for a full house, plenty of distractions. An audience, in case I needed to make a scene. But there were only two other customers, in a corner booth. A server leaned on the lunch counter, chewing gum, swiping her phone screen lethargically. From the kitchen, I heard laughter.

I'd chosen Dot's for the safety of a crowd, yes, but also because Zach would maybe be there. If things went badly with my father, perhaps Zach would stage an intervention. It was a lot to hope for, but I would take any lifeline I could find.

My father sat patiently across the table. Waiting, I

supposed, for me to speak first. I tried to outlast him, waging my own silent war. When at last he parted his lips to speak, I blurted, "I have to pee," and darted away. I hid in the restroom for as long as I thought I could. Splashed water on my face. When I emerged, I nearly collided with a busboy and his plastic tub of dishes. He sidestepped me with an apology and began to clean the table previously occupied by the other two customers.

"Excuse me," I said to the young man. "Does, um, Zach work today?"

But the boy in the apron just frowned. "You want his job?"

"Want his job?"

"Yeah, girl. He quit a while ago. I heard he moved."

I blinked. "*Moved?*" No, that wasn't possible. Zach was mad at me, sure, but he wouldn't leave town without saying goodbye. Would he? *You betrayed him, Vanessa. So: yeah, maybe he would.*

I walked back to my father's table in a daze. When I sat down, he reached for my wrist. "Cass, hon, are you okay?"

Cass. Hon.

Those words. I hadn't heard him say them – hadn't heard him say *anything* – in so long. And they resurrected memories I'd tamped down, packed away. The casual way he'd taken a shit on everything I loved. The long nights away from home that he never had an excuse for, the way he berated and gaslighted Mom when she dared ask him where he'd been.

I jerked my arm away, suddenly enraged. Just sitting there, calling me pet names. Like nothing had changed. Like he *belonged*.

He raised his palms. "Whoa, there."

"Not your damn horse," I snapped. He sighed – as if he had expected this, as if a bit of petulance was the price for seeing me – and that pissed me off, too. "Oh, *excuse* me," I added. "Already had your fill? You can leave any time."

He settled back against the booth. "I'm okay," he said. "Are you?"

"Does Mom know you're here?" I asked. "Because she *shouldn't*, and you shouldn't tell her. She's finally *happy*, you know." The word nearly jammed in my throat. It was true, in a broad sense, that Mom was happier now. But the last couple of months hadn't exactly been a sitcom.

"No," he said. "No, she doesn't know. I came for you. Just to see you."

"So you give a shit about *one* of us." I folded my arms. "That's nice. If you didn't want her to know, why did you park in the *driveway*? Captain *Obvious*. Come to think of it, how did you even know where to find us? Were you stalking us?"

"I knew you'd be upset," he said. He looked away, squinted at the afternoon sun. "You're right to be."

"*Thanks.*"

"I didn't think you'd accept my Facebook thing."

Thing. As if he wasn't an old pro at social media, with his photo albums and blog posts and hippie-ass girlfriend. Sitting here now in his back-to-the-land get-up, all hemp necklace and linen shirt and tortoiseshell glasses.

"My mistake," I said.

"You're…" He trailed off, and I wondered what he'd been about to say. *Hostile? Vicious? Bitchier than I remember?* "Can we just – talk, maybe?"

"Talk, if you want to," I said, arms wide. "You're here for a reason, I guess. What do you want?"

With a flicker of hope in his eyes, he leaned forward. "I've never stopped thinking about you," he began. He must have seen the daggers in my eyes, because he put his palms up once more, as if warding off an attack. "I know you must think I'm awful, Cass. I wanted to say some things. You don't have to say anything back. I hope you'll just hear me."

"Don't call me that."

My father looked at his hands. "You're graduating soon," he said. "I have a gift for you."

"I don't want it."

"Hey, hear me out," he said. "At least do that much?"

I put on my most defiant face. I knew how petulant I looked, but there'd be no better time to indulge my most base instincts. I was *angry.* I didn't realize how angry I'd been, or for how long. At him. At Mom. At the world. And now he sat right there, fooling himself that he had a chance to make things right. As if he hadn't gleefully detonated that chance years ago.

All he was now was a perfect target.

"Whatever," I said. "*Jonathan.*"

He flinched. "I – want to give you *Andromeda*."

I stared at him. "Your…*blog?*"

That made him laugh. He wasn't allowed to be light and full of humour. Not now, not ever.

"No, Cass— Sorry. *Vanessa.* Not the blog, though you can have that, too, if you—"

"Fuck your blog."

He sighed again, then nodded towards the parking lot. "The bus. That's what I meant."

"You're not serious," I said.

"I'm very serious."

"I don't want your shitty old van."

"Bus," he corrected. "And… Well, okay. That's up to you, of course. But she's yours. Always has been, from the moment I saw her. I just knew."

Bullshit. I'd read what he wrote. His *Niña, Pinta, Santa Maria,* his Hubble-on-wheels, his Star Bus. No – he was lying to me. He wanted something.

"She's all yours," he said. "Arecibo on wheels. A mobile skywatching installation."

"Arecibo's a *radio* telescope."

"Palomar, then. Griffith. Whatever." He pointed. "You see that skylight? Telescope goes right through there. You drive her out on the tundra, or into a canyon. No light pollution anywhere. You can see *amazing* things."

This I remembered about him. The way he romanticized the sky. The woman he was sleeping with had joked about his obsession. I wondered now if he'd fucked her in the back of the van he said he'd bought for me. I was certain he had.

"You can't buy your way back in," I said.

"I wouldn't expect your forgiveness to come so cheaply."

"You can't afford it," I muttered. "Trust me."

He let that one go. He was quiet as the server came by to refill his water glass. When she'd gone again, he said, "You're still all about Cornell, huh? Still the Sagan acolyte."

That caught me unprepared. "So?"

"Don't go."

I wrinkled my brow. "Excuse me?"

"Don't go," he repeated. He'd always hated the idea. But he'd never told me not to go, even when he was mocking me. "At least…not yet."

Don't go. I didn't tell him that there was an email in my inbox at this very moment from the institution he loathed. Subject line: *Wait list decision.* I didn't tell him it had been sitting there since March, that I couldn't bring myself to open it. That I'd decided maybe it was better not to know –

not yet, maybe not ever. *Don't go*, indeed. No, that decision had pretty much been made for me. "You have a better idea?" I asked.

"I do." He fanned his hands wide, like a Hollywood producer imagining a starlet's name in lights. "Take a year off. See the world. Don't rush into, like, six trillion dollars of personal debt."

"Gap years are a bad idea. Everyone says so." That wasn't necessarily true, but I wanted to be contrarian. It didn't matter what inarguable facts he threw at me, I wouldn't agree with him. Had he pointed at the sun and called it a star, I'd have argued that the sun, in fact, is a butt.

"Trust me, Ca— Vanessa."

"Trust you."

He nodded.

"Trust," I said. "*You. Really.*"

"When you're my age, you'll realize two things," he went on. "One: you can *always* go back to school. Cornell isn't going anywhere. They *like* money. They'll take you when you're old, too, I promise. And two: you'll *wish* you'd wasted a *minimum* of three hundred sixty-five days of your youth."

"That's why you ran away?" I asked. "Because we crushed your fun?"

His face fell. "I didn't mean it like that."

"Growing up was just too hard. You wanted to be young again. That it?" I couldn't stop going after him. It felt *good*.

"So you just shrugged us off, was that it? Extra weight you didn't need. Ballast. Toss the wife and the brat overboard, they're only holding you back from—"

"I didn't mean it like that," he repeated.

"How did you mean it?"

He looked like someone who had painted himself into a corner. "I only mean well."

"Right," I said. "You've always only meant well. Right?" I stared at him for a long time, until he looked away. "Did you really come all the way out here just to foist your shitty van on me and decide my future?"

"I only wanted to help," he said. Then he feebly added: "I *am* your fa—"

There it was. I wouldn't let him say the word.

"No," I interrupted. "You aren't. You never were." I leaned forward, wishing I had claws. "A father who wanted a snowball's chance in hell of forgiveness would have opened with an *apology*. Not a bribe. You said you had things to say. Well? What were they? I haven't heard anything yet."

"Just get behind the wheel," he offered. Still trying to sell me. "Drive to the Rockies. Down the Alaska Highway. Park somewhere under the stars. Sleep under the Milky Way. Watch the *aurora bor*—"

"*Jesus.* You don't stop."

He was flailing now. "You think college has things to teach you that life won't," he said. "I promise you're wrong."

"Oh, I don't know," I retorted. "Maybe it'll teach me to avoid the great American art of repeating your father's mistakes." His face paled, and I zeroed in. "Is that what I am? Some sort of sleeper agent? I'll get married, start a family, then – flip! – something in me will wake up, and I'll just drop them on the side of the road because I never got to swim with sea turtles in Costa fucking Rica?"

I was breathing hard when I finished. The server was watching from the counter; behind her, faces gathered in the kitchen window.

He was quiet for a long time. "So you don't want the bus."

"Not if you come with it," I said.

He shook his head. "That's up to you."

"I'm not driving you back to your dirty commune."

"I'll hop a Greyhound or something." He looked hopeful now. "Does that mean you'll take *Andromeda*?"

I held out my hand. "Keys."

His face brightened. He now looked like a man who had gotten what he came for, and I realized that the bus wasn't what I'd assumed. It wasn't a bribe; it was an offering. His penance, his absolution. Giving me the bus got him off the hook. For everything. He dug in his pocket for a ring of keys and slipped the Volkswagen key free. He beamed as he placed it in my hand.

"Stay right here," I said. I walked to the lunch counter

and asked the server for paper and a marker. She fished a paper children's menu from a folder and pressed a fat Sharpie into my hand. I could feel my father watching as I scribbled, my back to him. When I was finished, and without a word to him, I walked through the doors and into the sunshine.

In the parking lot, I unlocked the bus and climbed inside. The bus smelled faintly of weed and bodies, and I knew he'd lied. The bus wasn't for me. It never had been.

That's when I understood what Cece meant. *You're lying to yourself,* she'd said.

Cornell had never been about Carl Sagan. That was what I'd told myself, and it turned out I was a pretty convincing liar. No, Cornell was about one thing and one thing only: the biggest *fuck you* I could manage to give my father. All those sepia-toned memories of the deck, the stars – they'd papered over the things I'd forgotten. The awful things he'd said. The way he'd taken shots at me, as if I'd disappointed him by not romanticizing the same ideals he held. He didn't want a daughter. He wanted someone who would only ever look upon him with adoration.

A clone. I thought of the woman on his Facebook page. No. He'd wanted a *groupie.*

Had he ever wanted Mom? Me? How could someone ever just walk away from their family?

My father stared at me through the diner window,

shielding his eyes. He wore a perplexed expression, like a man who had scripted this whole exchange in advance, only for me to set fire to the script. I started the engine and issued a jaunty wave. Confused, he returned it, his hand lingering in the air.

As he watched, I leaned forward and slid the children's menu onto the dash, marker side out, where he could read what I'd written.

FOR SALE BY OWNER
CHEAP

His face fell, and he slumped against the booth, defeated. I felt a fleeting sense of victory, but then he pushed himself to his feet, and that rush turned sour with adrenaline.

Now I just had to get out of here. The transmission made a tortured, grinding sound as I shifted into reverse. Whether my father was an inept mechanic, or because I was so inexperienced behind the wheel, I couldn't tell. I backed out of the parking spot – thank goodness the lot was empty – then shifted into drive, handling the bus like an old pro, at least until I thumped over the kerb at the exit. Somewhere behind me, on the other side of a velvet curtain – Jesus, *velvet* – several heavy objects clattered to the floor. If I did keep the Volkswagen, the curtain would be history. And the bus would for damn sure get a new name.

Andromeda.

My father stood on the sidewalk watching as I drove his bus away.

Jesus, what an asshole.

35

ZACH

The bus to San Diego was half-full. Around me, people slept, or watched movies on little devices, or bobbed their heads to music. I watched the scenery slide by awhile, then opened my backpack, hunting for my sketchbook. Resting right on top were two yellow envelopes. I hadn't put them there.

I thumbed open the first one and found a sheaf of hundred-dollar bills. My skin drew tight like a glove, and I cast a glance across the aisle to be certain nobody had seen. No one had. Carefully, I riffled through the stack, counting. Fifteen bills. More money than I'd ever seen in one place. And there was a note:

Don't spend it all on pencils, Z.

The second envelope was bulky and fastened shut with a coppery paper fastener. I up-ended it and shook the contents, and Dad's dive compass slid into my open palm.

I'd always loved this compass, had begged Dad to let me

hold it. I turned it over in my hands now, traced my father's name and the date of his first dive, etched into the back. It bore the markings of that day: the case dented, scorched in places. Little scars chipped into the surface revealed the bright brass beneath. The glass shell was cracked and fogged over, but it still worked. The dial turned lazily, pointing northward, towards Orilly. The bold *S* indicated the highway ahead. San Diego. The future. *My* future.

All this time I'd thought the compass was lost in Dad's accident. And Derek had it all along. As I slipped it back into the envelope, I found another note:

So you can always find your way back home.
Love you.

It was signed by all of them: Derek, the girls, Leah. Beneath her own signature, in tiny letters, Robin had added *and Mama too.*

I wiped my eyes and put the envelopes away, then leaned against the window and began to sketch. I drew Derek in profile, in shadow; I drew the girls attacking a burrito, eyes shining. In Santa Maria, I sketched a pickup trundling through acres of strawberries, birthing clouds of dust; in Santa Barbara, the missions, stark against the summer sky. I drew the ocean, placid but for threads of white foam that erased themselves against the shore.

I drew Vanessa as I remembered her, sitting on the side of Dad's boat, legs dangling, her shoulders up. I worked on her smile for miles, trying to capture the way it hinted at things she knew that no one else did, secrets she'd never tell. It had been a mistake, I realized, to leave without seeing her one last time. To leave things like I had. And it was undeniably strange to be the one leaving Orilly, instead of her.

"Buddy, you get this?"

I looked up to see a guy leaning over the seat, holding out his phone. A little message floated there, above the game he'd been playing.

Emergency alert

Tsunami warning in this area. Avoid coast, find high ground ASAP. Check local media – NWS

"I don't have a phone," I said. "NWS?"

"I don't know, either," the man said. He stood up, holding out his phone. "Hey, anybody else getting this?"

"National Weather Service," answered a woman. "Did anyone tell the driver?"

But someone had. The driver steered off the highway and into a filling station. "Ten minutes," he announced on the loudspeaker. The door hissed open, and people disembarked quickly, rushing into the convenience store.

I shoved my sketchbook into my bag and slung it over my shoulder. The driver was circling the bus, headed for the pumps, when I approached and asked, "Are we going back?"

"I've got to call it in," he said. "I'll make an announcement when everybody's back on."

Inside the store, the passengers had gathered around the register. Behind the cashier was a TV, where a sombre-faced woman reported an earthquake in the Sea of Okhotsk. "That's about a hundred miles off the Hokkaido coast," she said. "USGS is reporting the magnitude as nine point two. The Tohoku earthquake, just a few years ago, was a nine point oh." She paused, listening to someone's voice in her ear, then continued: "We're waiting for confirmation from the ground. The event occurred forty minutes ago. This could mean the island is experiencing high waves or tsunami activity at this moment."

Over the next fifteen minutes, it was confirmed by an expert from the United States Geological Survey. *Tsunami.* The newscaster and the expert recalled the previous earthquake in Japan and the subsequent wave and critical damage it had caused.

"In that quake," she said, "warnings and advisories were declared for the western coast of the United States. Should US residents expect the same today?"

I felt the crowd of travellers lean forward, straining to hear the answer.

"Absolutely," the expert said, and several people exhaled in a nervous rush. "Coastal states have already been put on alert. Any waves generated by this seismic event would be expected to make landfall in a matter of hours."

The newscaster turned back to the camera and said, "The USGS has declared a tsunami warning, we can now confirm, for residents of Alaska, Washington, Oregon, California, and Hawaii. People should immediately seek shelter as far inland, and as high above sea level, as possible. Let me repeat this—"

CNN was replaced then by the haunting image of colourful vertical bars and a high-pitched tone. It repeated several urgent beeps, and a calm but firm voice stated, "This is not a test. Attention. Attention. This is the Emergency Broadcast System. Repeat: this is not a test…"

"Oh, Jesus," said the man who'd shown me his phone. He was transfixed by the screen, swiping through a news article. "It says nine point two is twice as powerful as the last big quake. Guys, it says it might not even be hours."

Nobody was listening to him. People were on their own phones; some charged towards the antique-looking payphone outside. I wondered if it even worked any more. Twice as powerful as the last quake, the guy had said. The last time I'd seen the Emergency Broadcast System message was 2011, when the Tohoku earthquake and tsunami caused warnings here, too. Orilly had been untouched, then.

But I couldn't help thinking about 2008, and that damned surprise storm. That storm had been a warning to me and Mama, but Dad didn't take it seriously. Hell, the storm had essentially given him a gift: an affordable boat.

But that was then. This was now, and now was going to be worse. Much worse.

I never should have left.

Over the incessant beeping of the television alert, I heard the cashier shouting into a phone. "My sister's stranded at the aquarium. I have to get her," he said. "I have to close up. You're going to want the pumps off." I presumed he was talking to his employer. He listened a moment, then said, "Thank you," and hung up.

"The Monterey aquarium?" I asked him.

He ignored me. To the remaining customers in the store, he called, "Folks, I'm shutting down. Make your final purchases, get yourself safely on the road and to high ground."

"If you're driving to Monterey," I said, "I'll cover your gas if you can drop me on the way."

The cashier finally looked at me. "Where?"

"Orilly."

He blinked. "Where?"

"Orilla del Cielo," I clarified. "That crappy little oil town north of Big Sur, on the way to Monterey."

I waited outside as the cashier finished closing the store. Everyone else filed onto the bus. The driver spotted me waiting and jogged over to ask if I was coming or what.

I nodded towards the cashier. "I'm catching a ride back the way we came," I said. "My family's there."

"You sure, kid?" he asked. "I'm going to turn inland to Bakersfield. We'll get there well ahead of any bad weather."

I didn't point out that an approaching tsunami was a hell of a lot more worrisome than mere bad weather. "I can't."

He nodded. "Yeah, all right. You be safe." Then he dashed back to the bus and shut the doors. I watched as the bus rumbled away from the pumps and onto the highway. It caught the sun, glinting gold as it receded.

As I waited, I pulled out Dad's compass. The *S* still leaned towards San Diego, but now all I could see was the needle pointing towards Orilly. I hadn't been gone more than a few hours, I realized, and already that damned town was dragging me right back. Just like it had done to Derek.

The cashier finished closing up, then waved me over to an old Honda Civic. I stared at it a moment, this chariot that would sweep me backwards in time, unravelling those precious few hours of my future.

In the car, he thrust out a hand. "Edgar, man."

"Zach."

"You don't have to pay gas," he said as I buckled in. "Nice of you, but I'm goin' anyway." His phone rang before I could protest, and he snapped it up: "Yeah? Yeah. No. Yeah, no, I am." He listened for a moment. "No, you shouldn't do that." Another pause. "Right. No, I didn't think about that.

Fast as I can."

He flipped the phone shut – one of the old clamshell models – then held it out to me. "You got people to call?"

Leah answered breathlessly on the fourth ring. She said, "Did you hear that, Z? Listen." There was silence for a moment, then she came back. "I held the phone up so you could hear, but they just went off."

"What did?"

"The emergency sirens," she said. "They started five minutes ago, but they just stopped." She paused, and I heard a low wail rise until it soared. "They're back." Before I could say anything, she rushed on: "You don't worry about us. I've got the girls, and your mama's here, too. My brother and his family are loading up at his house right now. Going to Dad's place in Paso. They'll be here any minute to pick us up. They've got room." She lowered her voice, presumably so the girls wouldn't hear. "Are you okay? Are you someplace safe?"

"Are they scared?" I asked.

Leah released a shaky breath. "They saw the news already," she confessed. "Zach, they're saying this time is bigger than the last one. Way bigger."

"Distract them," I said. "When you're on the road. Play punch buggy; they know how now. And tell them to watch out for a black Civic. I'll be waving."

"Z, a Civic? You don't—" She stopped. "Marcus is here. We've gotta go."

"Kiss them for me," I said, trying to keep my voice steady. "Mama, too."

"Z," Leah said. She didn't have to say more.

"I know," I said. I closed the phone and sat there quietly. Derek would have come back from San Luis Obispo, dropped the girls with Leah, then gone straight to the rigs. He was on shift tonight. I looked out Edgar's window, towards the horizon, but of course I couldn't see Derek's rig from so far south.

"Heavy stuff, man," Edgar said. "Water."

The trip north seemed elastic; time stretched, sagged in the middle. The highway began to jam up with other vehicles, drivers fleeing the coastline. Somewhere among them, I knew, was Leah's brother's van, carrying the people I loved. My heart had already left my body, soaring ahead over the roads, searching for them. I hoped they reached safety. I knew Leah would do everything she could.

In the meantime, I needed to focus.

I had to reach Derek.

And Vanessa.

"Edgar," I said. "Can I borrow your phone again?"

I called 411, asked for some numbers, and wrote them down in my sketchbook. I called DepthKor first, listened to the automated instructions, pressed numbers, and at last got connected to the rig Derek was assigned to.

But nobody there picked up the phone.

I ended the call, then took a deep breath and dialled the second number. It rang four times, then a recorded message said, "You've reached Aaron and Elise and Vanessa. Please leave a message, and—"

I hung up. Then I gritted my teeth and dialled the Bartlett house again. I hadn't wanted anyone to answer – no answer meant maybe they were already safely out of town, or at least on their way. But I needed to let Vanessa know I wasn't gone. That I was there. For her. And for my family.

The line rang twice, then was interrupted by a sharp triple tone. A recorded voice intoned, "We're sorry. All circuits are busy. Please disconnect and try your call again."

Shit.

By the time Orilly was in sight, the highway lanes had filled. Cars had spilled onto the shoulder, and speeds had slowed to a near crawl. Highway 1 was like a busy New York street from a movie, soundtracked with shouts and honking horns. Edgar swung off the highway at the first exit. I watched through the window as we rolled past a credit union. Its lighted sign read CONGRADULATIONS CLASS OF 2013, and it hit me: it was graduation day.

"Change of plans," I said, and pointed. "Take me there."

A few turns later, Edgar paused at the bottom of the hill. Through his rain-spattered windshield, I could see that this road, too, was clogged with vehicles. Anyone who hadn't left town, I knew, would be headed here: Costa Celeste, the half-completed resort on the highest hill in town. And, conveniently, the site of Palmer Rankin's graduation ceremony.

"So, uh," Edgar said, "I don't think I can get up there." He looked at his watch anxiously. "I really gotta keep moving, you know?"

"I can pay for gas," I offered again, but he waved me off.

"Here, wait. Give me your drawing pad." He scribbled a telephone number down. "I don't know you, and who knows, maybe you're a lousy human being, but still, you know? Just call me when this is all done and let me know you didn't get drowned here."

"I will," I said. Then I started climbing the hill towards the resort.

I hoped Vanessa would be there.

And I hoped desperately that she wouldn't be.

36

VANESSA

After I left the diner, I drove straight to the city impound lot in my father's stupid van-bus thing. Being arrested for driving without a licence would have undermined the impact of my dramatic exit. I hadn't driven more than three blocks before I noticed another driver turn to stare. I felt enormously conspicuous, rolling through town inside this blue monstrosity.

Sneaking into the lot in broad daylight wasn't the dangerous adventure I might have imagined. It should have been thrilling, but the place was abandoned. I could have driven the van right through the gate, and nobody would have noticed.

I crossed the lot towards Zach's father's boat. This had been one hell of a year. I'd turned on my mother. I'd betrayed Zach, shoved Cece out of my life. Cornell was gone, and nothing I'd worked for mattered. Tonight was graduation. Cece would give the valedictory address, a better one than I ever could have. I wouldn't be there to see it, but she didn't need me. Didn't want me. She had Ada now.

One hell of a year. One hell of a day, for that matter. I didn't know how I'd tell Mom about my father's abrupt appearance, or his goddamned telescope-on-wheels. For that matter, I still hadn't told her I intended to skip graduation. The whole event seemed meaningless, given how things had gone. And now, discovering that Cornell was little more than a veil for how I really felt about my father...

I boarded the boat and slipped into the wheelhouse. It was strange to be there without Zach. And now he was gone. *He moved*, the busboy had said. But when? Where? He hadn't taken any of his art. Every sketch still hung from the wall, like the residue of failed sorcery, as if Zach had attempted to resurrect his father and succeeded only in conjuring these paper ghosts. He wouldn't have left these behind.

And I knew, then, where he'd gone. He'd gotten into art school. He'd gone to San Diego. He'd escaped. Zach had *won*.

I stared through the open wheelhouse door at the blue Volkswagen. I'd lost my friends, burned bridges with Mom, and for what? I thought I'd done it for Cornell. For a dream.

But no. I'd done it all for a goddamned bus.

I felt hollowed out. Gutted.

I texted Cece.

She wouldn't answer, I knew. But I texted her anyway.

hi. it's your shittiest friend. are you there?

I waited, but the three little dots didn't appear. A minute passed, then two. My phone went dark in my palm, and I sighed and shoved it into my pocket. I leaned against the door frame and squinted up at the sky. It was going to be a disappointing day for a graduation, I thought, studying the swelling grey clouds lumbering towards Orilly.

Then my phone thrummed gently in my pocket. I pressed a button and it lit up, and there she was, back in my life.

i deleted your number.

I started to type, and then I didn't want to any more. I swiped to my contacts and dialled her number and agonized with each ring of the phone. There was the faintest little click on the line, and the ringing stopped.

"Hello?" I asked. A moment passed, during which I thought I heard a whisper of a sigh. "Cece?"

Silence. But the line was open. She was there. Listening.

"You were right," I said. She didn't respond to that, either, so I just lurched on. "You've always been right, about everything. You were right about what I did to Zach. You were right about the stupid college thing. I'm such an idiot—" I almost said *without you*, but I knew that would just set her off. *I'm not your damn sidekick*, she'd have shouted. *I'm not the Robin to your Batman.* I paused, recalibrated. "I'm sorry, Cece. That's all. Just…sorry."

More silence.

"I just saw my father," I said quietly. "I understand why I'm such a mess now."

The quiet persisted, but then my phone vibrated. She'd texted me. I tapped the message, and a photo appeared. A selfie: her starry green eyes beneath her graduation cap. A braided tassel, out of focus against her skin.

Her voice, tinny in my hand: "Did you get it?"

I put the phone to my ear again. "Cece? Yes, I got it."

"I look like a doofus."

Like that, we were back.

"You look beautiful. And smart."

"I just threw up. Twice."

"You're going to say all the right things."

"I don't know," she confessed. "Ada convinced me to bury some subtext in my speech. To make it easier on my family later, if I ever – you know."

"Trust me, when they see Ada, they'll *immediately* understand." I didn't know how to say the next part, so I just said it: "I'm not coming. To graduation."

Things had changed between us. They weren't irreparable – we were talking again, at least – but they were different now. Just a couple of months ago, she might have argued with me over attending graduation. But now she didn't react at all. She said, "I'll pick up your diploma for you. If you want."

I sank into the captain's chair and tugged one of Zach's blankets around my shoulders. "You're not mad?"

"I'm not mad."

"Cece," I said.

"I know."

"I'm a bad friend."

"I know."

That made me laugh.

"Well, as long as we both know, I guess."

"I mean, we both know *now*," she said. "One of us has known this for a long time."

"It's why you're valedictorian."

"You threw the match."

"You're really not mad?" I asked.

"I saw the news. About your mom. About all of them."

"You said his bad luck might rub off on me."

"It didn't."

"Cece."

"It *didn't*." She lowered her voice. "It was a mean thing to say. And dumb, and wrong. Anyway. The worst is over now. Right?"

I thought again about the Cornell email waiting in my inbox. I wasn't sure Cece was right about that.

"No," I said. All the things that had gone sideways recently – they were only getting worse. Every thing was bigger than the thing before. "No. I don't think so. I don't want to know what happens next."

This is what happened next:

I fell asleep in the captain's chair, wrapped in Zach's blanket. When I woke, it was to the soaring cries of sirens. I knew those sirens. Every month, on a Saturday, they were tested for five straight minutes, waking me too early from sleep. But today wasn't Saturday. Today was Friday.

Oh god.

I stepped out onto the deck, still wrapped in the blanket. While I was asleep, it had begun to rain. I could see the glowing husks of the oil rigs in the distance, but where the horizon was usually sharp, now it was smeary and indistinct.

My phone vibrated, and I glanced at it to find a notification I'd never seen before. The National Weather Service. *Find high ground.*

Above the notification, my phone displayed the time and date.

Graduation was less than an hour away. Mom and Aaron would be there already. By now they'd be worried, searching for me among my fellow students, all dressed identically. The ceremony – ironically, perhaps – was at the resort that Mom had fed my college money to. And now that resort was high ground.

VANESSA

Funny. A few hours ago, skipping graduation was just a thing I planned to do. And now, suddenly, that decision had life-or-death consequences. I shed the blanket and ran for the fence. On the other side, I threw the Volkswagen into gear. Zach's boat fell away in my rear-view mirror as I gunned it for Costa Celeste, and for the first time, I found myself grateful he was gone.

37

ZACH

Only in Orilly would the powers that be decide to host graduation at a building site. Costa Celeste's grounds were mostly dirt, turned into mud now by the rain. Diggers and dump trucks were scattered about the acreage. None looked as if they'd been moved in a while. The hotel itself was little more than a husk: ten storeys of steel and concrete, every floor exposed to the elements, sheets of plastic flapping in the wind.

The event hall, by contrast, glowed warm against the darkening sky. I remembered the newspaper story about Vanessa's mother: the council had intended to put the event hall to use as quickly as possible. Weddings, dog shows, trade shows. More money to throw at the forever hotel project.

The scene at the top of the hill was already near chaos when I arrived. The dirt lot was filled with parked cars, and people streamed about in confusion as the sirens continued to ring out below. I saw a shape flash across a high floor of the hotel, then several more. People had begun to scale the hotel's concrete stairs, searching for safety within the uppermost floors.

Vanessa could be among them, but I couldn't go there yet. Once I'd reached the top of the structure, I wouldn't be able to get back down. The stairs were clogged with people; the only other way down would be an unfortunate tumble. Inside the event hall, the main room had been arranged for the ceremony: a stage, rows and rows of chairs, ribbons and bunting strung everywhere. Gowns and mortarboards lay strewn about. Purses and jackets. An empty stroller, an abandoned stuffed bear. Everyone had already cleared out.

I ran outside. First I'd rule out the parking lot, then search for her in the hotel. Surely she was there. If she wasn't, I'd be trapped – but I'd be safe, too.

I leaped from the sidewalk to the muddy parking lot and misjudged badly. My feet went in two directions on the slick mud, and before I understood what had happened, I was on my face in the muck. I'd hit something hard – a broken slab of concrete, it turned out – but it wasn't until I tried to push upright that I realized I'd done something terrible to myself. When I was nine years old, I'd nearly killed myself playing Little League. During a night game, I charged after a high pop fly, lost sight of it, then overcorrected when I found it again. "It was like you hit an invisible clothesline," Dad had observed later. I'd come down hard on my face and shoulder. We spent that night at the hospital, where I was treated for a collarbone fracture and two cracked ribs.

This felt worse. Felt *serious*.

I tried to get up, but the sensation of bones grinding was awful. My stomach went shaky and sour. I thought I might vomit, and a moment later, on my knees in the mud, I did. My right side had gone cold and tingly, and then numb. I couldn't figure out what I might have done to myself, but my head felt cloudy. I thought, dimly, that I might be in shock.

I still had to find Vanessa. I turned towards the parking lot, tried once again to get to my feet. I wobbled, then leaned against a tall lamp-post. The people in the parking lot ran about, leaving little shimmering trails behind them. *Yes. You're in shock.* My knees turned to water, and I slid to the ground. I don't know how long I sat there, head swimming. Someone splashed past me, sending up a fan of mud and grit; someone else nearby said, low and cold, "Dear god, I can see it. *I CAN SEE IT.*"

Oh, right. The tsunami.

People scattered. Screamed. Faces blew by, blurry and strange. I didn't recognize anyone. Certainly none of them was Vanessa. With a few deep breaths, I managed to stand up, using the lamp-post for support, and blinked and rubbed my eyes until I felt my vision resolve a bit. Below me, I could see Orilly. It looked much larger now, and I realized that the tide had been drawn out, exposing more of the shoreline than I'd ever seen. Further away, against the horizon, I saw the lights of an oil platform, and then they winked out, as if erased. A moment later, another disappeared, too.

Please, I thought. *Please, Derek, don't be out there.*

Cars wheeled about in the lot, creating log-jams; drivers leaned on their horns. I looked up at the hotel and saw a huge crowd silhouetted between the floors, watching the sea. Things went quiet, or seemed to, and I heard someone shout nearby, though I couldn't make out the words. My stomach heaved again, and I went to my knees once more. A white roar filled my ears, dull and inoffensive, almost pleasant. I thought of Vanessa and Derek. Of Leah and Mama and the girls. Of Edgar the cashier. I wondered if he'd made it to the aquarium in time.

I closed my eyes.

The wave came to Orilly.

38

VANESSA

All night, we waited.

In the morning, as the sun rose, the damage brought people to tears. I stood on the roof of the hotel with Mom and Aaron. Cece was there with her parents and her *abuela*; she was holding Ada's hand. We were drenched. We were freezing. We hadn't slept. Orilly was unrecognizable. Palmer Rankin seemed to have slid sideways down the hillside, the whole structure slumped over upon itself; strewn all over the coast, sparkling in the sunlight like bits of glitter, were the wrecked remains of homes and shops. And cars. There were cars everywhere that cars shouldn't be: wrapped around half-uprooted trees, lodged deeply in the earth, upside down inside broken buildings. And water. So, so much water.

We were brought down from the roof by men and women in bright yellow gear. They loaded people into buses and trucks. Aaron ushered us into a line. We shuffled forward with other – *survivors*, I guess, would be the word, but it felt wrong. We shuffled forward with the others, and I remembered Aaron's story about the wind telephone. *I hope it never happens again*, I'd said. I thought about Zach's bad luck, how it seemed to have taken up residence inside me. I thought about the last thing I'd said to Cece on the phone.

I stopped shuffling and looked back at the devastation.

My fault, I thought. It wasn't, I knew that, but somehow – cosmically – I felt responsible.

"Vanessa?" Aaron said.

"I want to help," I said. I looked at the nearest woman, wearing yellow gear and holding a walkie-talkie. She gestured towards the bus door, waving me forward. But I turned to Mom. "I have to help."

Mom studied my face, and I wondered what she saw there. Guilt? Resolve? Whatever it was, she didn't hesitate. "We'll help," she said to the woman.

Later – after hitching a ride in a cramped pickup truck – we joined the group of volunteers at a makeshift operations centre. We stood among a few dozen volunteers and were quickly divided into six teams of eight. "San Luis and Monterey are both sending additional people," a man with a megaphone explained, "but for now, we're short. We're a lot short. The first few hours are critical. You see a survivor, you shout. Easy as that."

Mom and I were assigned to one team, Aaron to another.

I'd seen disaster-recovery efforts on television before. Medical tents everywhere, co-ordinated supply deliveries, whole systems of support. The Orilly teams disabused me of the notion that these things were ever as organized as they seemed. I turned to Mom and said, "I thought they issued megaphones and flashlights and boats and things."

Before she could reply, a boy a few years older than me said, "As if." The woman next to him – weary eyes, a lined face – added: "The real tech comes later. The first few hours are just turning over rocks, hoping for the best."

"Hope you aren't squeamish," the boy said. The woman – his mother? – whacked his shoulder.

We fanned out and began to work our way through town in a short, broken wave. I sloshed through deep puddles. The tired-looking woman warned against it. "Never know any more how deep they go," she cautioned. "I once saw a car cross a puddle like that during a Texas flood. *Bloop*," she said, making a nosedive motion with her hand. "Just dropped right out of sight."

"You've done this before," Mom said.

"We help when help's needed," the woman said. She kicked over a sheet of soggy plywood. "Last week I was in Mariposa. Controlled burn didn't want to be. Had a feeling when I heard about the quake we'd be looking at water damage again." She paused, surveying the rubble around us. "Couldn't have imagined this."

Her name was Adele, and the boy was her nephew, Bo. He was carrying a long wooden stake; I'd thought it was a walking stick until he demonstrated how to use it to prise up debris to search beneath. We all found sticks after that.

From the northernmost end of our group came a cry: "Got one over here!"

We swarmed. There, lying face down in a standing pool of black water, was a man in a hooded jacket, one leg turned at an impossible angle. Adele said, "Roll him," and Bo and another volunteer did so, and for one awful moment I thought it was Zach. The man turned over, and the shock of red I thought was Zach's hair wasn't hair at all, but a torn shred of red tarp.

That was the first body I saw that day.

Mom saw me blanch and put her hands on my shoulders. "Are you all right?"

I nodded. "I thought – I thought maybe it—"

"Your friend," she said.

"But it couldn't be. He's gone. He left town."

"You'll get used to it," Bo said, and he stabbed a red flag into the earth beside the body. "You really will."

Mom and I walked in silence after that, navigating the ruins, investigating collapsed structures. She still looked fearless, still resolved – but there was something else there, too, swimming just below her expression. We kept going, listening for more shouts, helping other volunteers search when they called for assistance.

Then Mom said, "We're done now. Okay?"

I squinted at her. "What?"

"This is what happens, Vanessa," she said quietly, gesturing at the wreckage around us. "This is life. You can't account for these things. They just come sweeping up, always from your blind side." She met my gaze. "You *have* to stop being mad at me."

I looked around us. *This* was where we were going to have this conversation? But immediately I understood. I'd refused to talk to her for so long, I'd put us in such a state that *only* a natural disaster could have brought us to this moment. And everything had happened so fast, I hadn't even had time to tell her I wasn't mad at her any more. That I'd figured out what – *who* – had really pissed me off. I'd moved on – and I'd left her in that uncertain, awful place we'd been in for months.

"I can't do this again," she said. She wasn't just talking about the earthquake, or the tsunami, or the possibility that we could have died without putting right the wrongs between us. "I just can't."

The last year of her marriage to my father had been just like this. Strained silences. A constant heaviness in our home. The sludge of my father's lies tracked all over the house.

They'd slept in different rooms without ever acknowledging it; he was always "just falling asleep" on the sofa. She'd complained he was never home – but when he was, they fought bitterly or treated each other like ghosts.

Then when she let me down, I'd done the same thing to her. I was my father's daughter. Through and through.

Before I could say anything, Mom said, "I called your father."

I blinked. "Like – today?"

"Before." She bit her lip. She'd learned that trick from a public speaking course. *It keeps me from speaking before I've measured what I intend to say,* she'd told me. "I did a terrible thing. To you. To all of us." Her eyes opened, focused on me. "I'm so sorry."

"You couldn't have known it wouldn't work," I said. Saying it made it real, but it had been real all along. Mom wasn't a malicious person. She'd taken the money expecting to return it, and then some. Aaron was right: it was time to let her off the mat. "You couldn't have."

"Everybody knew it wouldn't work." She drew a deep breath, started walking again. "We fooled ourselves."

"I made it about *me*," I said. "I thought you didn't want me to have the thing I wanted most of all. I thought you wanted to punish me for being like him." I stopped. "I *hate* being like him."

"Vanessa," Mom started.

"No," I said. "Mom, it was just college. I thought I knew why it mattered, but I didn't. Now I do, and it doesn't. Not for the reasons I thought." Then I tipped my head at her. "Wait. Why did you call him?"

She kicked a rock towards a puddle. "I…thought he could fix what I'd broken. Even if it meant…" Another kick. "Even if it meant he was in your life again. It…seemed like a fair punishment. For how badly I ruined your plans." She frowned, and I noticed more lines around her eyes than I remembered. Her laugh was mirthless. "I thought he'd write you a cheque. Maybe help a little with tuition, at least get you started."

I could imagine how that telephone call had gone. The things he'd have said to her. *Oh, look,* he would have said. *Of course you need someone to sweep up your mistakes. You haven't changed at all. Always looking to me to swoop in and fix your shit.* And she'd done that – thrown herself in front of the runaway train that was my father – for *me.*

If I'd ever doubted it, I was a fool. My mother fucking *loved* me. And my father… Maybe he never had.

So I told her the story of the diner, and the FOR SALE sign. She clapped a hand over her mouth in delight. "He named it *Andromeda*, if you can believe that," I finished.

She snorted. "He *would.*"

A fresh shout went up, this one from another team altogether. Despite the distance, the desperation in the cry was obvious. Mom and I broke into a run, followed Adele and Bo and the others, skittering down a hillside. At the bottom, Adele threw up an arm and said, "Whoa." I couldn't slow myself quickly enough, and I slipped on the mud and landed hard beside a body of water that shouldn't have been there. It was vast, a lake right in the middle of Orilly.

Adele pointed at a signpost in the middle of the water. "That sign. Do you know it?" It was the sign for Maddie's Market, still standing straight and tall – but submerged so that only the topmost letters were visible. "How tall would you say that sign is? Ten feet? Five?"

"Twenty," I croaked. "Maybe more."

"Holy shit," Bo said. "Okay, people, let's back it up."

Mom helped me to my feet as Adele said loudly, "Folks, this whole area has collapsed. We're on the edge of a very large sinkhole. Back to safer ground."

On the opposite side of the crater, the other rescue team was still loudly shouting. Bo shielded his eyes, scanning the water. Then he pointed. "There," he said.

"Oh my," Adele breathed.

Scattered across the centre of the lake were islands of wreckage. As I squinted, one of the islands moved. And even at this distance, even under these conditions, I recognized that island's body language. Something in the way it moved. I *knew* that island.

Oh god.

Zach.

39

ZACH

The first thing I noticed: I'd been unconscious way more than a few minutes. When I opened my eyes, the sun was coming up. Water pulled at my clothes; indistinct shapes bobbed past on all sides. *Tsunamis aren't this placid*, I thought. There was water in my eyes, my nose, my ears; salt and oil and dirt smeared in a paste on my skin.

The wave had come, and now I was here. What had happened? I remembered so little. Blackness. Colours that rippled around me, like they were coming from my own body, like oil gone iridescent in water. For a moment I thought I'd heard my father's voice.

And then I'd broken the surface and fought for air before I went under again. Except I didn't go under. I flailed in the water, surrounded by debris, until I found something to hang on to. I couldn't swim away. My right side was still… broken, or something. The wires and connections were all severed. I thought I'd been sucked out to sea, so I tried to kick in the direction I thought home might be.

But only one leg worked. The other exploded as if I'd been jabbed with a thousand needles. My leg was stuck fast, and struggling only made the pain echo up my spine.

"Hello?" I shouted, but no reply came. I gathered my strength, raised my voice: "*Help!*"

Only the sound of water, slapping against debris, against me. I clung to my bobbing hunk of debris – what appeared to be part of an infant's car seat, I noticed with a kind of dim horror – and tried to be grateful. That I was alive. That I was above the water, not below. And I was. But only just.

I was still wearing my backpack, I realized. There wasn't much in it, but it was ballast now, nothing more. Clinging to the car seat, I struggled to remove the bag, then unzip the pocket. My sketchbook was still inside, the pages turning to mulch. The envelope of cash. Clothes. I reached inside and removed the other envelope; then I released the bag. It sank out of sight.

I removed Dad's compass from the second envelope. I rested it on my arm and stared at its face. It had survived Dad's accident. I hoped that it – that we – would survive this, too.

Water lapped against my face, into my mouth, and woke me. Immediately, I heard the voices. Behind me, I thought. Was that west? South? I looked to the compass, but my bad arm had slipped below the water after I passed out. The compass was gone, lost at last to the sea below me.

There wasn't time to mourn it, however. *Voices.*

I tried to rotate my body towards the sound, but my leg held fast. Even the barest movement lit my nerves like a bundle of fuses, and I gritted my teeth until I tasted blood. I was hurt, and badly. I tried not to think about open wounds, in this water. The infections would kill me before I had a chance to drown.

The voices were distant, but not quiet. People, speaking loudly. In a boat? But I didn't hear the sound of oars, the flap of a sail, the hum of an engine.

My throat was raw. I tried to call out, but my voice was little more than a croak. How long had I been unconscious this time? Only minutes before, it seemed, I'd had the full use of my lungs. My body was falling apart, systems failing all over the place.

I could make out the voices now, or snatches of them. "*Sudden drop-off,*" one said. "*Stay away from the water.*" So they were on land. Which meant I wasn't lost at sea. I was in Orilly. I had to be. Which meant...

Orilly was underwater.

I couldn't seem to generate a loud enough shout to draw their attention. But I could splash. I kicked hard with my good leg to keep myself afloat, then slapped the water wildly with my good arm. *Make all the noise you can*, I thought. *Make a scene.*

In other words, be exactly the person I wasn't.

And it worked.

A shout went up, and then more cries filled the air.

40

VANESSA

The phone didn't even ring. As soon as I pressed the green button, I heard the awful triple tone in my ear. *Your call cannot be completed,* a voice said. I disconnected and shoved the phone back into my pocket and looked helplessly at Mom. "I can't get them," I said. "His family needs to know. They must be going crazy."

Mom put her arms around me. "I'm sure they're safe. And your friend is going to be okay."

Behind her, Bo trudged cautiously into the water, plunging his long wooden stake into the mud beneath his feet. Adele stood beside us and watched as he waded deeper, and then, abruptly, he dropped out of sight beneath the water. A moment later he came surging up, coughing. When he clambered out, his clothes and skin were streaked black with grime and muck.

Zach was in that shit up to his eyeballs.

"Hang on!" I shouted towards Zach, so small out there. "We're coming!"

Bo, stripping out of his wet jacket, muttered, "Don't make promises you can't keep," and Adele smacked him again.

Over the next few hours, a rescue plan took shape. An aluminium boat arrived, towed behind a four-by-four pickup. Mom took charge alongside Adele, co-ordinating the effort. When the boat was put into the water, it sent tall ripples surging outward. "Careful," Adele warned. "Every ripple could drown him. He looks like he's barely staying up."

"Send me," I said. "Less weight in the boat, less displacement of water. I'm the smallest person here." Which wasn't exactly true – Mom was perhaps a little shorter than I was, and sparrow-boned – but I was going.

Instead, Adele went. Mom stood beside me on the shoreline, and we watched as Adele paddled slowly towards the centre of the sinkhole. She glided gently alongside Zach and slowed the boat. When she tried to lift him into the boat, I clapped my hands over my mouth; the sound that came from Zach was gravelly and barely human. My eyes filled with tears.

"He's stuck," Bo guessed.

When Adele returned, she looked sadly towards me.

"He's going to be okay," I said. "He *is*."

Zach was pinned. "He guessed it might be concrete," Adele said. "He's got one leg free, and he can feel rebar."

She'd left Bo's long wooden stick out there with Zach, taught him how to use it to push against the debris. It wouldn't be enough to free him, but it would help him stay above the surface. "Maybe that way we won't almost drown him next time."

"Concrete and rebar, that's structural," Mom said. "Could be a collapsed wall. A roof."

"And if that's the case," Adele agreed, "we won't get that boy out of there until the real equipment gets here. If they can even do it."

"There's no *if*," I snapped. "We're not leaving him. He's my—" I was nearly hyperventilating. He was *out* there, small and alone. "He's my best friend."

"Honey," Adele said. But I didn't want to hear her sympathy. She wasn't angry, and I hated that. For her, this was just one more sad story in a long line of them. One more terrible disaster filled with them. But it wasn't for me.

I stalked away, and Mom and Adele let me go. But a moment later Bo followed.

"She's seen this before," he said. I didn't reply, and he sat on the trunk of a wrecked sedan. "Aunt Addie was in the Peace Corps, like, thirty years ago, or something." He told me the story: Colombia. A volcano. Mudslides. It was the first time she'd seen real disaster, the first time of many she would join rescue efforts. "There was a girl. She was young."

"What happened?"

"Her house collapsed," he answered softly. "On top of her. They found her on her knees, chest deep in filthy water. Her eyes turned almost black. The only way to get her out was to amputate her legs, but the shock would have killed her."

My voice sounded hollow in my ears, and I repeated my question. "What happened?"

"Nothing she wasn't afraid of," Adele said. She'd walked up behind me. Mom was with her. Adele looked sternly at Bo. "You shouldn't tell her this story."

"She made it, though?" I looked up at Adele hopefully. She didn't answer, but the facts were written on her face. I turned away from the three of them. I couldn't see Zach, not from where I stood.

The wind had picked up, turned the water choppy, and I flashed back to the bus ride. College fair. All his drawings that day were so clear to me now: the sea, its hungry mouth, those bright teeth; the oil rigs, probing the earth like fat ticks. Somewhere out there, trapped in the black water, was a boy who believed the sea had taken something from his family. A boy who knew that the sea was never sated, that it would only take and take, again and again, until it had taken everything he had.

And now it had come for him.

Specifically for him.

I rubbed my eyes with the sleeve of my jacket, then turned back to the group. "He's *alone*," I said. "He's *alone* out there."

Adele shared a look with Mom, and Mom nodded.

"Yeah, okay," Adele said. "Take the boat."

41

ZACH

The sun moved across the sky, then vanished behind a bank of clouds. It began to rain again. I was beyond cold; my whole body trembled as I leaned on the wooden pole Adele had brought. I didn't know how much more I could take. My leg throbbed painfully. I was getting tired.

After Adele had left, things had certainly picked up on the shoreline. The voices were more or less steady now as people shouted directions to one another. There were more of them than there had been this morning.

This morning. I'd been in the water, as best I could estimate, nearly twenty-four hours already. I'd be one hell of a prune by the time they got me out. If they got me out. I'd always been regarded as the unlucky kid in town, but it was more than that, I thought. Bad luck is a tame thing. It trips you up when you're confident, deals you the wrong cards at the right moment. What I had was more insidious than that. It took Dad away, drowned Mama in memories. I had no idea if my family was safe right now, or even alive.

Bad luck was a high inside pitch when you swung low and away. *This* was going to kill me out here on the water, alone, within shouting distance of strangers. I thought about the last things I'd said to my family. And the last time I'd talked to Vanessa, it had gone about as badly as it could have gone.

Maybe it wasn't bad luck. Maybe it was a curse.

Curses are vengeful.

This felt something like that.

The rowing boat returned as darkness fell, gliding slowly across the water like a Viking funeral longboat. I imagined myself lifted out of the water and laid in its belly. Imagined what the flaming arrows, fired from shore, might look like from that vantage point. Sizzling through the sky, sparking and popping as they arced high and then plummeted towards my—

Wait.

There was a light in the rowing boat, gently illuminating the person who swept a paddle from one side to the other. As the boat creaked closer, I realized I was hallucinating. Because it looked like Vanessa.

"Zach. Come on, Zach, snap out of it."

My eyes flew open, and Vanessa was right there, leaning over the side of the boat, struggling with my arms. Confused, I looked down and saw something magical: a life jacket. She was trying to fit my arms through it without losing her grip on me. I helped, despite my shaking limbs, and the difference was immediate. I hadn't realized how exhausted my muscles were until I relaxed them and sagged into the embrace of the jacket.

"Where…did you—" I began.

"Hold still," Vanessa said, and she lifted a contraption out of the boat next: four lengths of wood, hammered together like a window frame. Lashed to each board were hefty orange buoys, the same kind that had been laced into the rotted, old fishing net on Dad's boat. She lowered the frame over my head, like a squared-away wooden collar. "Now hang on to this," she said. "Does that help?"

The contraption lifted me a couple of inches above the water.

"Y-yes," I stammered.

"It's the best they have right now," she said. She gripped my good hand. "They're working on it. We'll get you home."

She said it earnestly. She had a trustworthy face. But I could see a flicker of something else there, something she was trying to keep pushed down where I wouldn't notice it. I knew what it was. I felt the same thing.

Maybe I wouldn't get home at all.

* * *

I slept again. When I came to, things were worse. My face was hot, but my body was frigid. My hands had begun to throb mercilessly.

Vanessa had tied the rowing boat to my little raft and was sitting there, watching me. "I was starting to float away," she explained. "How are you feeling?"

My voice sounded like broken glass. "O-okay."

"You're sure?"

"Peachy," I said. I tried to smile, but it hurt. "Y-you?"

Her chin quivered, but she didn't cry. "Are you scared?"

I nodded. "I'm s-sorry I didn't say good-b-bye."

"Don't think about that."

It was getting colder. The sun had already gone down.

"You'll be back in San Diego before you know it," she said.

"D-didn't even m-make it halfway there."

"You will. It'll be sunny and warm. You'll do all those life-studies classes with naked ladies."

"Naked old guys, t-too," I said. I swallowed hard. My tongue felt bulky. "My h-hands hurt."

She leaned as close to me as she could and put her hands on mine. "You're freezing."

"It's g-going to be hard," I said. My teeth were chattering now. "To g-get me out." She didn't say anything to that. I wondered how badly things were beyond my little lake. "How b-bad was it?"

"I don't want to say. You have enough to deal with."

"People d-died, th-then."

She nodded. There were lights on the shore behind her. Her hair glowed, but her face was draped in shadow. I wished I could see her face. I wished I could draw her. Just like this.

Sunrise was hours away. It might as well have been years.

"V-Vanessa." I hesitated, then said it: "I'm really s-scared."

She squeezed my hand. I didn't tell her that it hurt. She bent down and kissed my forehead, then each of my eyes. I could feel myself slipping away again. The sound of the water, the wind, the voices – it all knitted together into a blanket of static.

"It's going to be okay," she said softly.

I wanted to believe her.

42

VANESSA

Zach woke me just before dawn. I'd fallen asleep in the boat, and I woke with a frantic start. He was looking at me, but not; there...but not. His eyes fluttered between open and shut. His lips were an alarming shade of blue-grey. He wasn't trembling any longer; he was *shaking*. Hard. Hard enough that his little raft was beginning to prise itself apart.

"Do...y-you b-believe in...g-god?" he asked.

This wasn't good. "Zach, hang on," I said, and kneeled in the boat and shouted towards shore: "*Now! We have to get him out NOW!*"

He continued without waiting for an answer. "M-Mama," he said. "Sh-sh-she b-believes."

"Of course she does," I said, but he didn't seem to hear a word I said. He looked off to the right, away from me, as if he could see someone else there. His eyes were unfocused, his pupils liquid and vast.

"Sh-she w-would pray for m-me," he said. "Even th-though I d-didn't."

I put my hands on his face. "You're going to be okay," I said. But I didn't know if he would be. I was trying hard not to break down in front of him, but I was losing him. He was falling apart, right here in front of me. "You're going to be *fine*."

"Y-you have to t-tell her," he stammered, "th-that I l-love her. T-tell all of th-them. The g-g-girls."

"Zach, no," I said.

"V-Van-nessa," he said. "I'm g-going to d-die."

The words were so final, so heavy. His lips were swollen. Blood had dried in the cracks. His tongue was swollen, corrupting his speech even as he struggled to speak.

"They're going to get you out," I urged. "You have to hang on. You have to just *hold—*"

He looked right at me then, lucid and sharp-eyed, and clearly said, "Vanessa. I'm going to die."

"*No*," I insisted.

Zach's face seemed to fog over again. His head lolled forward and collided with the raft. "I..." he began. "I-I w-want—"

"What, Zach? What do you need?"

I'd only ever seen him strong. Stoic. Carrying everyone else's load, without complaining. But now...he looked like a lost little boy. His shoulders shook. "M-Mama," he rasped. "I just w-want...m-my mama."

I turned my face away so he wouldn't see me weep.

* * *

He drifted in and out of consciousness. Each time he woke, he was further away, less aware, more frayed. I wasn't certain he knew I was there any more. I clung to his life jacket so hard my hands hurt, afraid he'd shake himself right off the wooden raft and pitch forward in the life jacket and drown. I shouted myself hoarse, but nobody came. They didn't understand. We'd run out of time.

The sun was up when he woke again, and for a moment, he was his old self. Despite everything, he smiled at me.

"What, Zach?" I asked.

"Don't you feel it?" he asked. His voice was crisp and bright. "Something's different."

His eyes closed, and he went limp in the water, and I screamed towards shore.

What happened next felt like a dream.

Through the fine mist of rain, I saw a white truck skid wildly down the hill towards the makeshift rescue station Adele and Mom had established. The door burst open, and a man whirled out, shouting, yanking bulky bags from the truck bed. I recognized the voice, distant but powerful, and the shock of red hair.

Derek steamed across the water in a boat with a small out-board motor. Adele and Bo were with him. Derek was wearing his dive suit, and Adele worked furiously in the bow of the boat, unpacking the bags of gear he'd brought.

"Two days!" Derek bellowed. "Two *goddamned* days!"

I burst into tears at the sound of his voice.

He barked orders. "I'm going down," he said, reaching for his air tank. "Your job," he went on, nodding towards Adele and Bo, "is to get him out of the water and into the boat. Then you get him to shore. Don't wait for me."

His confident, angry facade faltered as he got his first look at Zach. His mouth opened and closed. Finally, he said, "Oh, Z." Then he drew a deep breath. "Gonna get you out of here." He climbed down into the water, then patted the side of my rowing boat. "I'm glad you're here with him."

To Adele, he said, "You be ready."

He put the regulator between his lips and sank below the surface.

Word of the rescue effort must finally have spread. While Derek was below, a siren squawked, and an ambulance picked its way through debris to the shoreline. Two medical techs emerged with a stretcher, then waited at the water's edge.

Adele threw her hands up. "Where were they yesterday?"

I could see the sickly green glow of Derek's lantern moving about. He wasn't down long before he surfaced.

"It's a slab," he said, yanking his regulator out. "I think his leg's cr—" He looked at me. "It's not good," he corrected. "If I had a couple more divers, we could probably shift it. Hand me that crowbar."

Bo hefted the bar and passed it over to Derek. Then Derek said, "Vanessa, you hang on to this," and handed me something else. "It was our dad's. Zach must have dropped it."

I wiped grime from the compass. Water had gotten through the cracked glass and sluiced over the needle, but it still worked. "He's going to be okay, right?"

"You keep talking to him," he said to me. "He'll need the distraction."

Derek submerged again. I could see his shadow, faintly, in the glow of his light. He was down there a while, and then several things happened simultaneously: there was a deep, muted groan from below the water, and a storm of bubbles raced to the surface, and Zach popped out of the water like a cork, then lurched sideways against the wooden raft. It had held together, right until the end.

Bo went into the water then and lifted Zach up from below; Adele got her hands around him and pulled. I gasped at the sight of Zach's injuries as he rose out of the water: his hands and stomach were bloated, and one arm swung limp at his side. His right leg was folded in places that bones are not meant to fold. His jeans were shredded, revealing swollen and gashed skin beneath.

He was talking again, perhaps dimly aware that things were happening. It sounded as if he was reciting his home address, though I could barely understand him.

With a final heft, Bo shoved Zach upwards, and Adele yanked him into the boat. Zach uttered a terrible, primal cry of pain as he tumbled inside. Adele yanked the cord on the outboard, and Bo swam towards my rowing boat. "Get ready!" Adele shouted towards the shore. *"We're coming!"*

I turned towards Derek, but he wasn't there. His lantern glowed deep below the water, and a column of bubbles swept to the surface.

Bo grabbed the side of my boat and saw the alarm on my face. "What?"

"Derek's down there, he's *still down there*—"

PART FOUR

AFTER

43

VANESSA

I arrive at the hospital a little too early. The familiar door to his room is closed, a curtain drawn over its little glass window. I wait in a little alcove with chairs and a television. Leah is there with the girls. Robin and Rachael run to me, and as they squeeze me from two directions, I give Leah a smile.

"Waiting?" she asks. "We were just in a few minutes ago. He's doing okay. Some pain today, more than usual."

I wrinkle my nose. "Poor guy."

Robin asks Leah if they can watch television, and both girls sit down and fiddle with the remote until they find cartoons.

"You doing all right?" Leah asks.

"I think so."

"This town," she says. "It takes so much."

"Yes," I agree. For the first time, I really understand.

* * *

When I check his room again, the door stands open, and I peek inside. I can see him on the hospital bed, mummified in casts, tethered with clear tubes. His room is quiet, and I wonder, not for the first time, how he manages to keep his sanity.

"Hi," I say.

Derek can't move his head. "Vanessa?"

"Who else?"

"Weren't you just here?" He exhales. "No. Leah was just here."

"And the girls," I say. "They're in the waiting room. Don't worry." I cross the room and stand beside his bed, and pat his hand. "I heard today was difficult."

Derek rolls his eyes. "They tell you not to worry, don't sweat, the pain goes away. They don't tell you first it'll double or quadruple before it does."

"I brought you some books," I say, holding up a bag.

He offers a sideways grin. "Maybe when they let me move my arms again I'll read 'em."

"I thought I could read a bit. Or Leah, maybe."

"Yeah?" He considers this. "Maybe. Nothing funny. I can't laugh."

"You see the pictures?" I ask him. "Of the town?"

"Leah and I watched some of the news together," he says. "It's hard for me to see. I keep thinking back, how many things had to go wrong, how many things had to line up just right, for me to even find Zach." His voice is shaky. "After the wave, everything was chaos. They airlifted us off the rigs, you know. To Monterey. You know it took two days for me to get back to Orilly? The truck was okay. And that's how I heard about Zach. On the radio in my truck. Lot of chatter, and someone said his name. I hadn't even been worried about him. Far as I knew, he was at his school, far enough from the coast to be safe. But he wasn't. I *should* have been worried. I should have been trying to call every two minutes until I found him. And look what happened," he finishes. The colour has seeped out of his face. "Look what…"

"Hey," I say. "Hey, come on."

He clears his throat, then winces. He tries to change the subject. "You, uh, hear anything else? About anything?"

"They're saying that they're going to fill the hole. I guess they don't know if it'll be safe to rebuild there. I sort of hope they leave it wild, you know? Even if it does mean people have to find a new place to live."

"Let me tell you what," Derek says. "Orilly? She's a working town. No patience for wasted space. In a couple of years, you'll never know what happened there."

I sit with him for a while, and we talk about the girls, about their mother. It's all easy and light until I notice Derek's eyes are wet. "They don't tell you this, either," he says. "Flat on your back, can't go anywhere, you have all this time to *think*. I don't normally have this kind of time." He hesitates. "All I can think about is Zach. The way he looked. The way he sounded. I just…" His eyes flick to meet mine. "You know?"

I squeeze Derek's hand. "I know. Me too."

44

ZACH

Vanessa finishes reading the news story aloud, then puts her phone away. She leans forward. Her hair is swept back into a ponytail, revealing the eyelets in her ears. I like it this way, but I don't say so.

"None of it," she says. "Really? You don't remember?"

I shake my head, then change the subject. "I'm sorry. For leaving like I did. I didn't say goodbye."

She tells me we have already discussed this. But I don't have that memory, either.

"You went to school," she says, "and then you came back. You never said why."

"Because." I shrug. "Everyone I love is here."

She kisses me.

I am okay.

By that, of course, I mean that my body will recover. "Okay" is subjective. This is "okay": my right leg has a steel pin in it now, running from my ankle to my knee. "You might set off the metal detectors at the airport," my physical therapist warned me. But she doesn't know I've never been on an airplane. I don't see much reason to start now. The doctors installed a thing called a halo, which is this series of metal rings that surround my leg, with spokes that radiate inward and jut into my bone, holding everything together as I heal. Vanessa thinks I look like an android. I'm happy to still have a leg. I'm told it may not work as well as it used to, that I might need a cane for the first six or eight months. This seems both a small price to pay and a fitting reminder of everything that's happened in the last year.

Well, a reminder, at least, of the things I can actually remember.

I remember searching for Vanessa at the resort. I remember falling in the parking lot. Four cracked ribs, they tell me, along with a separated shoulder and broken humerus; my chest and arm are wrapped in a stiff plaster shell.

I remember the sound of the wave as it came for us.

But that's all. I don't remember anything else before waking up here, at the hospital in San Luis Obispo, the nearest hospital that wasn't already overcrowded. I'm told many times how fortunate I am. "A few more hours in the water," my doctor said, "and we'd be looking at hypothermia, possibly gangrene. You probably wouldn't have made it."

ZACH

The sea took my father. It came for Derek and for me, and it almost succeeded. But we are, I've come to understand, a family of divers. Mama has submerged herself in her memories; unwilling to live only in a world in which my father does not, she moves between both. And so did Derek, who, despite his best efforts, did not kill himself attempting to save me. The two of them taught me something without ever saying a word: that their love isn't afraid, that it'll brave the deepest darkness to stage a rescue attempt.

Dad's boat is gone. I try to imagine it adrift somewhere at sea, for as long as it might have remained afloat. Perhaps, I think, my father will be reunited with it. Perhaps they'll chug slowly towards the horizon, each of them made whole, together and content at last. It is a nice thought.

We lost our house, but then, so did almost everyone in Orilly. DepthKor, Derek's employer, was generous enough to assign our family a small house in the oil district, where the seasonal workers live. Leah tells me it's even nicer than the duplex Dad worked so hard to provide for us, which makes me a little sad. The girls visit and tell me how nice it is to live in the new house; Leah's there with them, at least until Derek can come home. I ask if Mama likes it, but they don't have the right words to answer me. It's all right, I tell them. I know.

Vanessa is here every day. She rants about the newspapers getting the details wrong. She reads me stories about how the federal agencies have taken charge of the recovery and rebuilding efforts. The sinkhole that I'd been trapped in has been drained; the hole was nearly six hundred yards across at its widest, she tells me, and ninety-four feet deep. When I've had enough of disaster literature, she reads to me from *The Varieties of Scientific Experience*.

I'm lucky, everyone says, and I think about that. My brother prised a house off my leg, then dropped it on himself and broke his back – but he's alive. The admissions officer at Fleck wrote to tell me they'd hold my spot, and wished me a speedy recovery. My family's safe and dry. Every day, Vanessa appears in my doorway.

Lucky.

Imagine that.

45

VANESSA

The skywatching group meets near Annette, thirty-five miles east of Paso Robles, on a vast and empty plain between craggy hills and farmland. The seasons have changed, and the hillsides have gone orange and gold. Not that I can see the colours; from here, the city lights are muted by the mountains, and the night skies are rich and black.

The meet-up is part science club, part hippie commune. There are weekend stargazers and serious astronomers alike. Scattered all over the field are clusters of people with tents and telescopes. Some drink wine. Someone's playing a guitar.

The irony is not lost on me. *Take a year off*, my father had said. *Just drive around, look at the stars.* Here's something I've learned in the last few months: even an asshole can be right once.

Mom waits until I've parked the Volkswagen, then unbuckles and climbs into the back, already yawning. "Coffee," she mutters. "Where did you put the coffee?"

She brews us each a cup on the portable stove, then sits in the open door of the bus, taking in the scene. "This is… kind of cool," she reluctantly admits. "I might envy you. Don't get me wrong. I'm never going to sleep, not until you come back home."

The Annette meet-up is my dry run and something Mom and I agreed on. She'd join me for a short overnight trip, ostensibly to put her mind at ease. In the morning, we'll sleep late, and I'll drop her in Orilly before I leave again. I'll drive north first, spend a month or so in the Northwest, then head east before the snow comes. Aaron and I had pored over a map, plotting a course that would take me through as many of the darkest Bortle sites as possible; that meant spending half my gap year right here in the West, venturing into the least populated regions of Nevada and Utah.

"I wish Cece had taken a gap year, too," Mom says, not for the first time. "I'd feel better knowing you had someone with you."

"I'm going to be fine," I tell her for the fiftieth time. "And I'll see her when I get to New Haven. She's got her own stuff going on."

Cece was desperate to co-ordinate my visit with Ada's, ensuring we wouldn't overlap, and that I wouldn't cramp her style. She'd been texting me for days:

you have to give me DATES, nessa.

WHEN ARE YOU COMING

To which I'd replied:

I'll see you when I see you.

THE ROAD WILL NOT BE RUSHED.

"I know, I know." With a sigh, Mom sinks onto the bed. "I'm just saying."

Outside the bus, the field is utterly dark. A shadow approaches, holding a flashlight with a red bulb. "Cool set-up," the new arrival says, taking in the bus. "Did you *build* this?" She's a few years older than me, hair tucked in a loose bun beneath a kerchief. "Tell me it has a name."

Mom elbows me, but I'm embarrassed to answer. So Mom gives the girl a smile and says, "It's my daughter's bus. She named it *Voyager Three*."

The girl laughs. "Of course you did. It's perfect."

She invites us to join her group, and we do for a little while. They're knotted around telescopes, taking turns at one another's eyepieces. Someone's brought a gorgeous Celestron – but before I can ask to try it, I spot the Meade.

"Is that…?"

The girl is Tallulah, but she goes by Tally. She introduces me to her friend, Geoffrey, who owns the Meade. "Not every day you get to look through a fifteen-thousand-dollar scope," she says. "He'll let you try it. Won't you, Geoff?"

He does, and the sky is crisp and alive, both larger and smaller than I've ever seen it. A sigh escapes my lips, and I hear Geoffrey laugh. "Everybody makes that sound when they look through this beauty," he says. "I should name it that sigh." I laugh, a little uncomfortably, but he goes on: "It's the sound people make when they see the stars for what they really are."

I look up from the Meade. "And what are they?"

"Why, they're us," Tally says.

I usher Mom over. "I'm afraid I'll break it," she says of the Meade, but Geoffrey says, "No, dear, the view's more likely to break *you*." Mom bends over the eyepiece, then snaps upright: "*Oh my god.*" She whirls to face me, accusingly. "You never told me it was like *this*."

"You never asked," I say, but she's already returned to the eyepiece.

The hours unspool, and it only gets darker. The meet-up will last all night, and Mom is having more fun, I think, than she'd anticipated. Tally offers her a glass of wine, then takes her around to meet new people. While she's occupied, I slip away, back to the Volkswagen.

I roll open the skylight, set up OSPERT's tripod. With my eye against the silicone cup, the sky gives up its secrets effortlessly. Against such darkness, Saturn is sharper than I've ever seen. I can almost track the little freckle of Titan's shadow upon her rings. The skies, the stars, all these wonders: for so long I'd been afraid my father had marked them as his own, that I had no right to them myself. But it wasn't true. It never had been.

It occurs to me then that the email from Cornell is still in my inbox, unopened; I haven't thought about it since graduation day. Does that mean I've made my peace with that lost dream? Was it ever the dream, really? Cornell is, after all, only a school. Here, beneath this vast, dark sky, it's hard to believe I ever could have been satisfied dreaming so small.

I wonder about Zach in San Diego. It's the middle of the night, but maybe he isn't sleeping. He has a cell phone now, and I take out my iPhone to text him. But outside the bus, in the dark, a murmur passes through the crowd, and I wonder what they've seen. I step down into the field and crane my neck upward in time to see the winking marble that is the International Space Station as it drifts smoothly past.

The phone is smooth and cool in my hand. Without thinking much about it, I slip it back into my pocket and leave it there. The night is humming, alive; a glowing screen would threaten that. I stretch out on the grass, drenched in the dark, and watch as the universe wheels overhead. This is everything I've ever ached for. Everything else falls away, and I understand, for the first time, that the skies belong to me.

They always have.

ACKNOWLEDGEMENTS

While writing is often a solitary pursuit, publishing a novel is no such thing. To that end, I owe a great deal of thanks to many people.

I am most grateful to Connie Hsu, my editor at Roaring Brook Press, for bringing out of me a book that might otherwise never have existed, and for pressing and shaping it into the novel she knew it could be. And to Seth Fishman, my agent at The Gernert Company, who lined up all the pieces so that this book could happen.

My thanks to Jennifer Besser and everyone else at Macmillan and Roaring Brook who pitched in to make this book what you hold in your hands. Aimee Fleck, Brian Luster, Tom Nau, Jennifer Sale, Kristin Dulaney, Jill Freshney, Lindsay Wagner, and Morgan Rath: thank you for everything you brought to this project. Special thanks to Megan Abbate for her steady hand and quick attention throughout.

Catherine Frank edited some early drafts of this novel, for which I'm deeply appreciative. Felicia Gurley, Monica

Villaseñor, and Daniel H. Wilson each read early pages and drafts and steered me away from certain death more than once. Thanks to Sarrah Figueroa and Philip Elizondo, who double-checked some of my inadequate Spanish. Any mistakes that live on in this novel are entirely my own.

Writing a novel set on the California coastline was a daily journey back to the years I spent in Morro Bay and San Luis Obispo, but my depiction of California should be taken with several spoonfuls of salt, as I've taken a few liberties. Orilla del Cielo, you'll be startled to hear, does not exist. The disasters that befall the town, however, bear similarities to some real events: the wind telephone, for example, is a real thing. It's in Otsuchi, Japan, and has been visited by mourners since the 2011 earthquake and subsequent tsunami in Tohoku. And in 1985, the eruption of Colombia's Nevado del Ruiz volcano trapped thirteen-year-old Omayra Sánchez in water for three days before she succumbed to her injuries.

For this novel's devotion to the stars and the sense of wonder they provoke, I must thank Ann Druyan and her late husband, Dr Carl Sagan, for their lifelong ambition to share that wonder. Their work on the *Voyager* project and its Golden Record are timeless. *Voyager 1* entered interstellar space on or around August 25, 2012, some thirty-five years after its launch. The probe will continue its mission until around 2025, when it will finally run out of power; the probe itself, however, will keep right on going. It will likely outlast the existence of our entire species.

And finally: for eighteen months, this novel required much of my attention, which would not have been possible without the support and love of my family. Felicia, thank you for stealing me away – or sending me away – to the movies when I'm exhausted, and reminding me that I can do this; Akiko, thank you for the homemade chicken and dumplings, and for reminding me that I work too hard; Emma, thank you for the tickle-fights and snuggly *Star Trek* marathons and afternoons spent sharing hot chocolate and reading together. Without you all, this would be no kind of life.

First published in the UK in 2019 by Usborne Publishing Ltd., Usborne House,
83-85 Saffron Hill, London EC1N 8RT, England. www.usborne.com
Published in arrangement with Roaring Brook Press, a division of
Holtzbrink Publishing Holdings Limited.

This is a work of fiction. The characters, incidents, and dialogues are products of the
author's imagination and are not to be construed as real. Any resemblance to actual events
or persons, living or dead, is entirely coincidental.

A CIP catalogue record for this book is available from the British Library.

ISBN: 9781474962766 J MAMJJASOND/19 05310/1

Printed in the UK.